REDCOATS-ish

Jeff Martin's War of 1812

By Jeff Martin

Dedicated to Gary and Gayle Martin, my parents.

Their encouragement and support made this book possible. So blame them

Published by Renegade Arts Canmore Ltd trading as Renegade Arts Entertainment Ltd
Office of publication: 25 Prospect Heights, Canmore, Alberta T1W 2S2 Canada

Renegade Arts Entertainment is Alexander Finbow Alan Grant Doug Bradley John Finbow Nick Wilson and Jennifer Taylor.

Visit our website for more information on our titles www.renegadeartsentertainment.com

ISBN: 978-0-9921508-6-0
First edition printed August 2014

Written and drawn by Jeff Martin

Letters, logo and cover design by Jeff Martin

Editor and publisher Alexander Finbow

Printed in Canada by Friesens

RENEGADE
ARTS ENTERTAINMENT

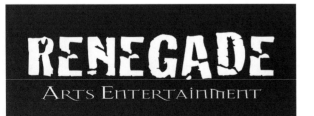

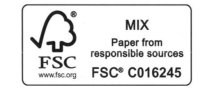

MIX
Paper from responsible sources
FSC® C016245
FSC
www.fsc.org

note from the frontline

ntil my time studying history at the University of Alberta, all I knew about the War of 1812 was that it started in 1812 and the White House burnt down. After taking it on myself to learn more about the war - because the sign of a history nerd is doing historical research that has nothing to do with your actual classes - I decided that it ould be ideal for comic adaptation. Why? Because of the rampant and borderline cartoonish levels of incompetence displayed by nearly everyone involved. It was great. en I started trying to write it. I got far too deep into a research rabbit hole to productively write anything resembling a comic script, so the project was shelved for the time ing.

few years later, at the 2012 Edmonton Expo, I ran into Alexander Finbow as Renegade was unveiling the Loxleys and the War of 1812 graphic novel. After a favourable rtfolio review and an invitation to pitch something related to an existing Renegade property, I found myself revisiting the tale of George Morton and John Pink, incompent Canadian militiamen. George and John's adventures first appeared as a weekly series on the Renegade Arts Entertainment website, which meant that I didn't have to try cram the entire war into a specific number of pages. That allowed me a unique opportunity to delve deeply into some of the lesser known details of the war, like the Battle Maguaga and Major Adam Muir. Those were some of the most rewarding, if infuriating, elements of the story to research. I didn't want to focus too heavily on the histori-figures, I wanted them to be important but infrequent cameo characters, because so many of them were ultimately very impressive human beings. There are already lots stories about soldiers who are GOOD at stuff. So let's see some guys who wouldn't have come close to being recruited if the standards were higher than "anyone who can rry a musket." George and John personify a war that nobody was good at until it was almost over... although it remains to be seen if they're ever any good at soldiering.

ff Martin
dmonton
ly 2014

For more cartoons from Jeff, visit RenegadeArtsEntertainment.com and www.heat.rentathugcomics.com

3

Foreword March!
by Jay Bardyla

I had the privilege of working on a short story with Jeff back in 2009 that appeared in an Edmonton produced anthology called MERCY SEAT: CHILDREN ARE CRUEL. I'm not sure how we got paired up as the tone of my story was certainly not something that seemed instantly suitable for Jeff's art style. "Back in the day" Jeff's claim to fam was his self-published comic called RENT-A-THUG which was about gangsters. Gangsters without legs.

It's not that Jeff's characters were legless... well, they kinda were. His character styling meant that everyone looked somewhat like a Weeble with feet and it was funny large due to the absurdity of situations, coupled with the visual imagery of egg-shaped people with guns being badasses.

I suspect I selected Jeff to draw my overtly dark tale as a way to distract the reader. He didn't draw the people in my story the same way he did in his own comics (he gave my characters more of a proper anatomy). His soft, rounded, cartoonish style easily led readers down a path far enough away from the reveal of the story that more than on reader was concerned for my personal well-being. Mission accomplished.

I knew Jeff was teaching himself how to draw and I also knew Jeff was really, really smart. His depth of knowledge was frightening at times, especially when it came to two topics that I conversed with him about on occasion; world history and professional wrestling (they're more similar than you might initially think). It's with that breadth of knowledge, coupled with his desire to make comics, that I knew Jeff would find a way to make something very different and very good.

My suspicions were confirmed when Jeff moved into his next creative endeavour, HEAT, a series about an intergalactic prison wrestling federation. While the concept itself should be enough to garner some attention, for me it was the evolution of Jeff's art that blew my mind. Sure the stories were fun and funny, but his dedication to refining hi art, learning the tricks of the trade to be a better artist while maintaining his unique individual art style, was more than admirable. The challenge of storytelling fight scenes that used unique body pretzelling holds and that often moved at crazy quick speeds was a monumental undertaking, but Jeff figured it out. He studied, he researched and h drew and drew and drew. The end results of all that work are in part what you hold in your hands now.

Of course the art is only one part of any great comic story. As cool, slick or fun as any comic appears, without some good writing to back it up people won't come back for the rest of the story. If you've spent any time in conversation with Jeff or have read any of his previous works, you would have learned about a word that is near and dear

4

Jeff's heart; snark. In the settings of war, one would think that the kind of snark being spoken would be gritty, angry, and violent. Thankfully our lead characters, George d John, have none of those attributes so their snark is far more entertaining with a strong focus on avoiding two things, marching across the wilderness and being shot at. nowing people today it would make sense that there would be at least a few Georges and Johns in the war, so it's quite refreshing to see this alternatively accurate depiction the War of 1812.

the end of the day all of this creativity would be for naught if there wasn't someone willing to put this out into the world and promote it. I don't think Alexander Finbow, megade's maestro (or overlord, depending on your perspective), ever thought that his company would inspire and host what has been produced here, but I am glad they d. It is a testament to their flexibility and fearlessness as a publisher to print something outside of their original mandate. With continued support these comics will reach new audience of readers and show them a different take on Canadian history. It will also help to inspire the next generation of writers and artists to believe that there is still om for unique concepts and fresh styles.

Kudos to all those involved and to you as well. With an open mind and, possibly, a nice glass of scotch, this will go down rather nicely for you. Enjoy.

y Bardyla is the owner of Happy Harbor Comics
e enjoys scotch. He reads comics too.

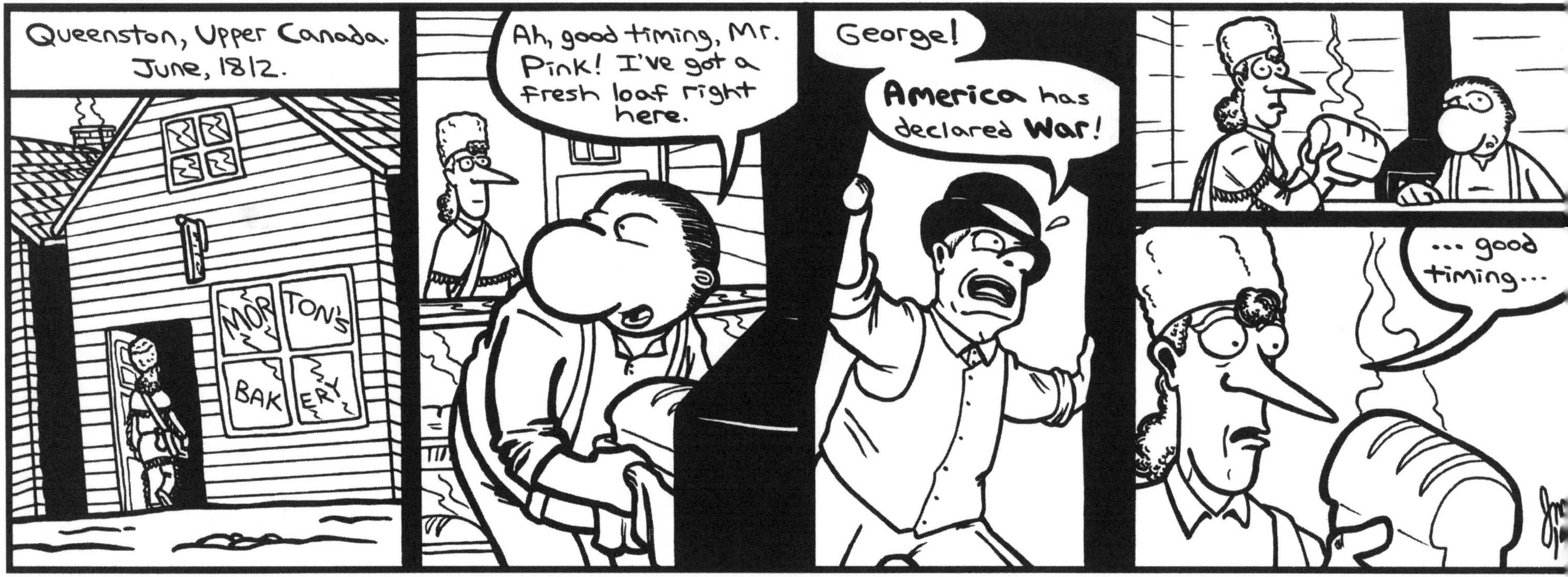
Queenston, Upper Canada.
June, 1812.
MOR TON'S
BAKERY
Ah, good timing, Mr. Pink! I've got a fresh loaf right here.
George!
America has declared War!
... good timing...

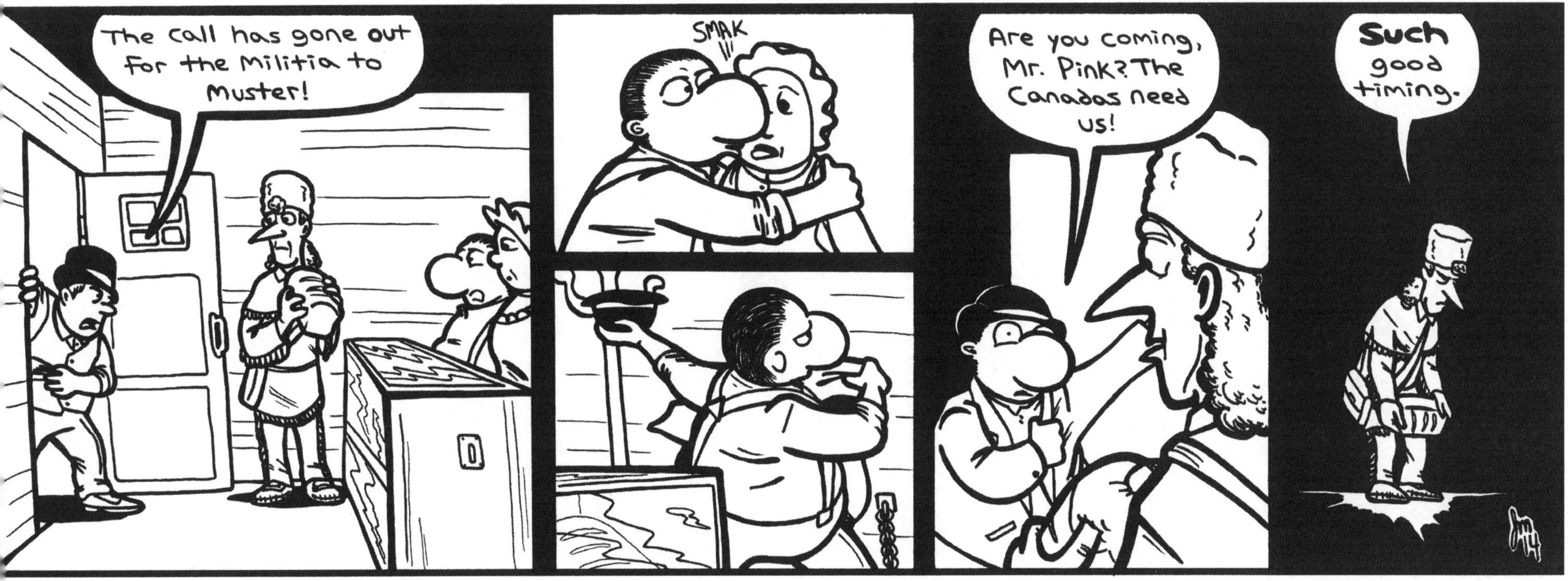
The call has gone out for the Militia to Muster!
SMAK
Are you coming, Mr. Pink? The Canadas need us!
Such good timing.

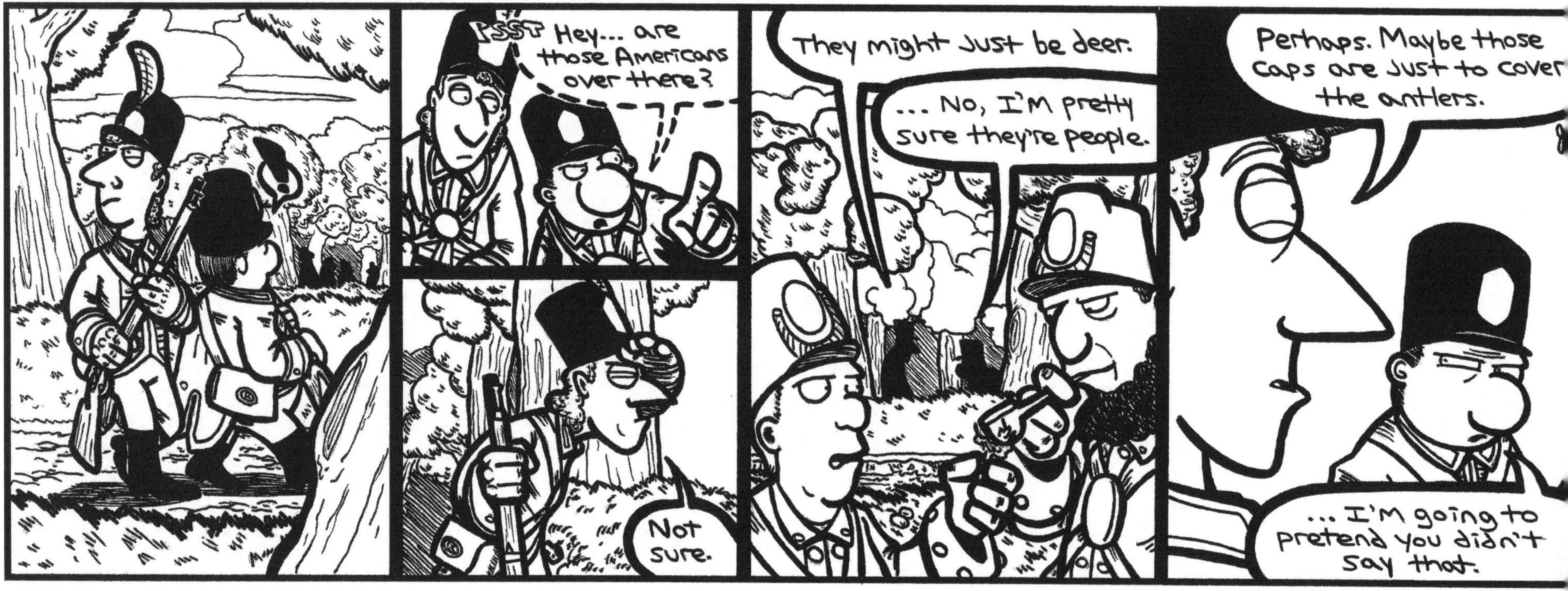
PSST
Hey... are those Americans over there?
Not sure.
They might just be deer.
... No, I'M pretty sure they're people.
Perhaps. Maybe those caps are just to cover the antlers.
... I'M going to pretend you didn't say that.

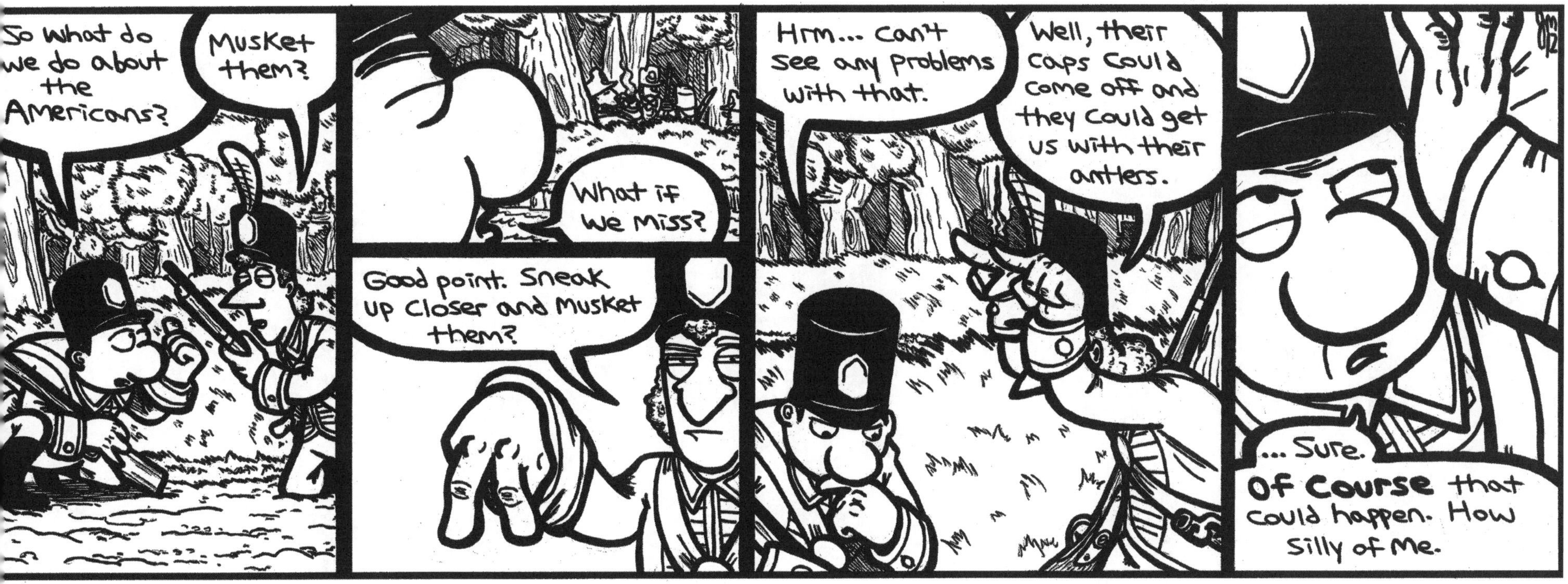
So what do we do about the Americans?
Musket them?
What if we miss?
Good point. Sneak up closer and musket them?
Hrm... can't see any problems with that.
Well, their caps could come off and they could get us with their antlers.
...Sure.
Of course that could happen. How silly of me.

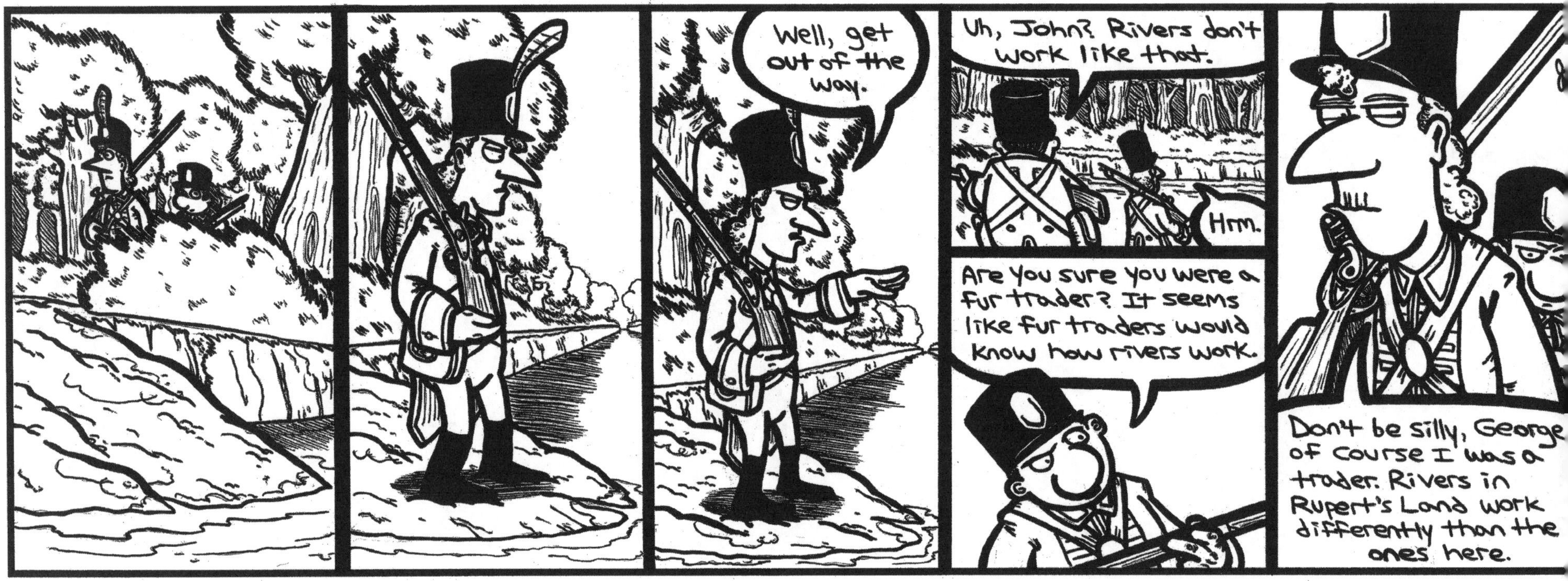

Well, get out of the way.
Uh, John? Rivers don't work like that.
Hrm.
Are you sure you were a fur trader? It seems like fur traders would know how rivers work.
Don't be silly, George of course I was a trader. Rivers in Rupert's Land work differently than the ones here.

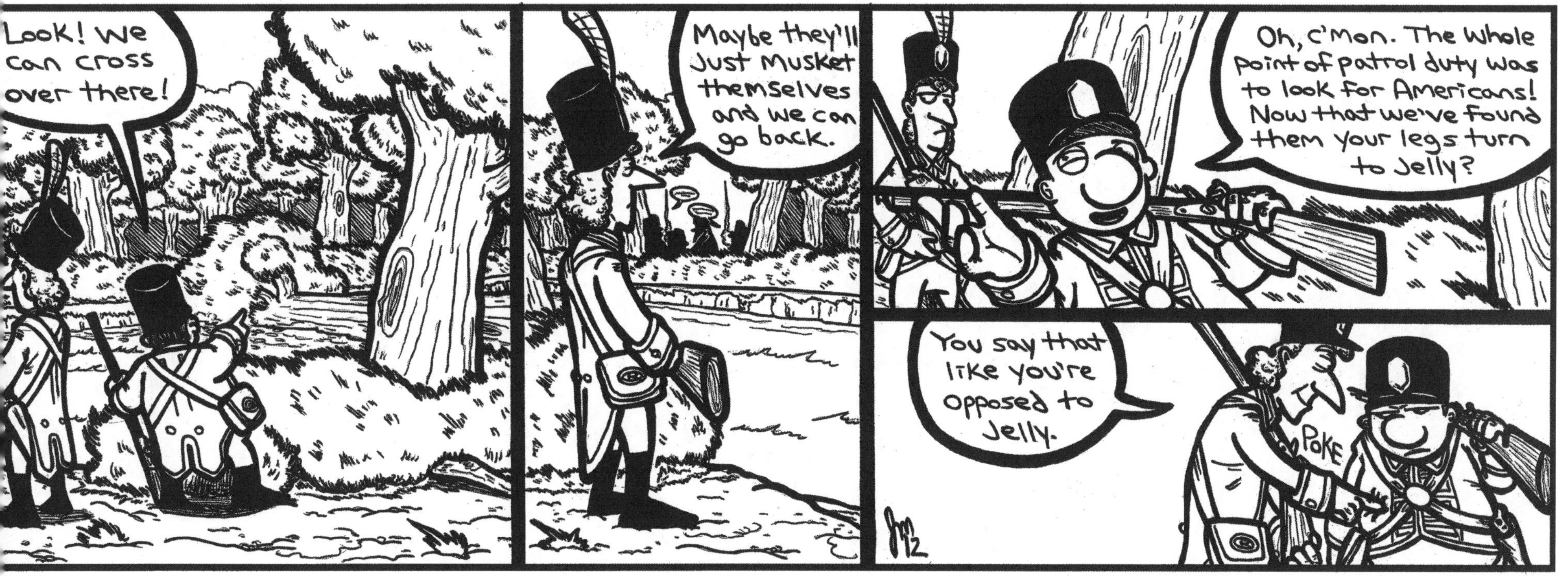
Look! We can cross over there!
Maybe they'll just musket themselves and we can go back.
Oh, c'mon. The whole point of patrol duty was to look for Americans! Now that we've found them your legs turn to Jelly?
You say that like you're opposed to Jelly.
POKE

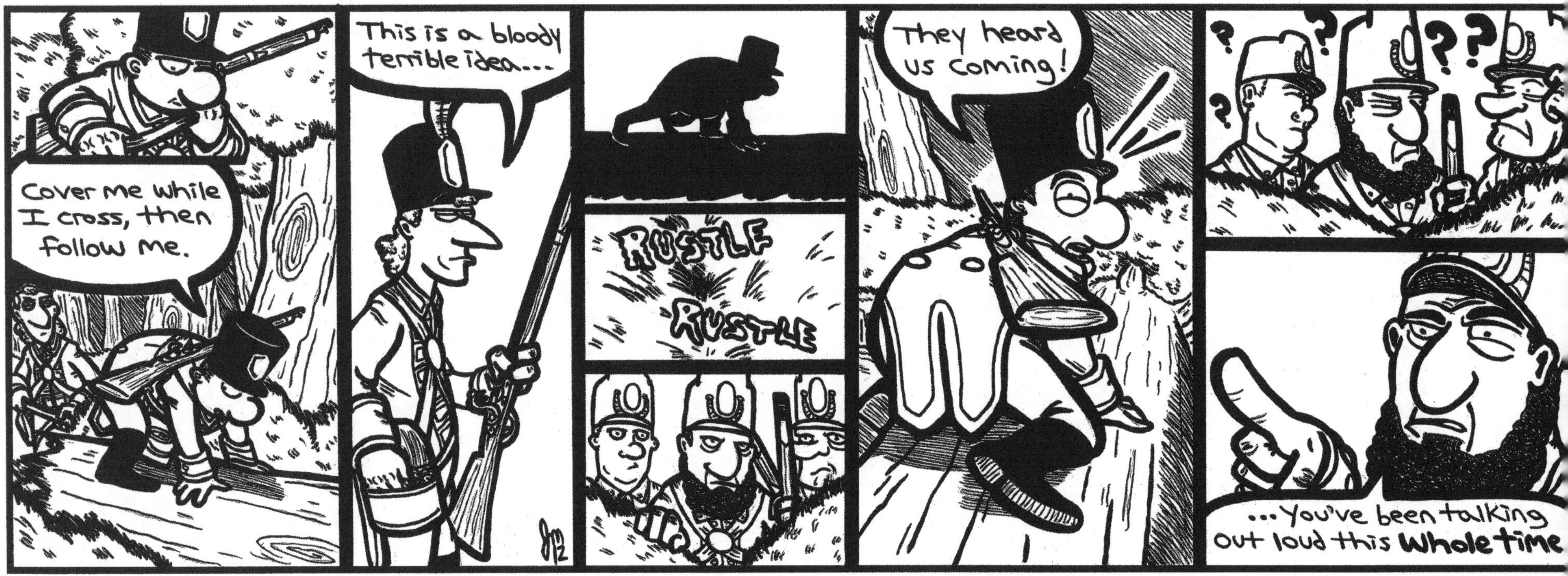
Cover me while I cross, then follow me.
This is a bloody terrible idea...
RUSTLE
RUSTLE
They heard us coming!
?
?
??
...You've been talking out loud this **Whole time**

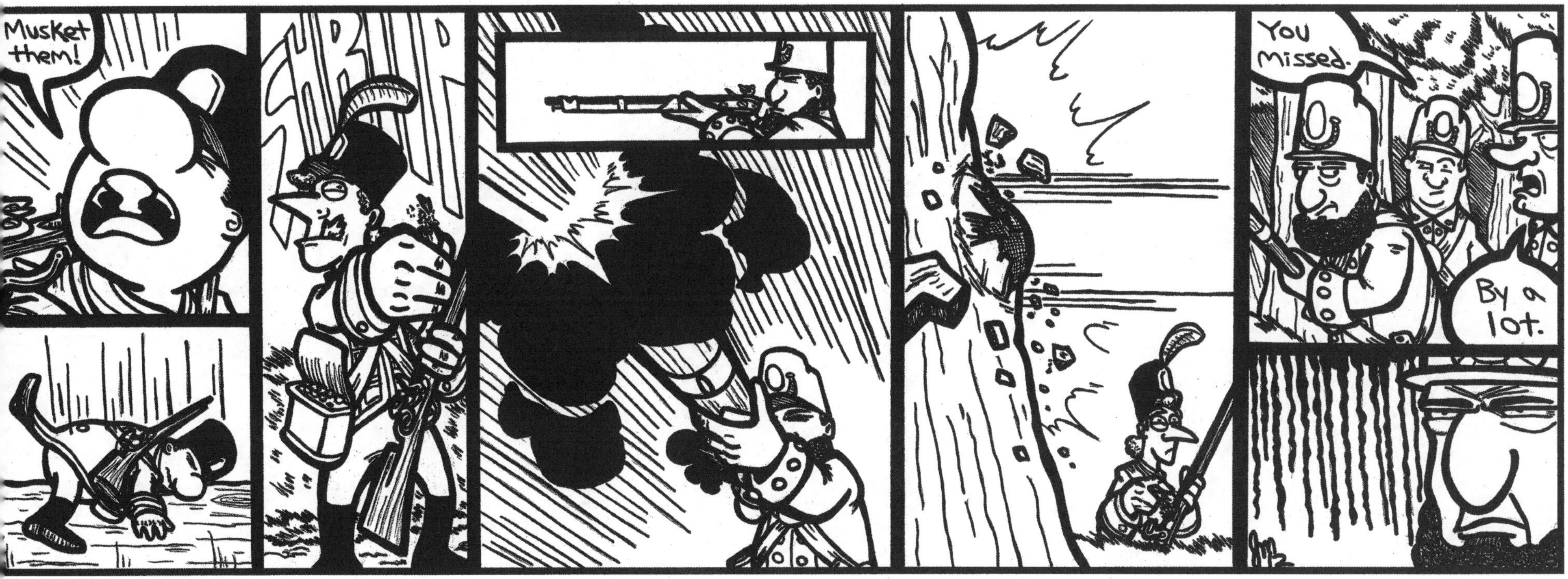
Musket them!
THRIP
You missed.
By a lot.

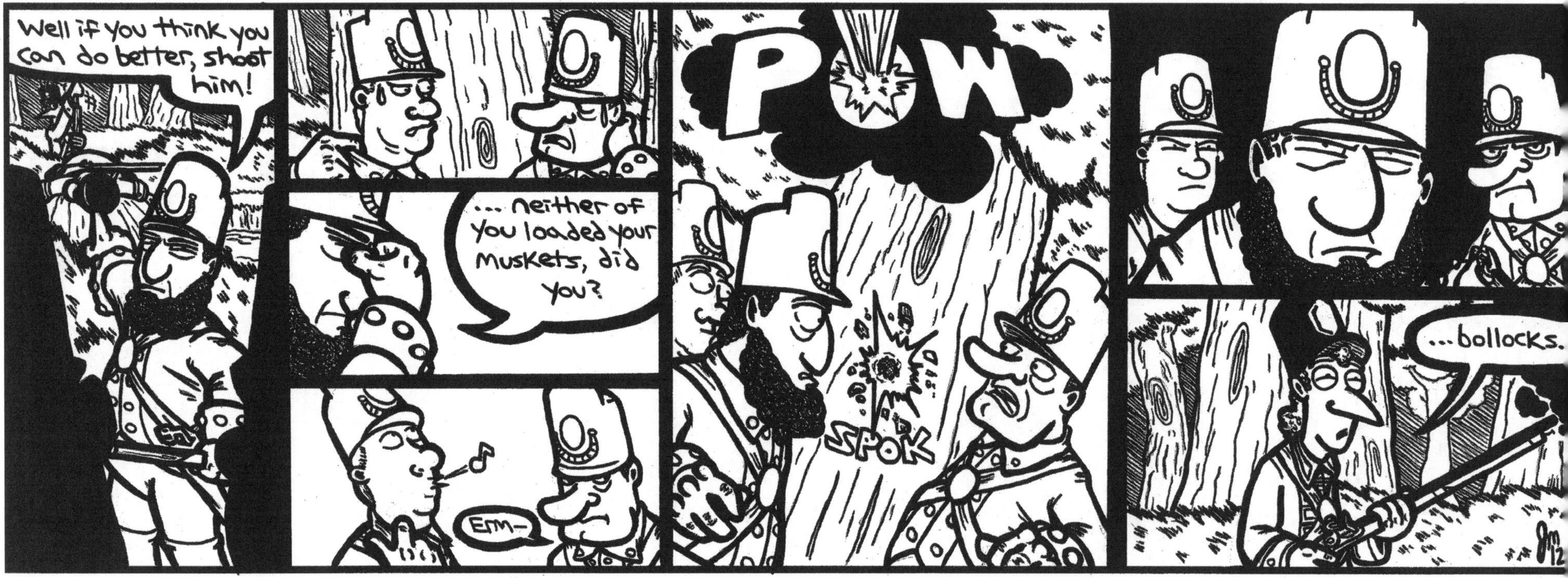

Well if you think you can do better, shoot him!
... neither of you loaded your muskets, did you?
Erm—
POW
SPOK
...bollocks.

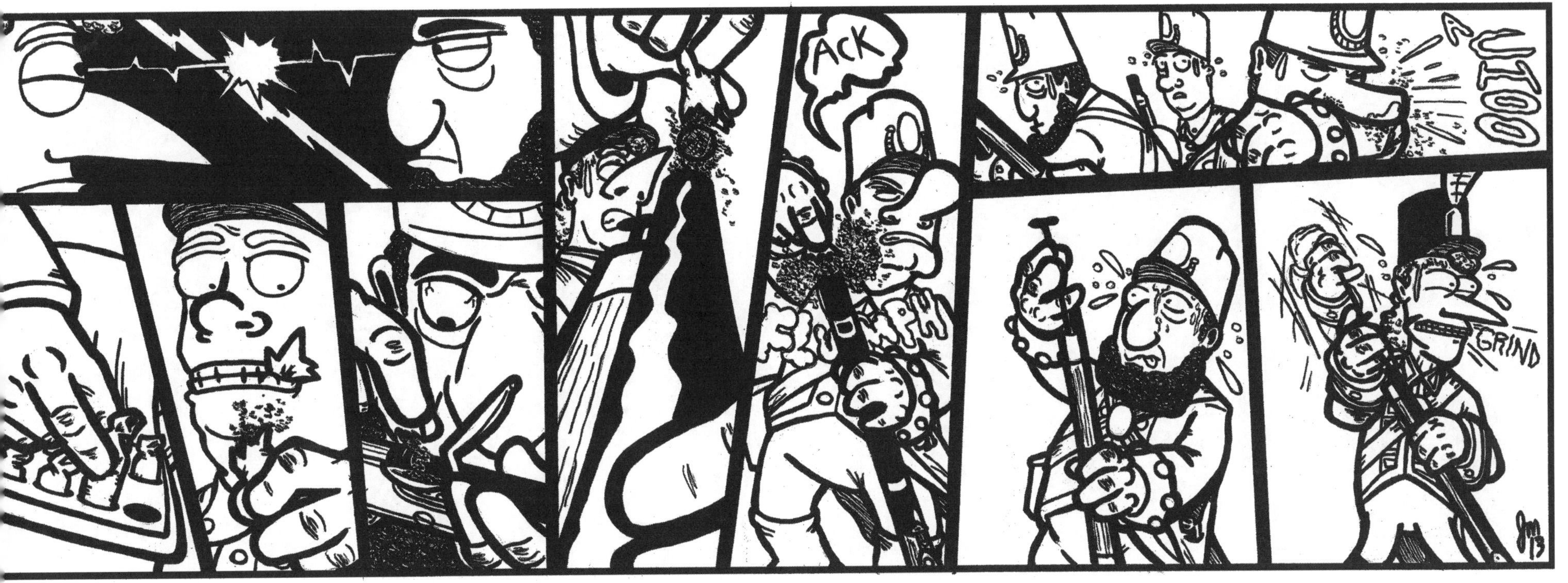
ACK
GRIND

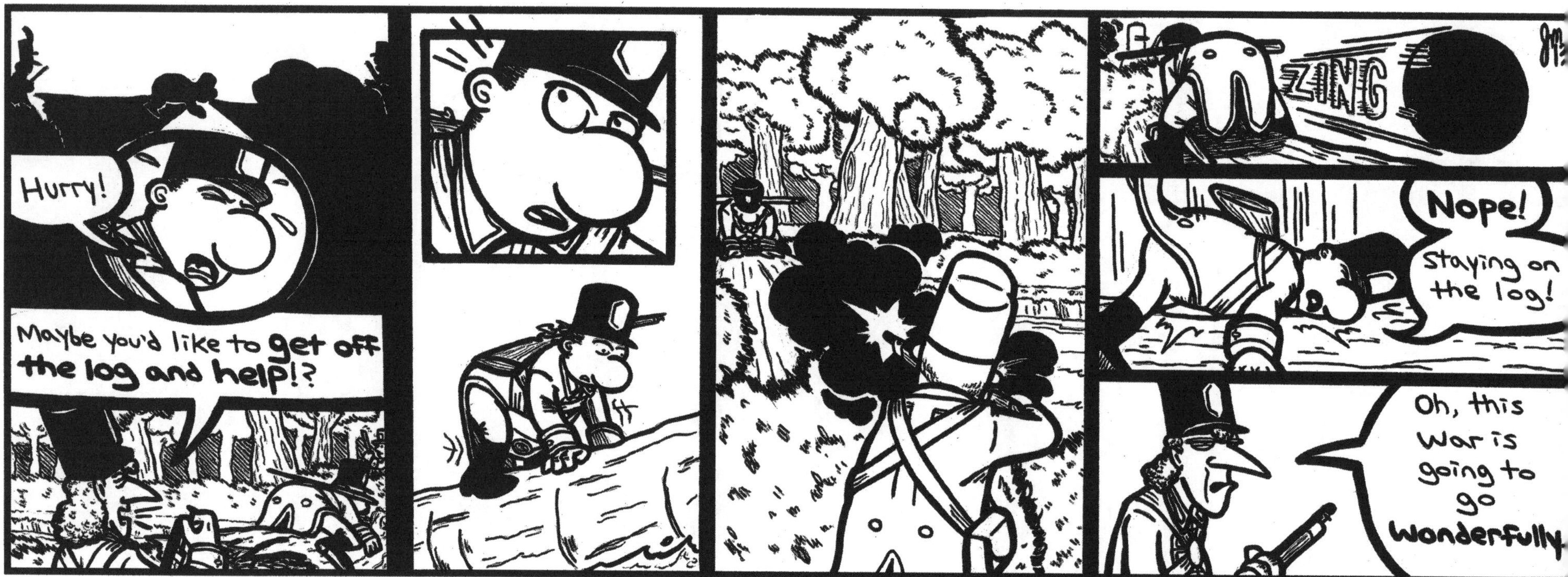
Hurry!
Maybe you'd like to get off the log and help!?
ZING
Nope! Staying on the log!
Oh, this war is going to go wonderfully.

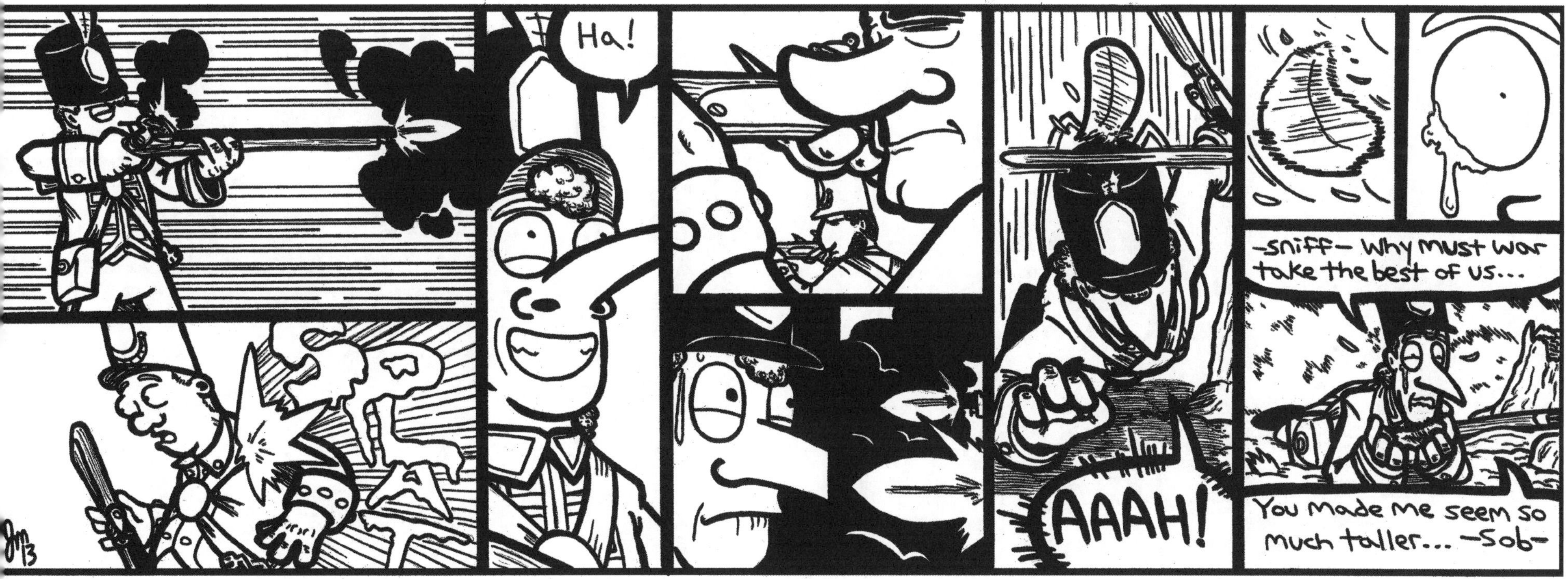
Ha!
AAAH!
-sniff- Why must war take the best of us...
You made me seem so much taller... -Sob-

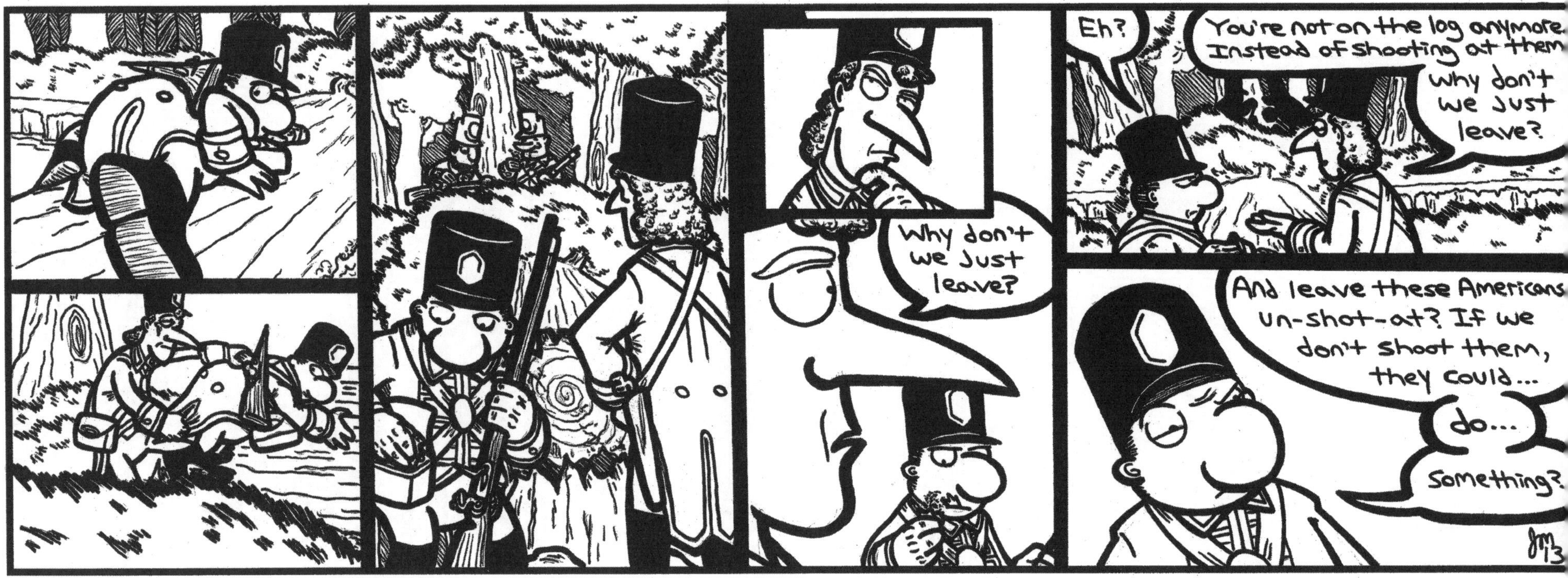
Why don't we just leave?
Eh?
You're not on the log anymore. Instead of shooting at them why don't we just leave?
And leave these Americans un-shot-at? If we don't shoot them, they could...
do...
something?
JM 13

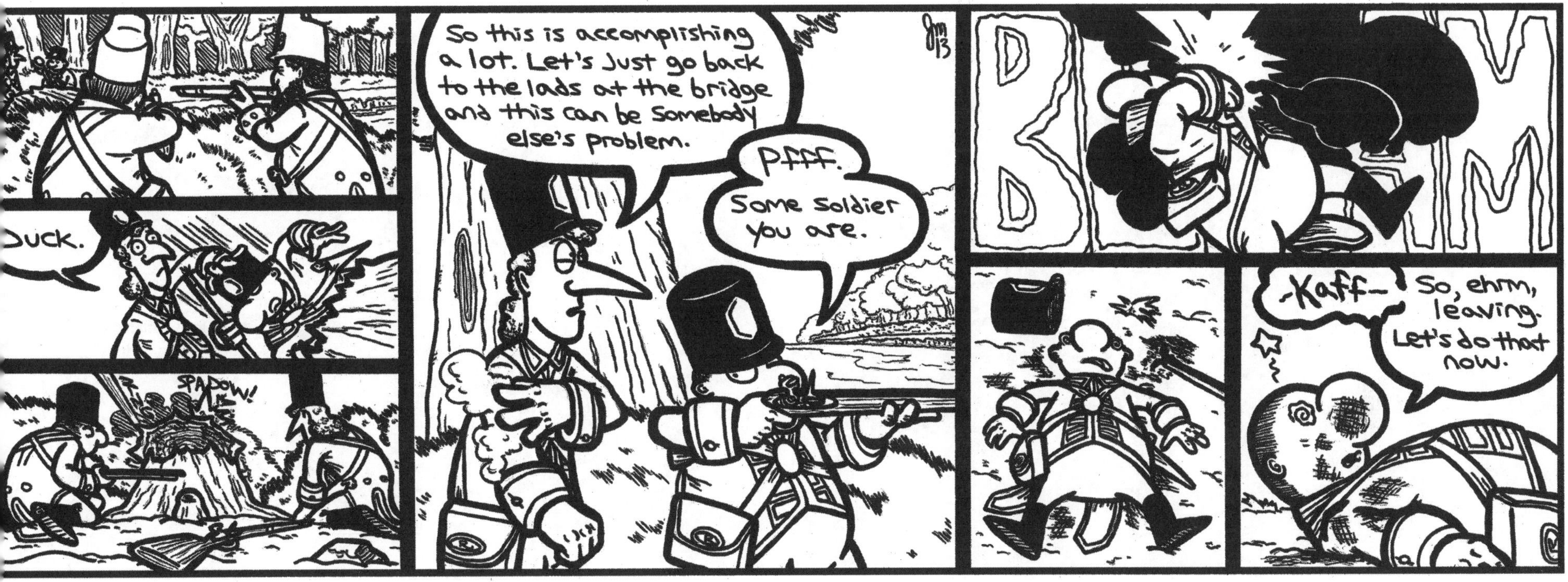

Duck.
SPADOW!
So this is accomplishing a lot. Let's just go back to the lads at the bridge and this can be somebody else's problem.
Pfff.
Some soldier you are.
-Kaff-
So, ehm, leaving. Let's do that now.

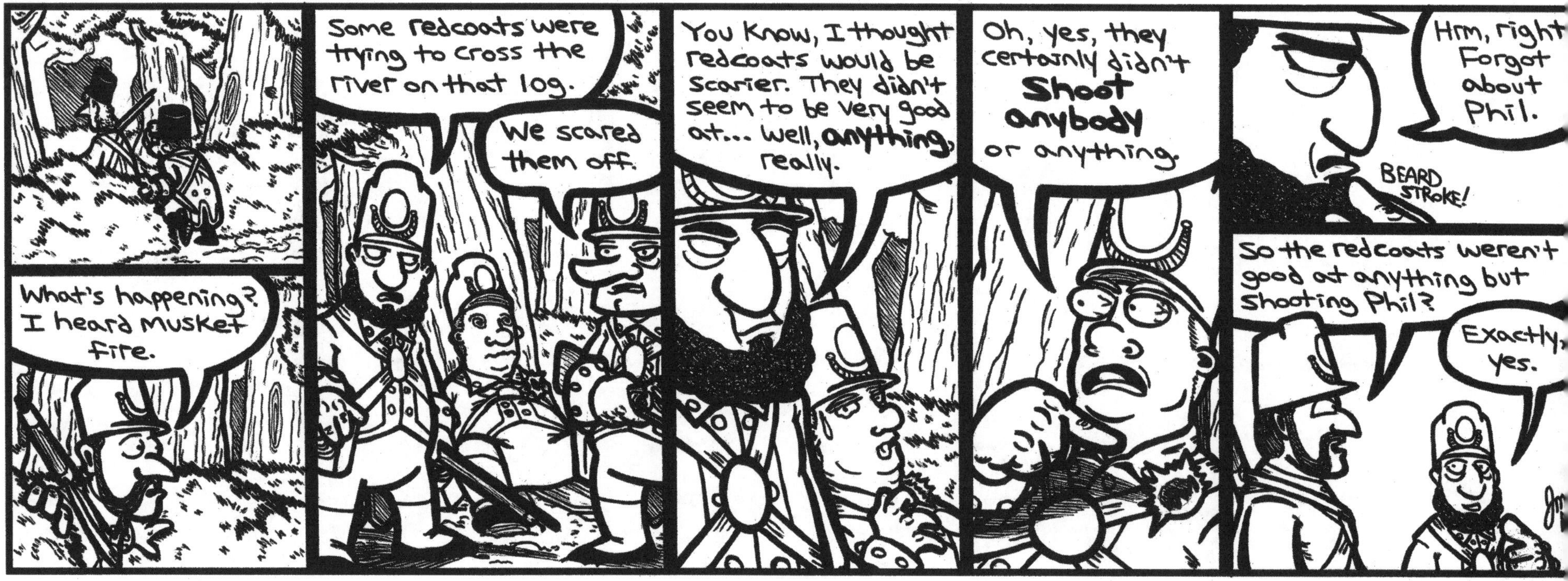
What's happening? I heard musket fire.
Some redcoats were trying to cross the river on that log.
We scared them off.
You know, I thought redcoats would be scarier. They didn't seem to be very good at... well, anything, really.
Oh, yes, they certainly didn't shoot anybody or anything.
Hrm, right. Forgot about Phil.
BEARD STROKE!
So the redcoats weren't good at anything but shooting Phil?
Exactly, yes.

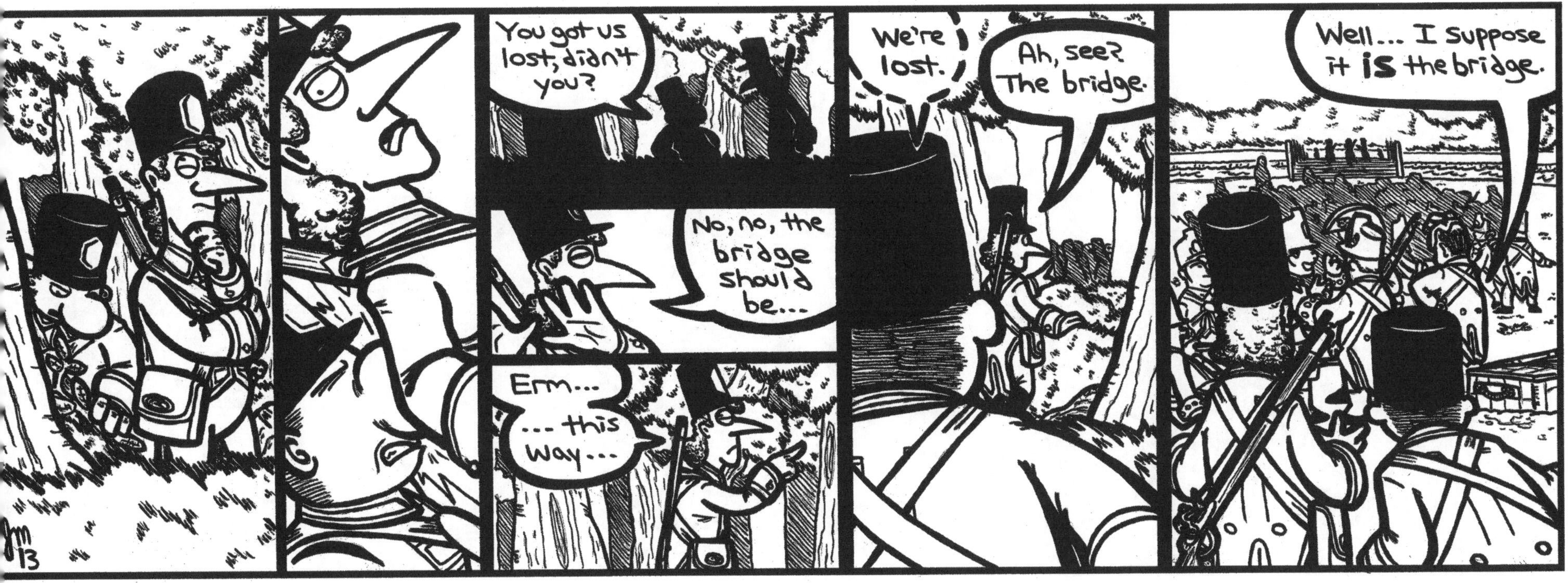
Jm 13
You got us lost, didn't you?
No, no, the bridge should be...
Erm...
... this way...
We're lost.
Ah, see? The bridge.
Well... I suppose it IS the bridge.

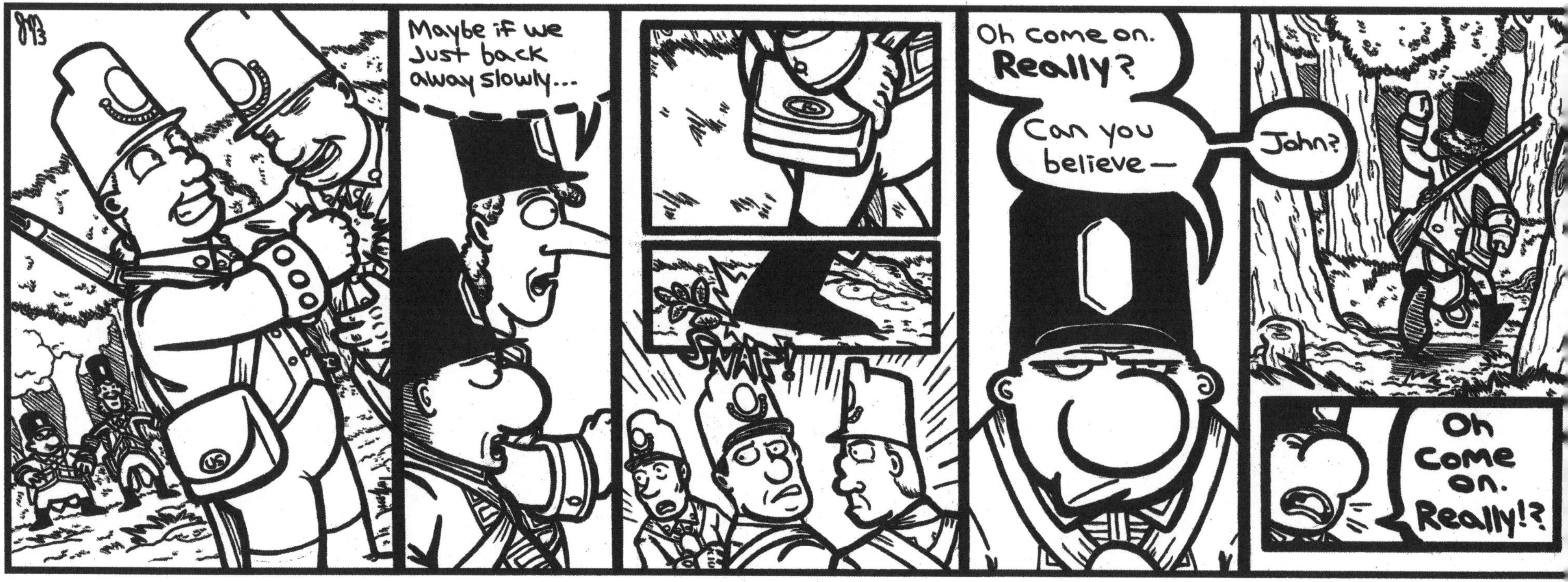
JM 13
Maybe if we Just back away slowly...
SNAP!
Oh come on. Really?
Can you believe—
John?
Oh Come on. Really!?

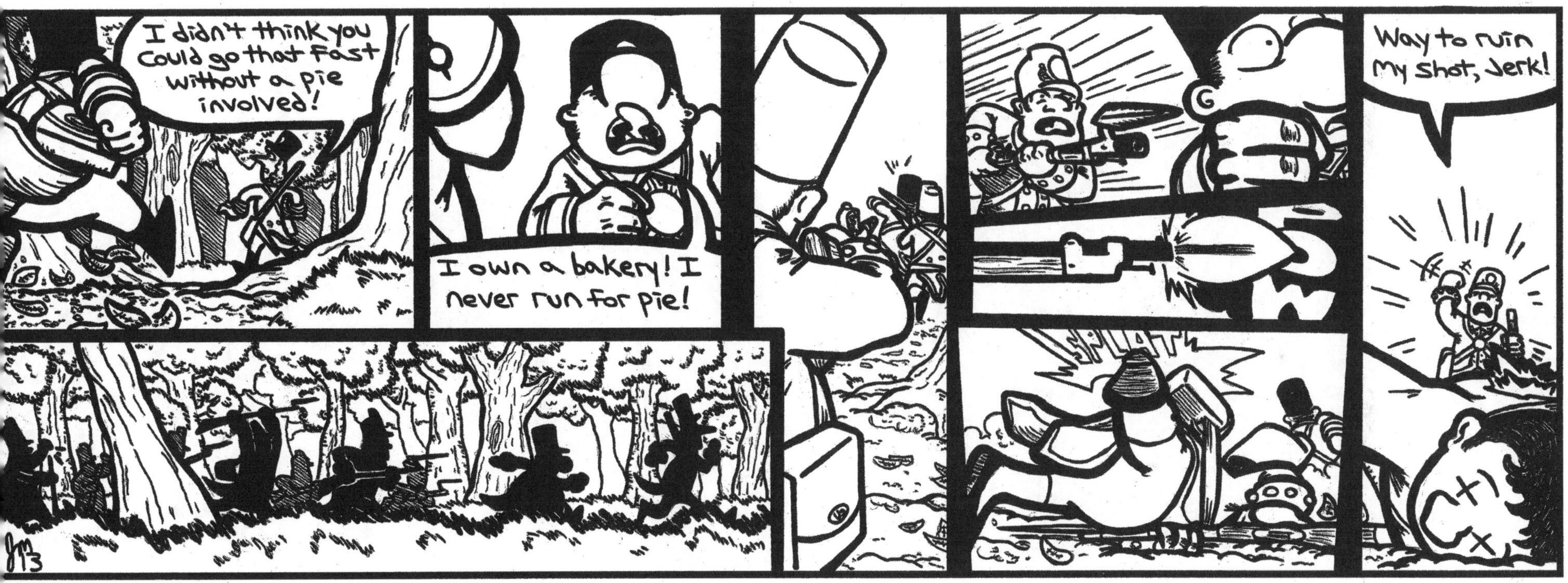
I didn't think you could go that fast without a pie involved!
I own a bakery! I never run for pie!
Way to ruin my shot, Jerk!

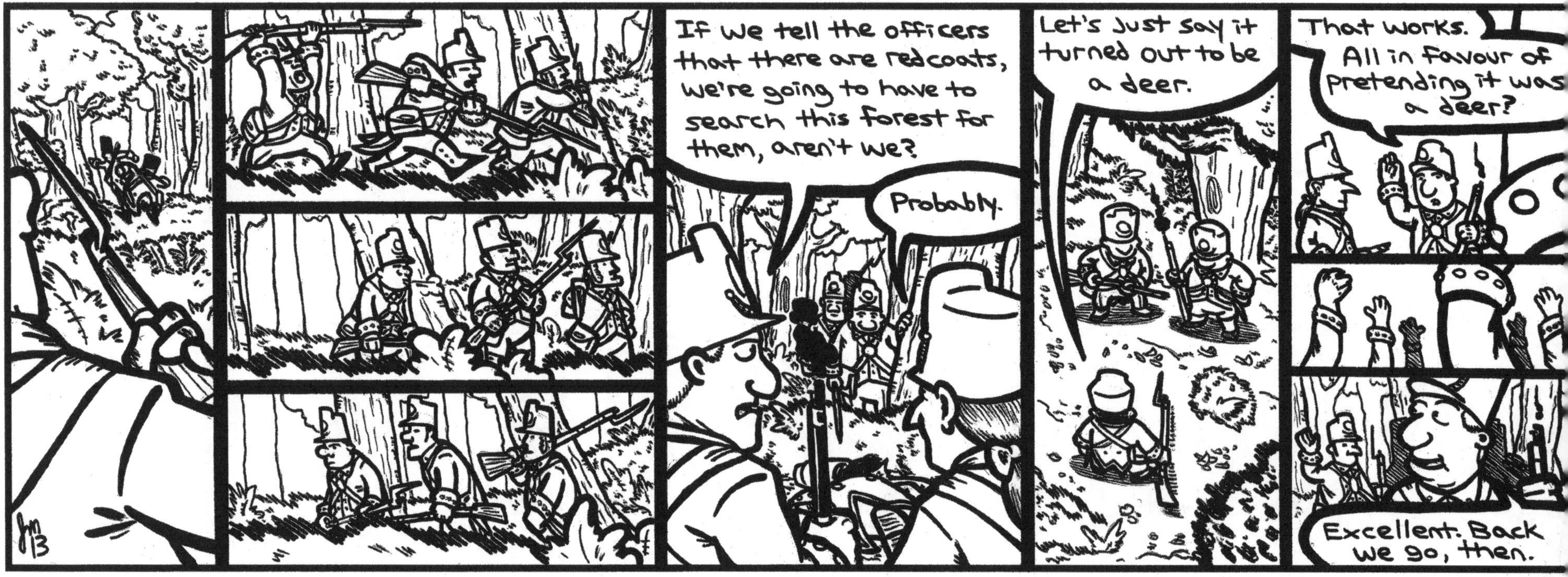
If we tell the officers that there are redcoats, we're going to have to search this forest for them, aren't we?
Probably.
Let's just say it turned out to be a deer.
That works. All in favour of pretending it was a deer?
Excellent. Back we go, then.

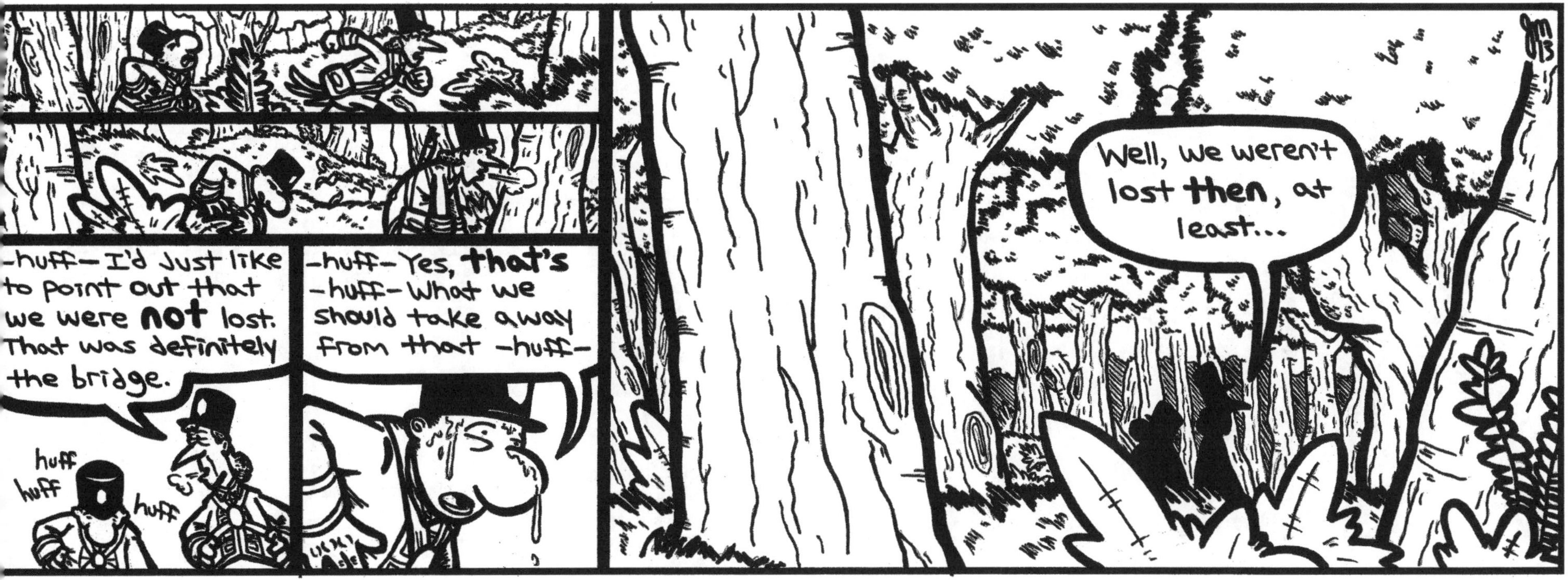
-huff- I'd just like to point out that we were **not** lost. That was definitely the bridge.
huff huff
huff
-huff- Yes, **that's** -huff- what we should take away from that -huff-
Well, we weren't lost **then**, at least...

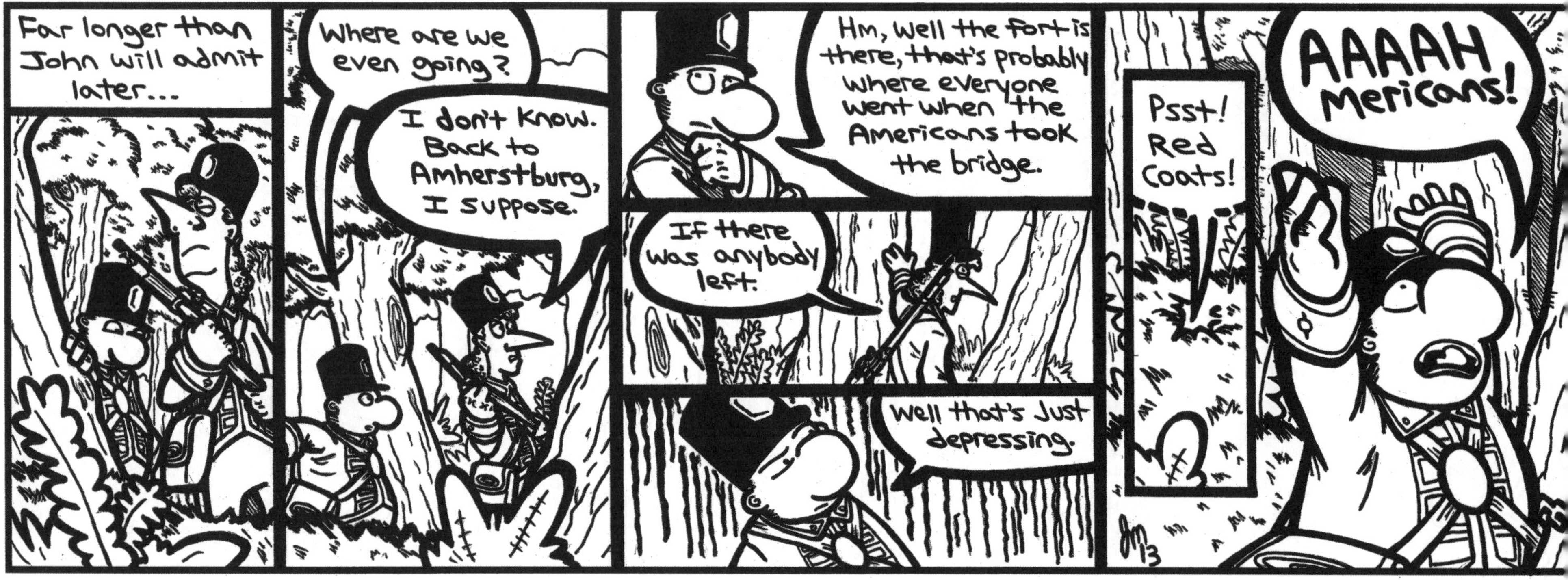
Far longer than John will admit later...
Where are we even going?
I don't know. Back to Amherstburg, I suppose.
Hm, well the fort is there, that's probably where everyone went when the Americans took the bridge.
If there was anybody left.
Well that's just depressing.
Psst! Red Coats!
AAAAH Mericans!

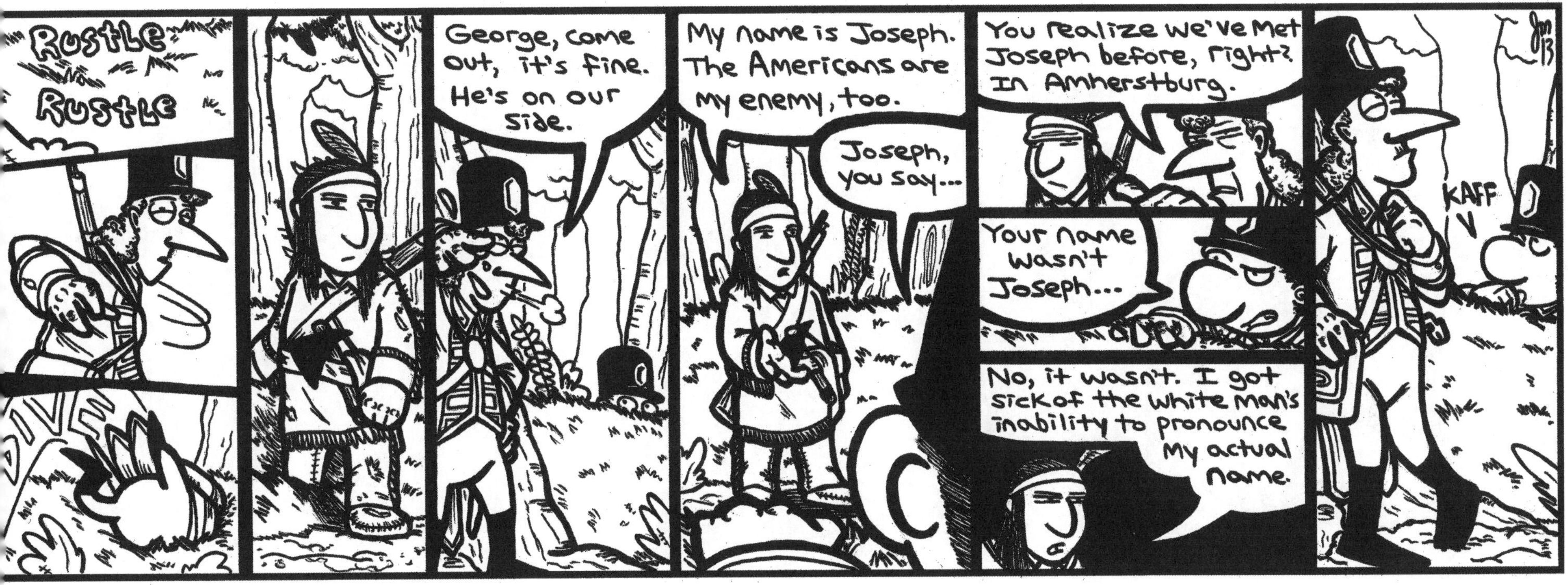

Rustle
Rustle
George, come out, it's fine. He's on our side.
My name is Joseph. The Americans are my enemy, too.
Joseph, you say...
You realize we've met Joseph before, right? In Amherstburg.
Your name wasn't Joseph...
No, it wasn't. I got sick of the white man's inability to pronounce my actual name.
KAFF

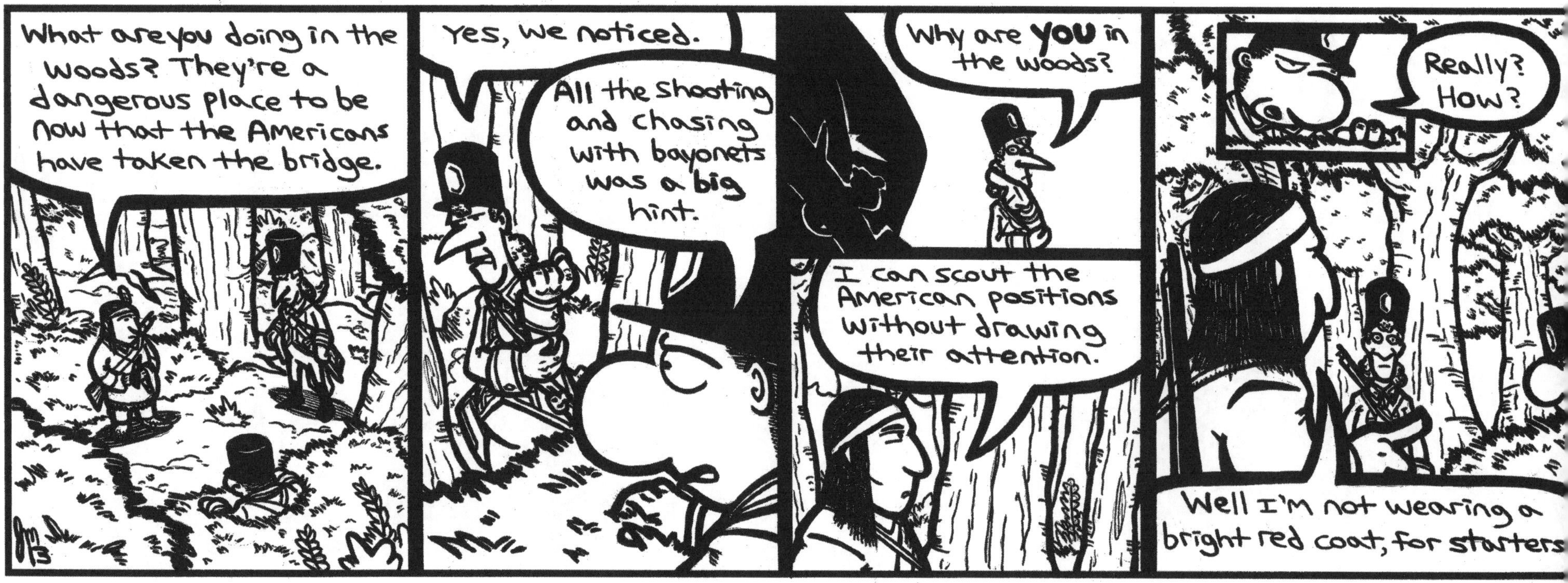
What are you doing in the woods? They're a dangerous place to be now that the Americans have taken the bridge.
Yes, we noticed.
All the shooting and chasing with bayonets was a big hint.
Why are YOU in the woods?
I can scout the American positions without drawing their attention.
Really? How?
Well I'm not wearing a bright red coat, for starters

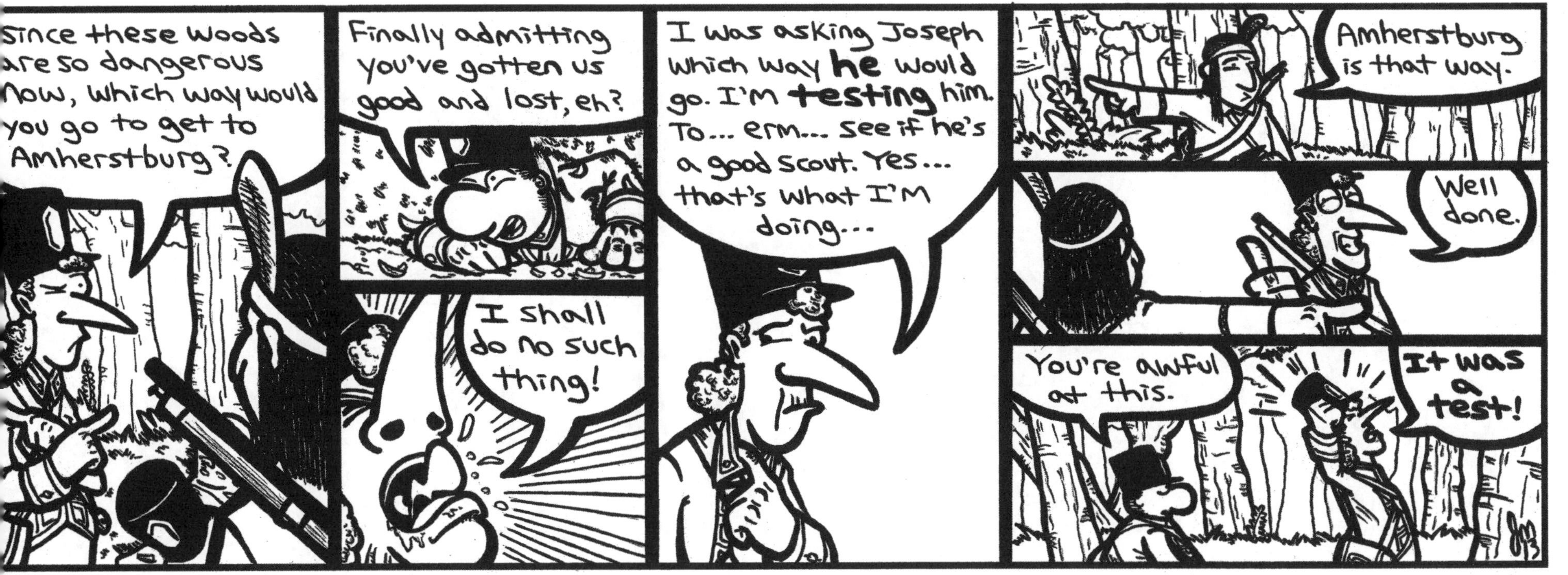
Since these woods are so dangerous now, which way would you go to get to Amherstburg?
Finally admitting you've gotten us good and lost, eh?
I shall do no such thing!
I was asking Joseph which way **he** would go. I'm **testing** him. To... erm... see if he's a good scout. Yes... that's what I'm doing...
Amherstburg is that way.
Well done.
You're awful at this.
It was a test!

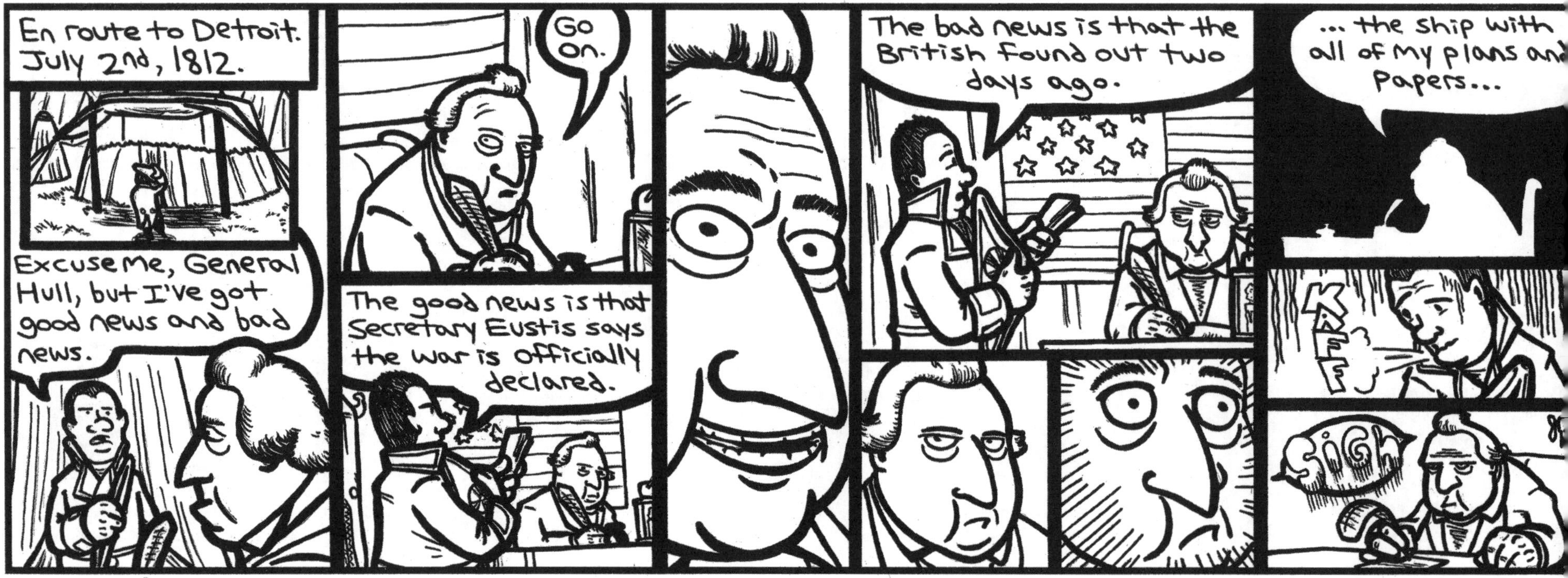
En route to Detroit. July 2nd, 1812.
Excuse me, General Hull, but I've got good news and bad news.
Go on.
The good news is that Secretary Eustis says the war is officially declared.
The bad news is that the British found out two days ago.
... the ship with all of my plans and papers...
KAFF
Sigh

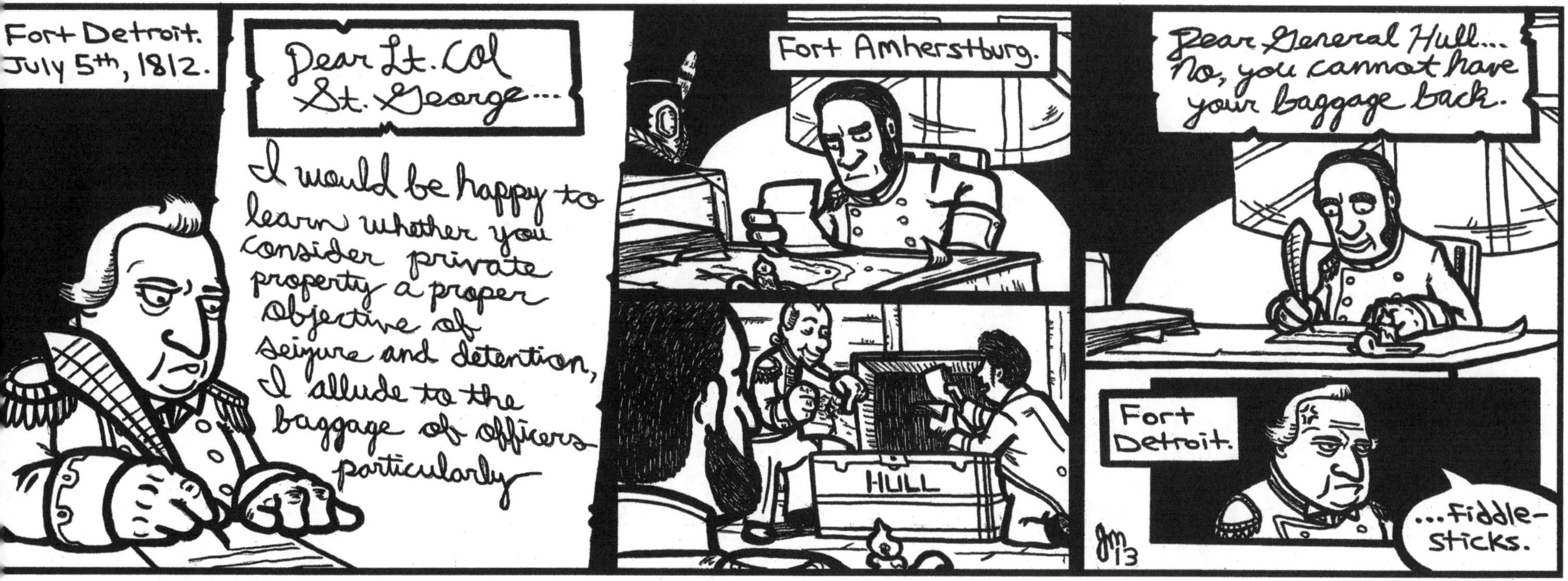
Fort Detroit. July 5th, 1812.
Dear Lt. Col St. George...
I would be happy to learn whether you consider private property a proper objective of seizure and detention, I allude to the baggage of officers particularly
Fort Amherstburg.
HULL
Dear General Hull... No, you cannot have your baggage back.
Fort Detroit.
...fiddle-sticks.
JM 13

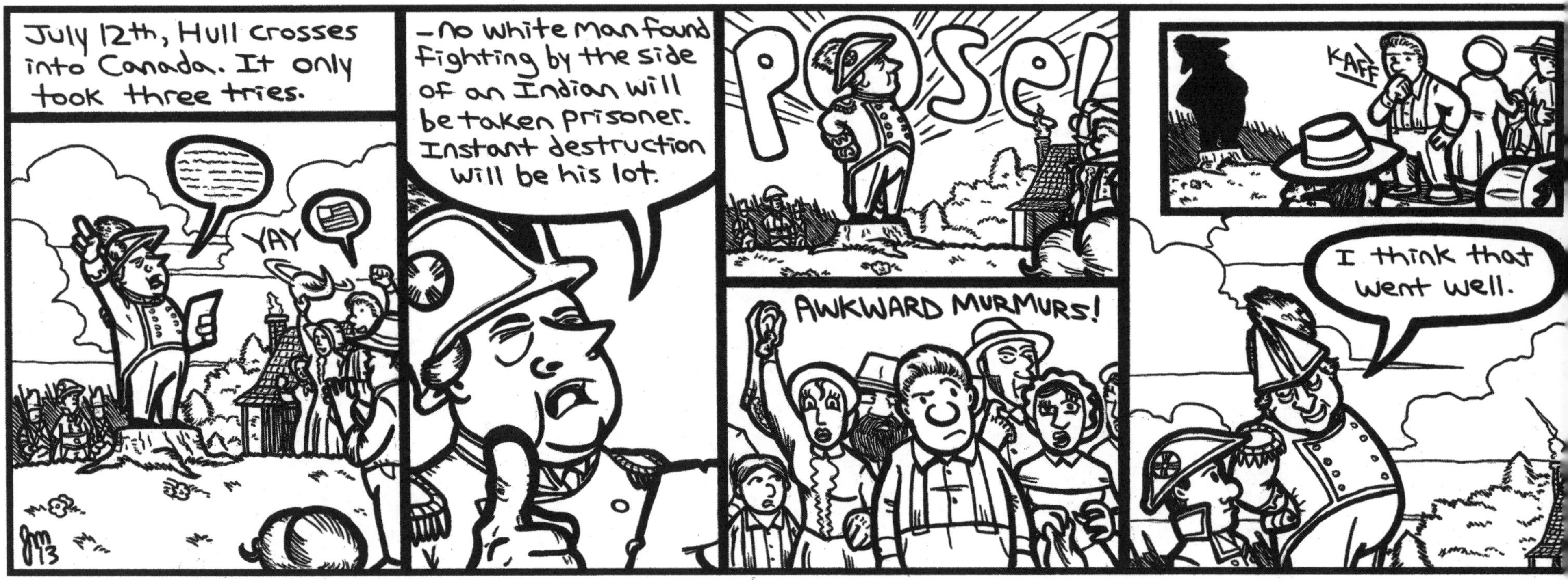

July 12th, Hull crosses into Canada. It only took three tries.
YAY
—No white man found fighting by the side of an Indian will be taken prisoner. Instant destruction will be his lot.
POSE!
AWKWARD MURMURS!
KAFF
I think that went well.

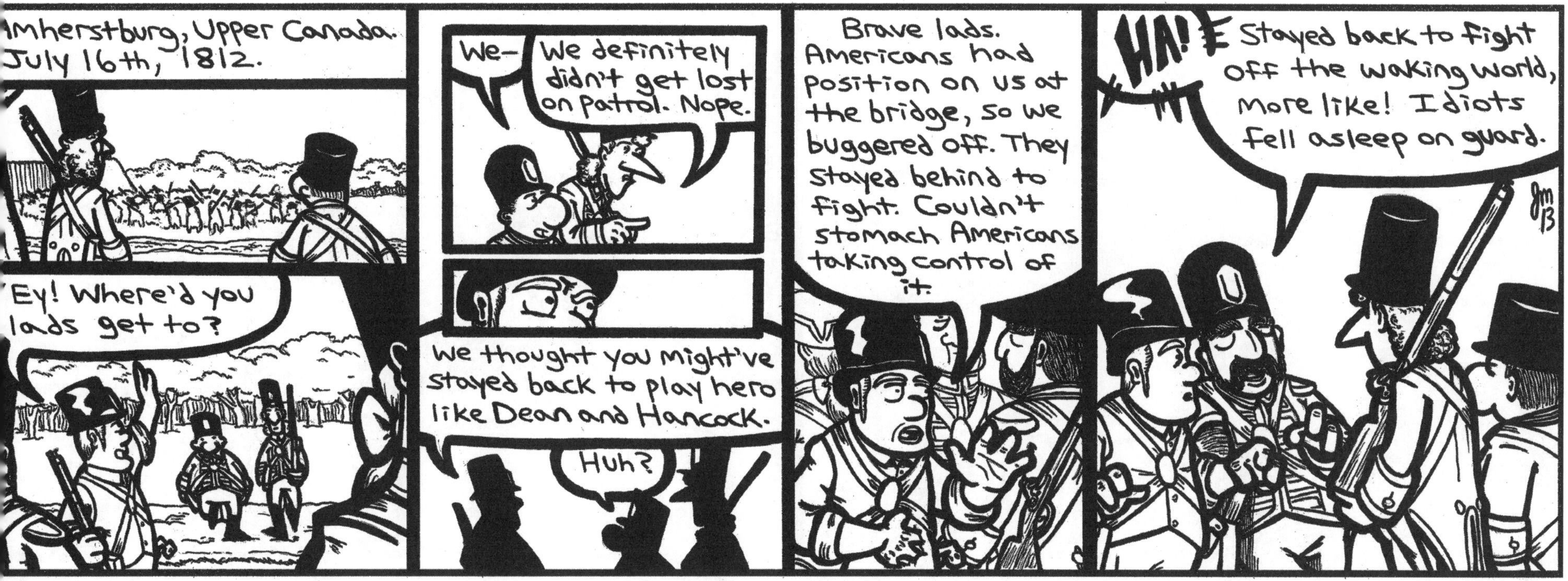
Amherstburg, Upper Canada.
July 16th, 1812.
Ey! Where'd you lads get to?
We–
We definitely didn't get lost on patrol. Nope.
We thought you might've stayed back to play hero like Dean and Hancock.
Huh?
Brave lads. Americans had position on us at the bridge, so we buggered off. They stayed behind to fight. Couldn't stomach Americans taking control of it.
HA!
Stayed back to fight off the waking world, more like! Idiots fell asleep on guard.
JM 13

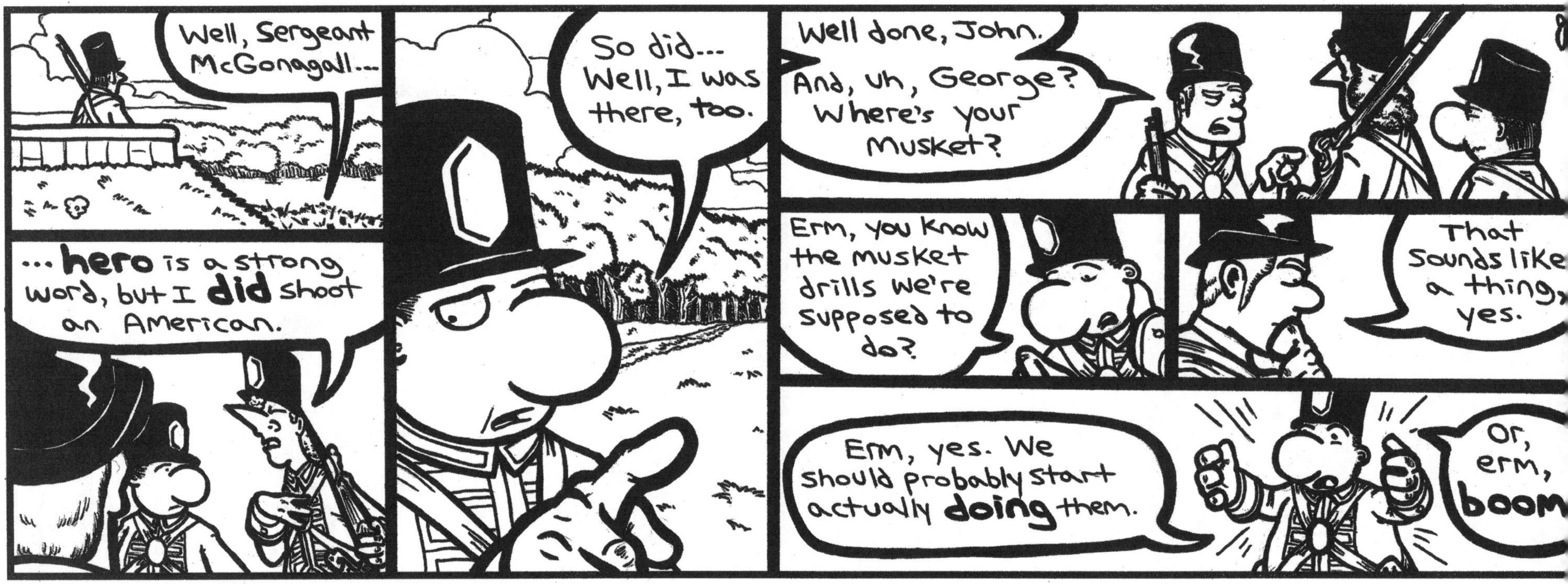
Well, Sergeant McGonagall...
...hero is a strong word, but I did shoot an American.
So did... Well, I was there, too.
Well done, John.
And, uh, George? Where's your Musket?
Erm, you know the musket drills we're supposed to do?
That sounds like a thing, yes.
Erm, yes. We should probably start actually doing them.
Or, erm, boom

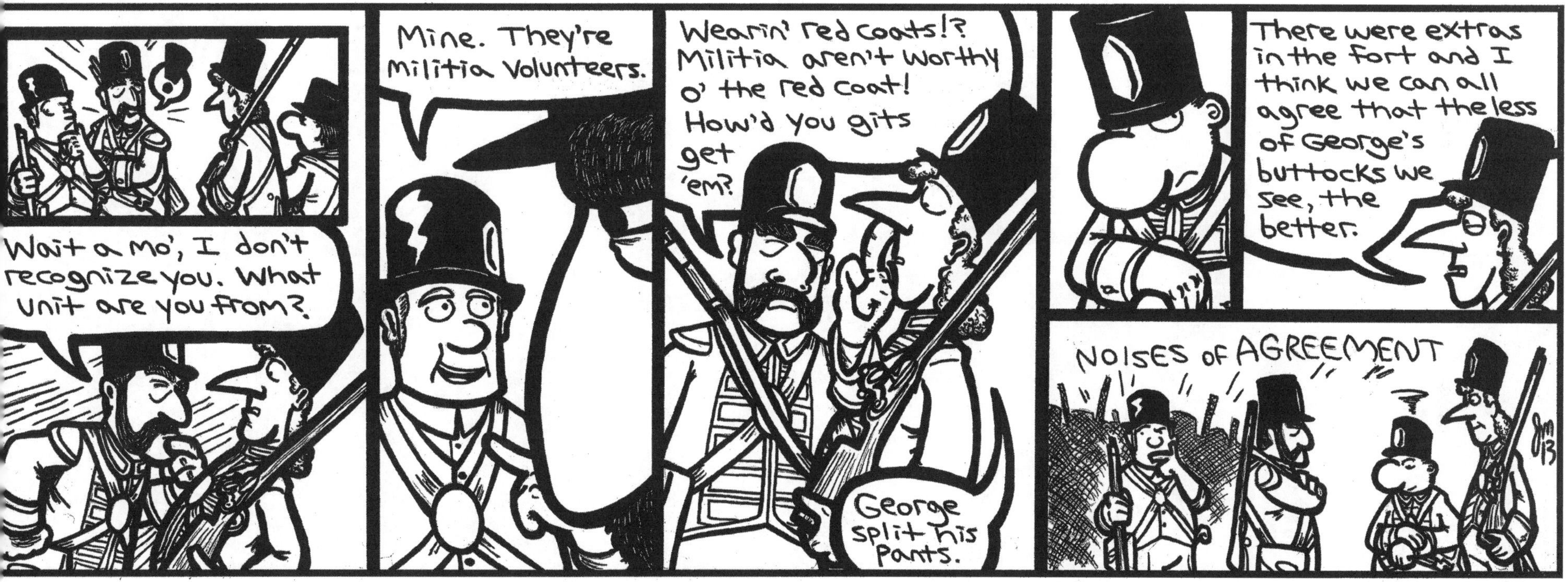
Wait a mo', I don't recognize you. What unit are you from?
Mine. They're militia volunteers.
Wearin' red coats!? Militia aren't worthy o' the red coat! How'd you gits get 'em?
George split his pants.
There were extras in the fort and I think we can all agree that the less of George's buttocks we see, the better.
NOISES OF AGREEMENT

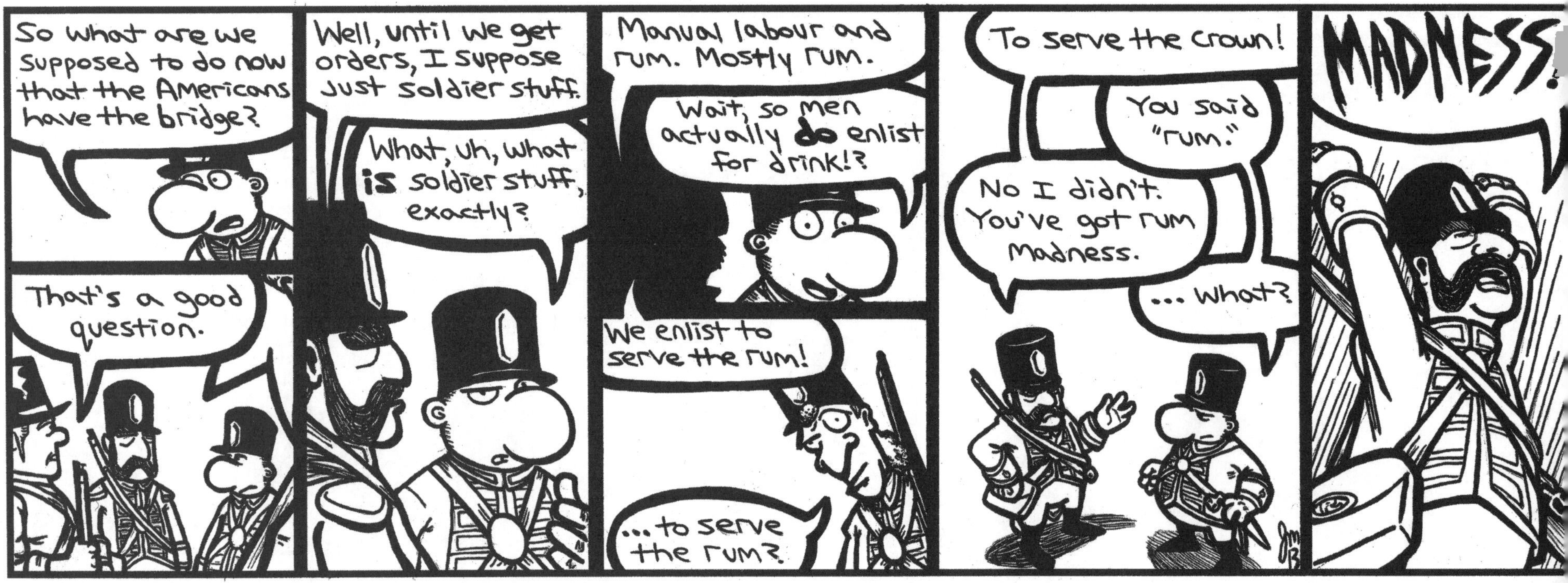
So what are we supposed to do now that the Americans have the bridge?
That's a good question.
Well, until we get orders, I suppose just soldier stuff.
What, uh, what **is** soldier stuff, exactly?
Manual labour and rum. Mostly rum.
Wait, so men actually **do** enlist for drink!?
We enlist to serve the rum!
...to serve the rum?
To serve the crown!
You said "rum."
No I didn't. You've got rum Madness.
...what?
MADNESS!

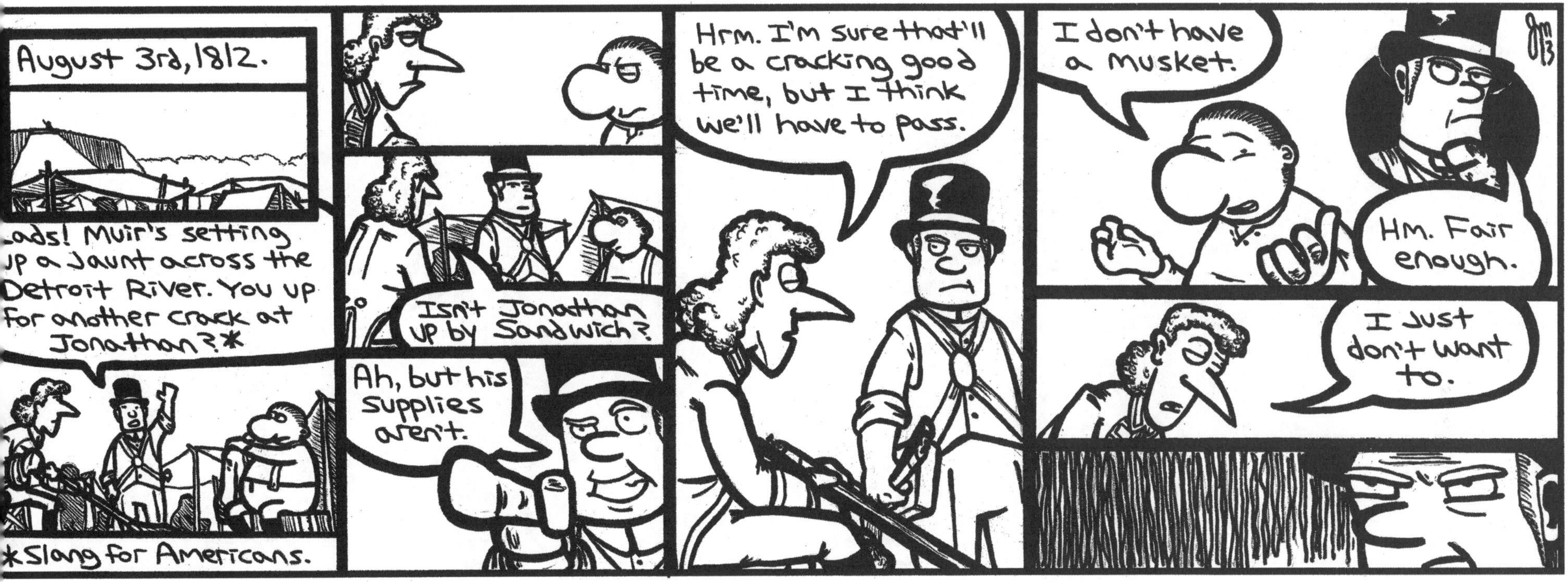
August 3rd, 1812.
Lads! Muir's setting up a jaunt across the Detroit River. You up for another crack at Jonathan?*
*Slang for Americans.
Isn't Jonathan up by Sandwich?
Ah, but his supplies aren't.
Hrm. I'm sure that'll be a cracking good time, but I think we'll have to pass.
I don't have a musket.
Hm. Fair enough.
I just don't want to.

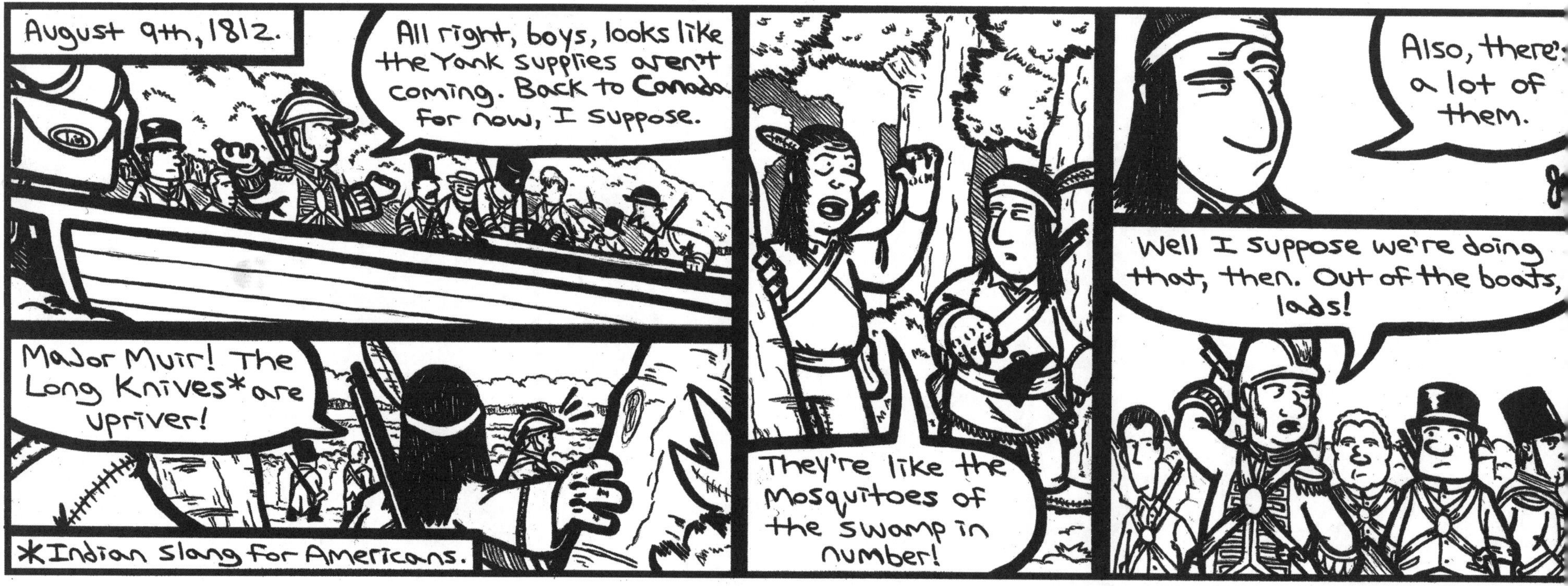
August 9th, 1812.
All right, boys, looks like the Yank supplies aren't coming. Back to Canada for now, I suppose.
Major Muir! The Long Knives* are upriver!
*Indian slang for Americans.
They're like the Mosquitoes of the swamp in number!
Also, there's a lot of them.
Well I suppose we're doing that, then. Out of the boats, lads!

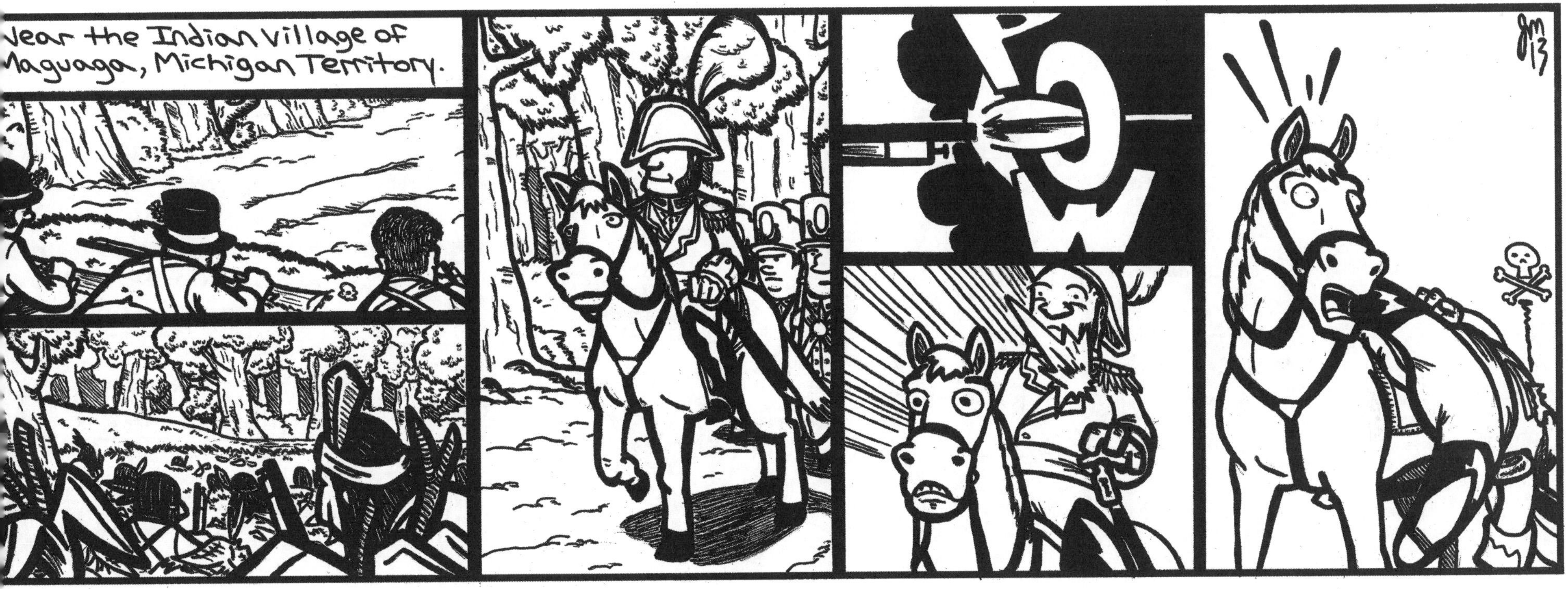
Near the Indian village of
Maguaga, Michigan Territory.
POW

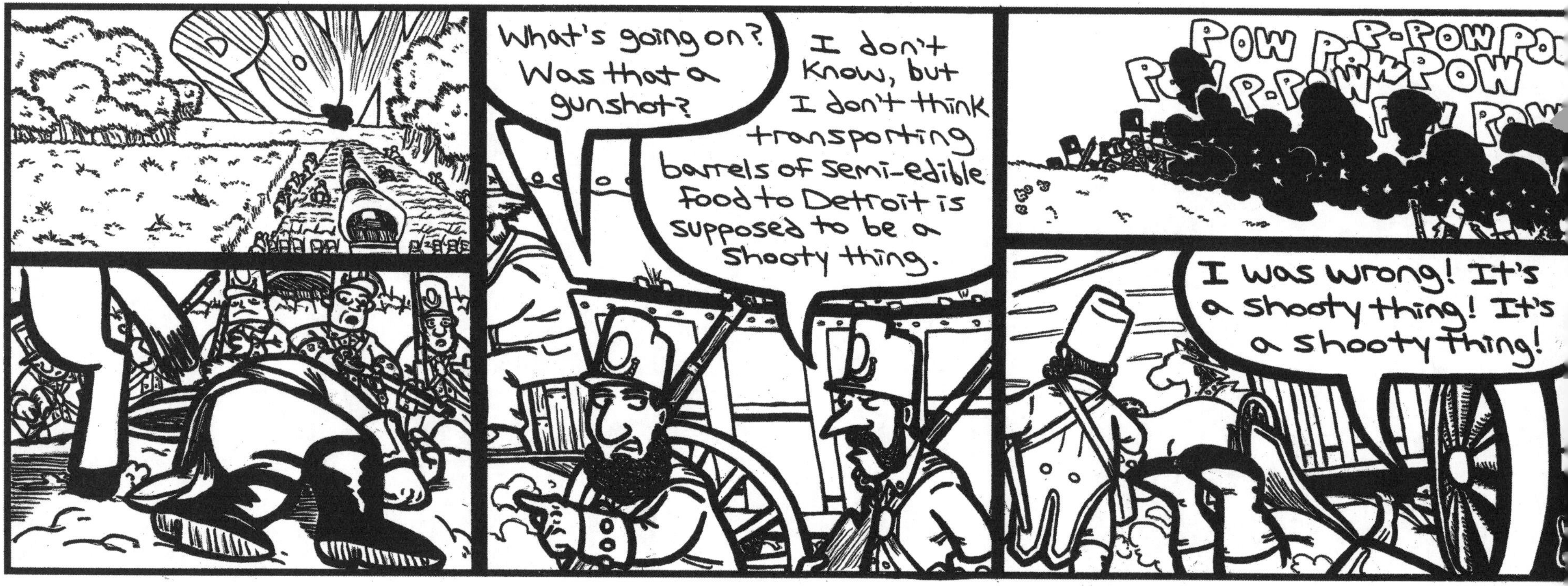
What's going on? Was that a gunshot?
I don't know, but I don't think transporting barrels of semi-edible food to Detroit is supposed to be a shooty thing.
POW P-POW POW
I was wrong! It's a shooty thing! It's a shooty thing!

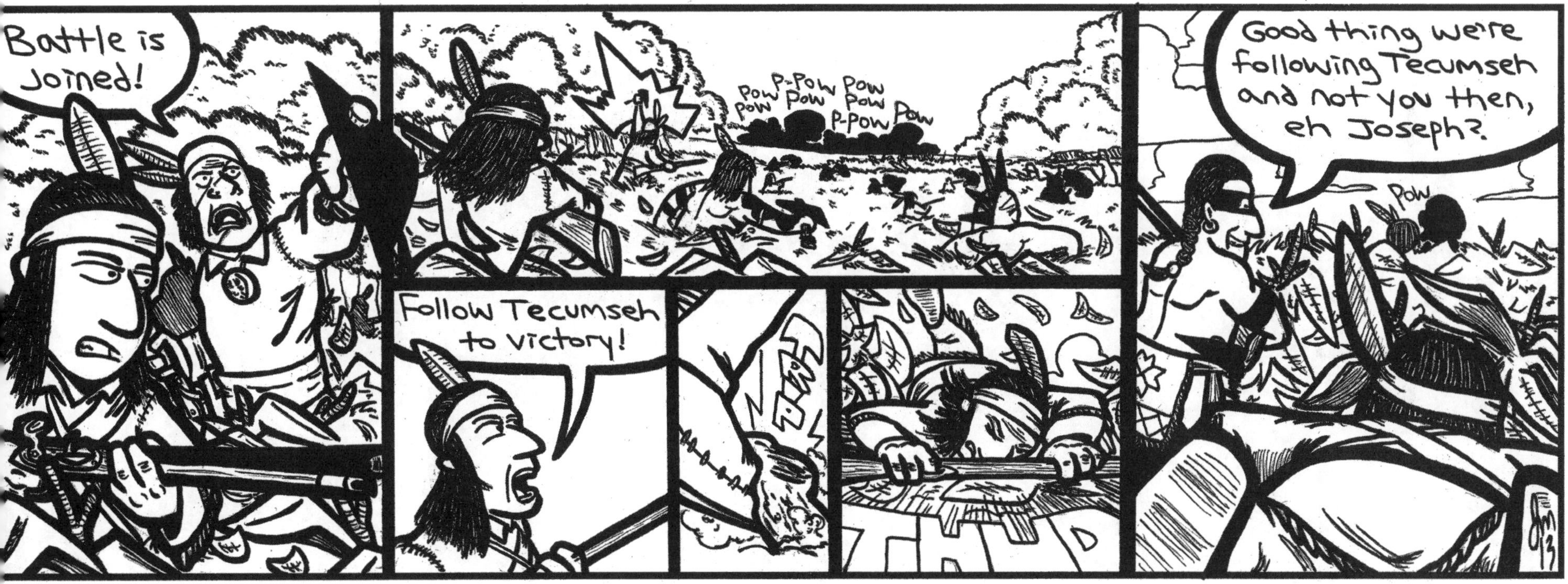
Battle is Joined!
P-POW POW POW POW POW POW P-POW POW
Follow Tecumseh to victory!
THUD
Good thing we're following Tecumseh and not you then, eh Joseph?
POW

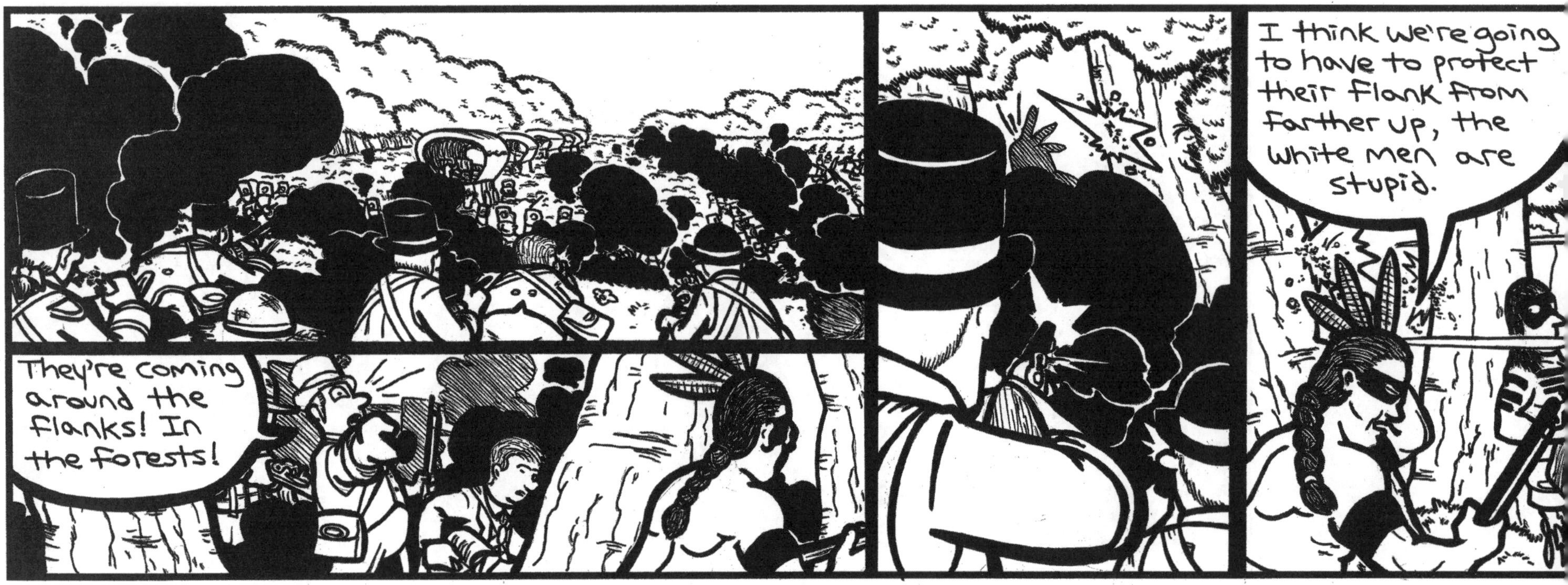
They're coming around the flanks! In the forests!
I think we're going to have to protect their flank from farther up, the white men are stupid.

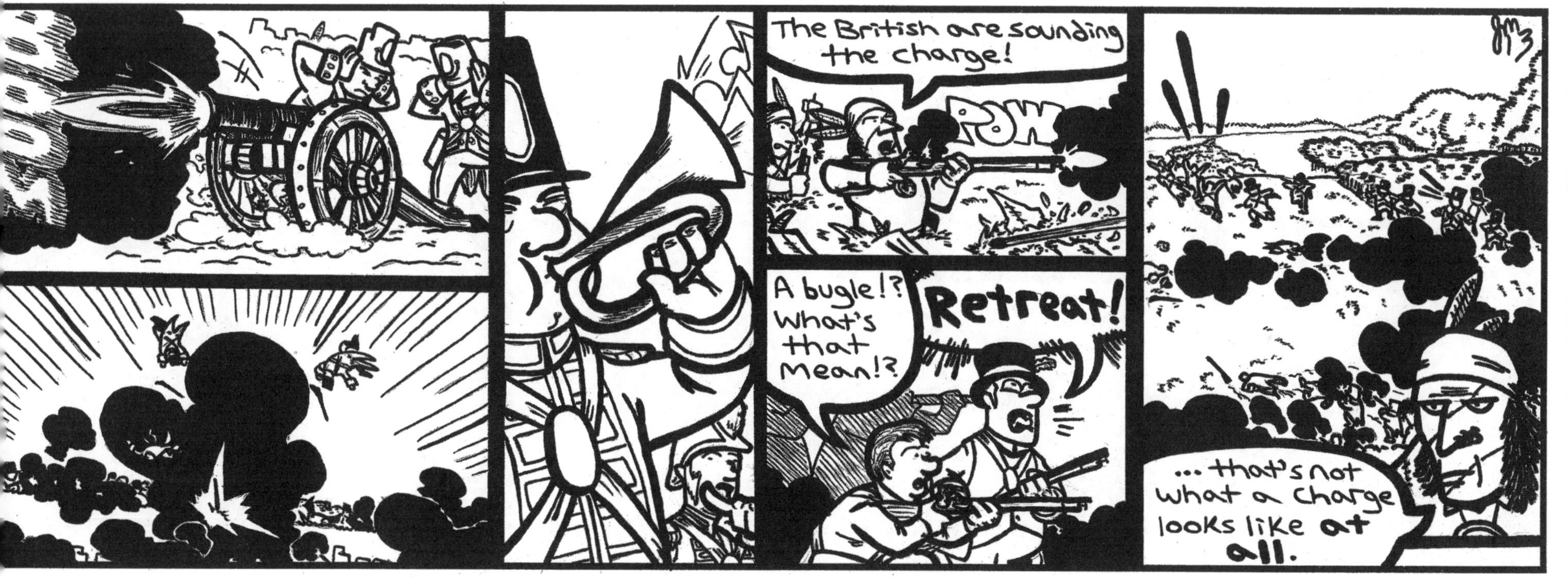
The British are sounding the charge!
POW
A bugle!? What's that Mean!?
Retreat!
!
... that's not what a charge looks like at all.

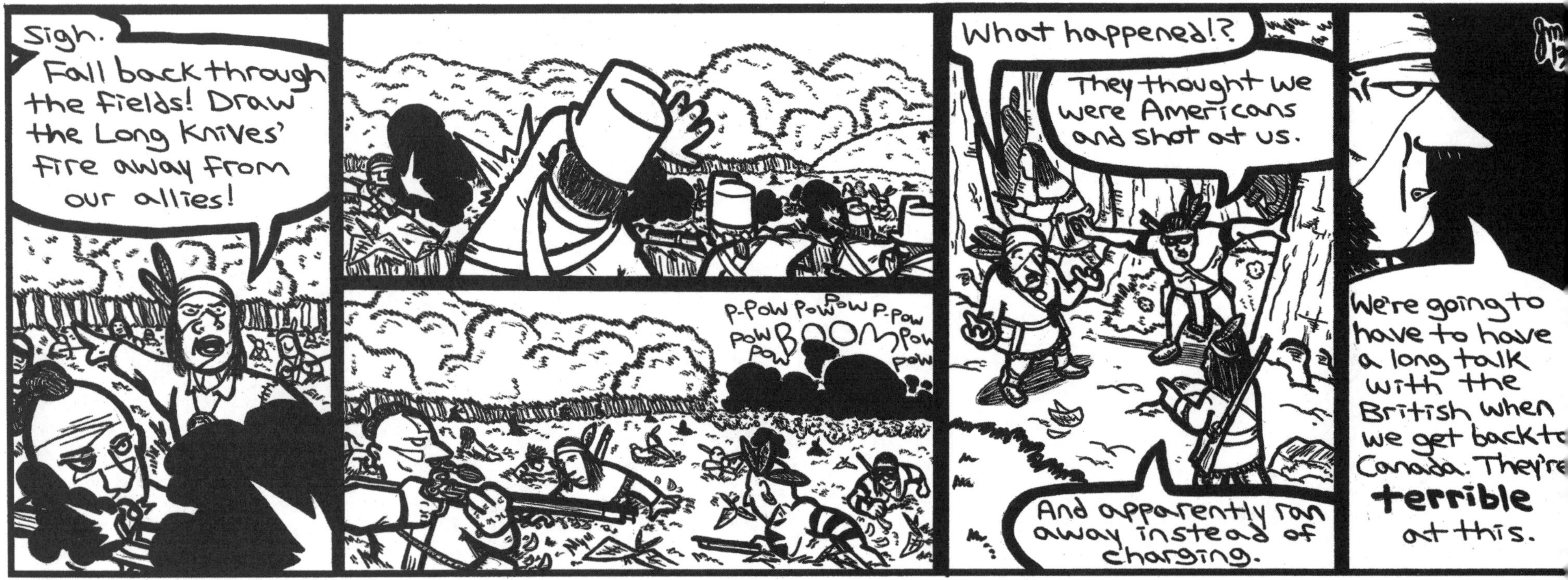
Sigh.
Fall back through the fields! Draw the Long Knives' fire away from our allies!
P-POW POW POW P-POW POW BOOM POW POW POW
What happened!?
They thought we were Americans and shot at us.
And apparently ran away instead of charging.
We're going to have to have a long talk with the British when we get back to Canada. They're **terrible** at this.

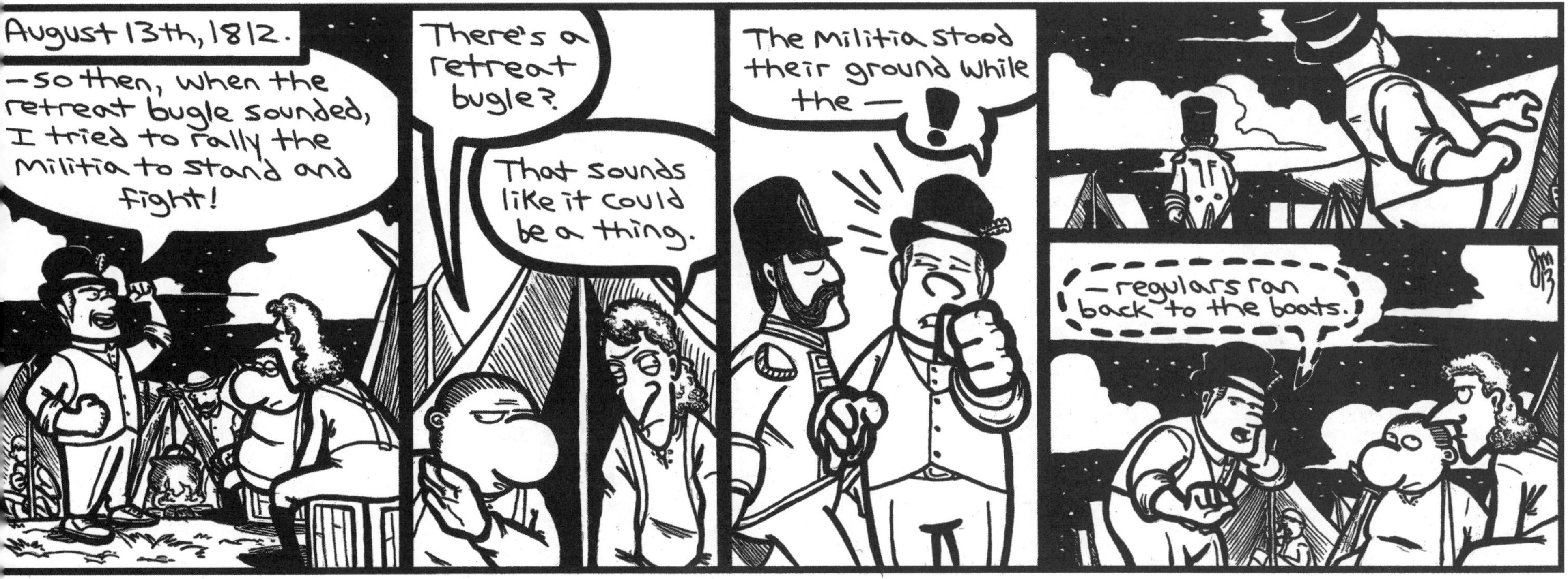

August 13th, 1812.
—so then, when the retreat bugle sounded, I tried to rally the Militia to stand and fight!
There's a retreat bugle?
That sounds like it could be a thing.
The Militia stood their ground while the —
!
—regulars ran back to the boats.

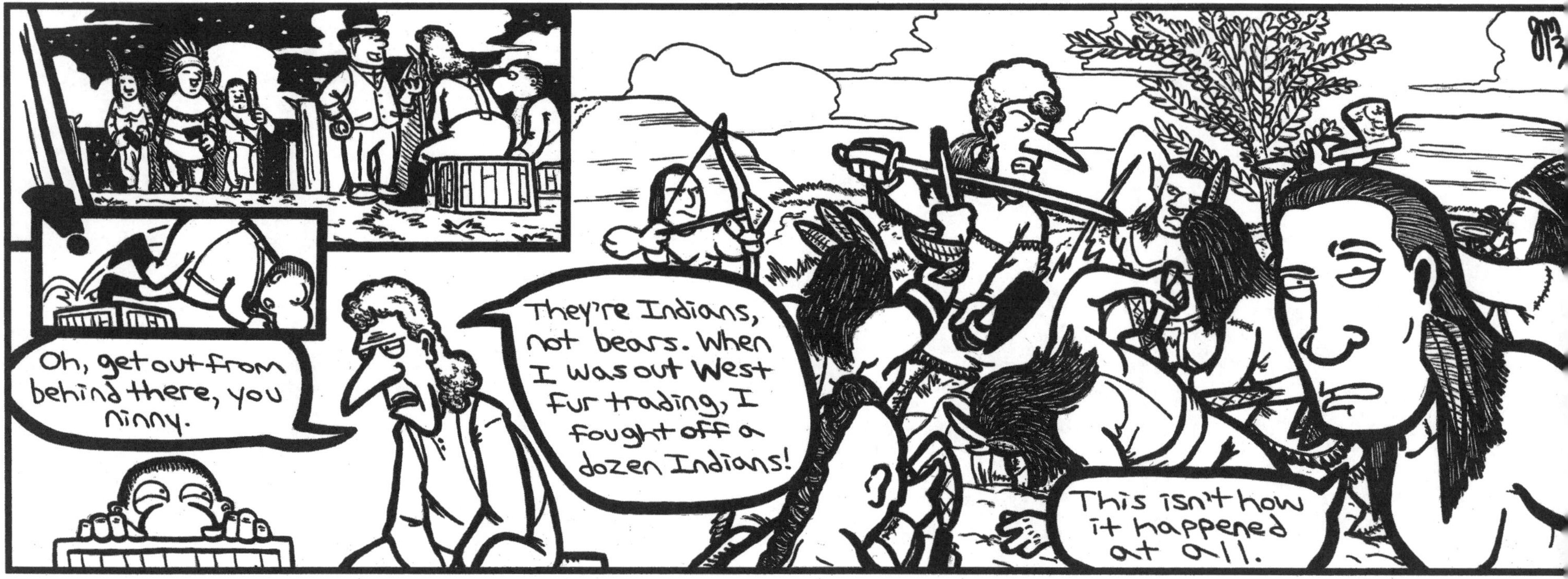
Oh, get out from behind there, you ninny.
They're Indians, not bears. When I was out West fur trading, I fought off a dozen Indians!
This isn't how it happened at all.

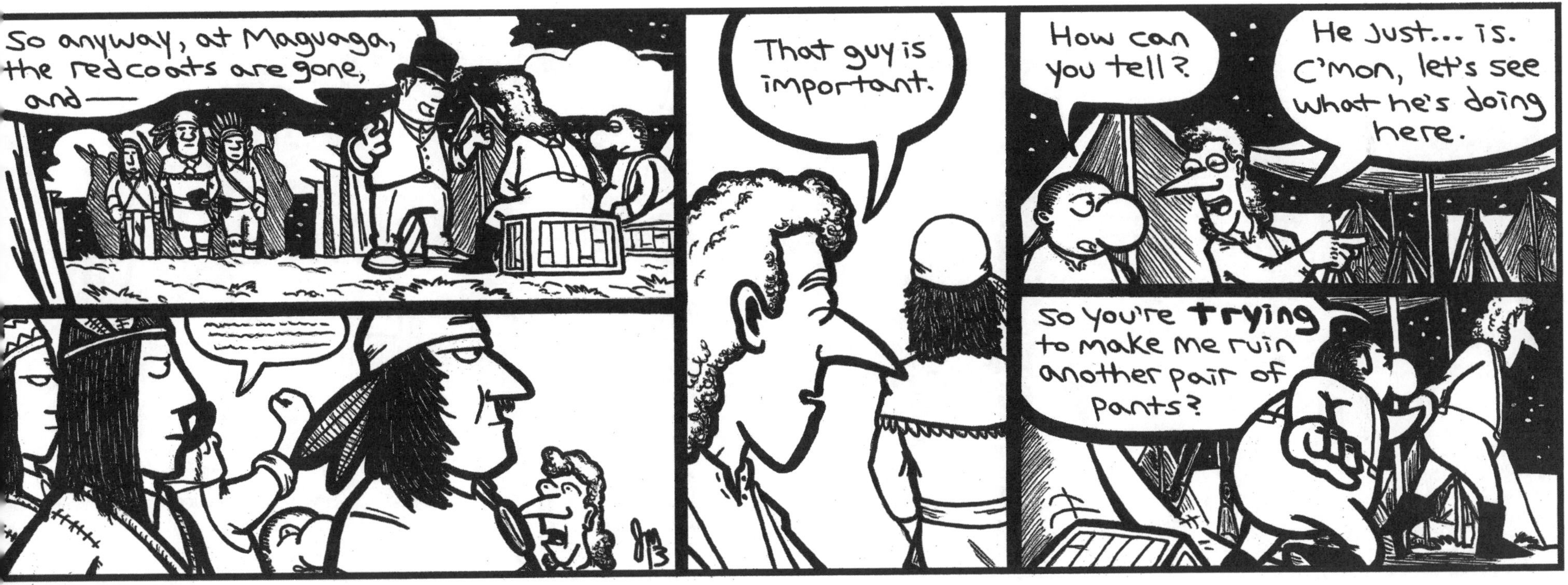
So anyway, at Maguaga, the redcoats are gone, and—
That guy is important.
How can you tell?
He just... is. C'mon, let's see what he's doing here.
So you're trying to make me ruin another pair of pants?

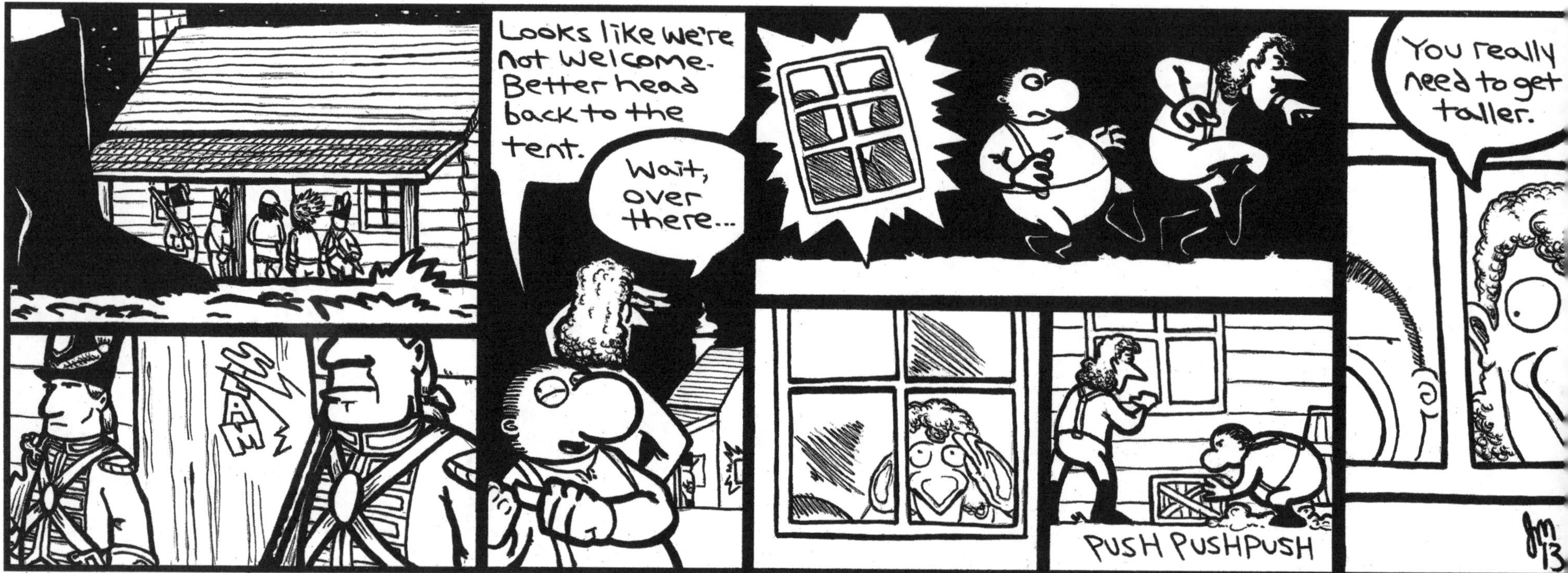
SLAM
Looks like we're not welcome. Better head back to the tent.
Wait, over there...
PUSH PUSHPUSH
You really need to get taller.
JM '13

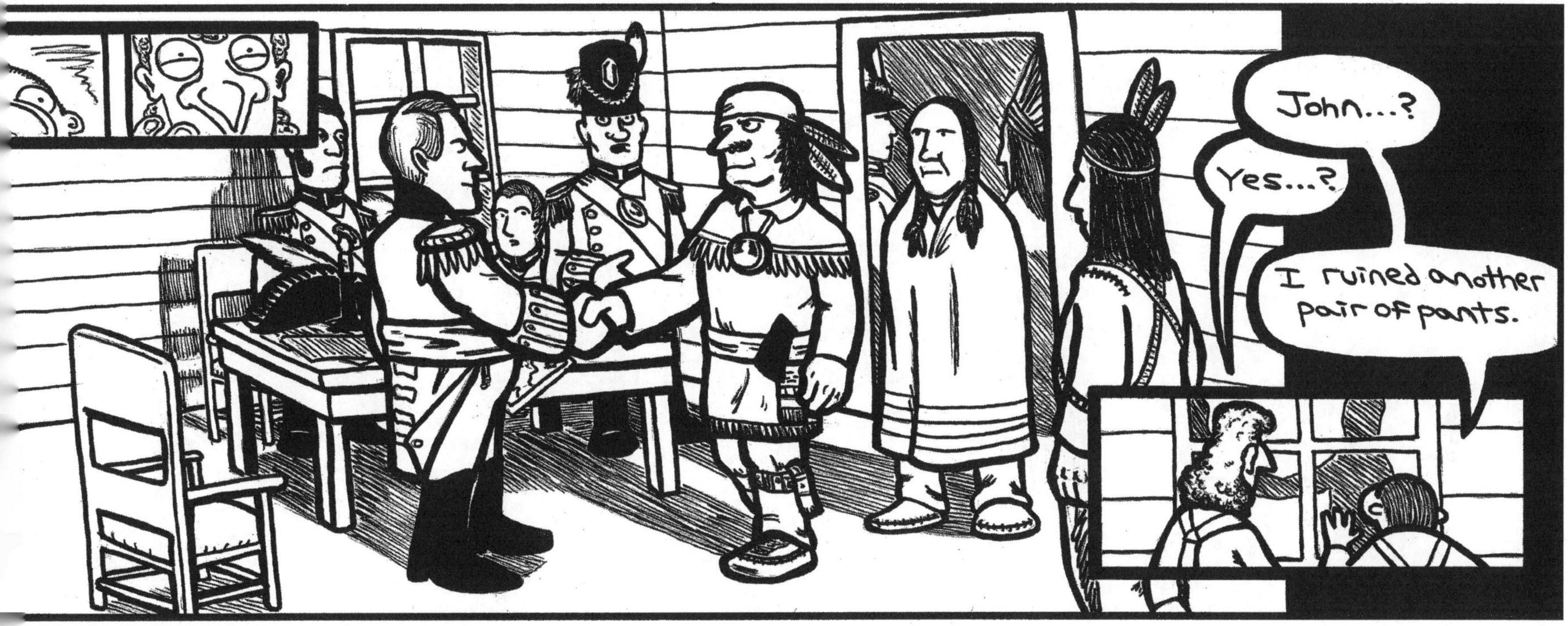
John...?
Yes...?
I ruined another pair of pants.

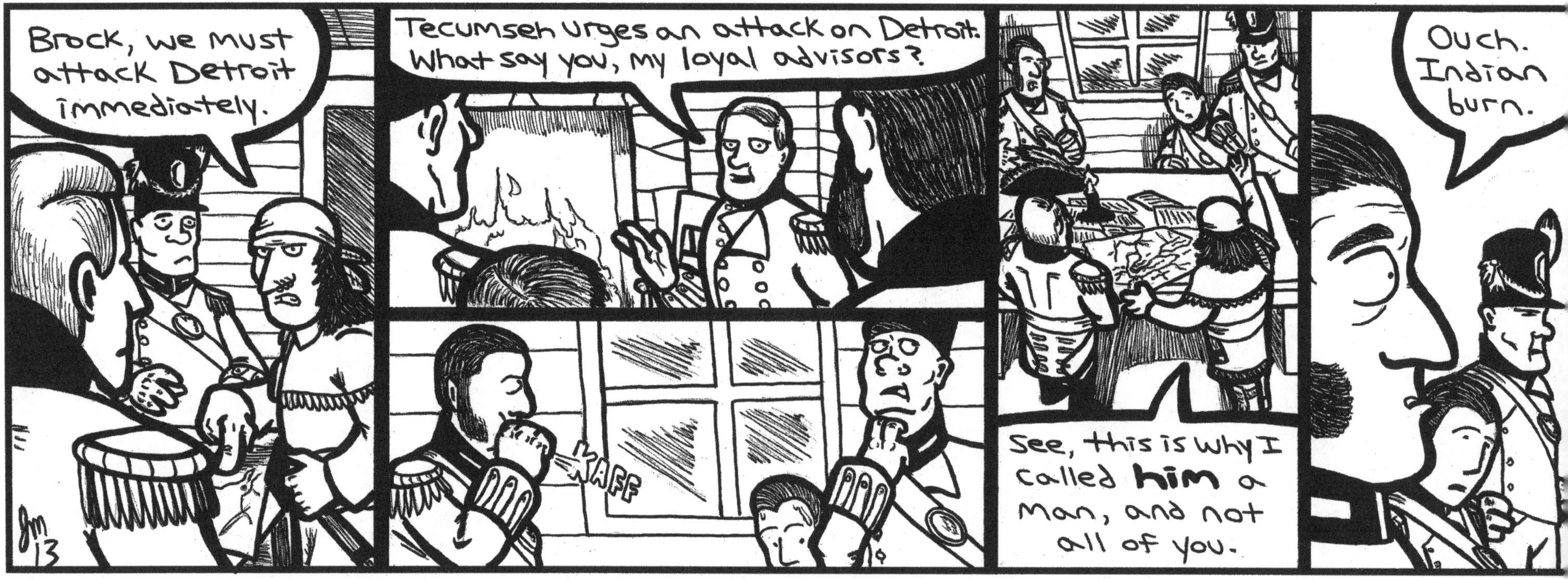
Brock, we must attack Detroit immediately.
Tecumseh urges an attack on Detroit. What say you, my loyal advisors?
KAFF
See, this is why I called **him** a man, and not all of you.
Ouch. Indian burn.
Jm 13

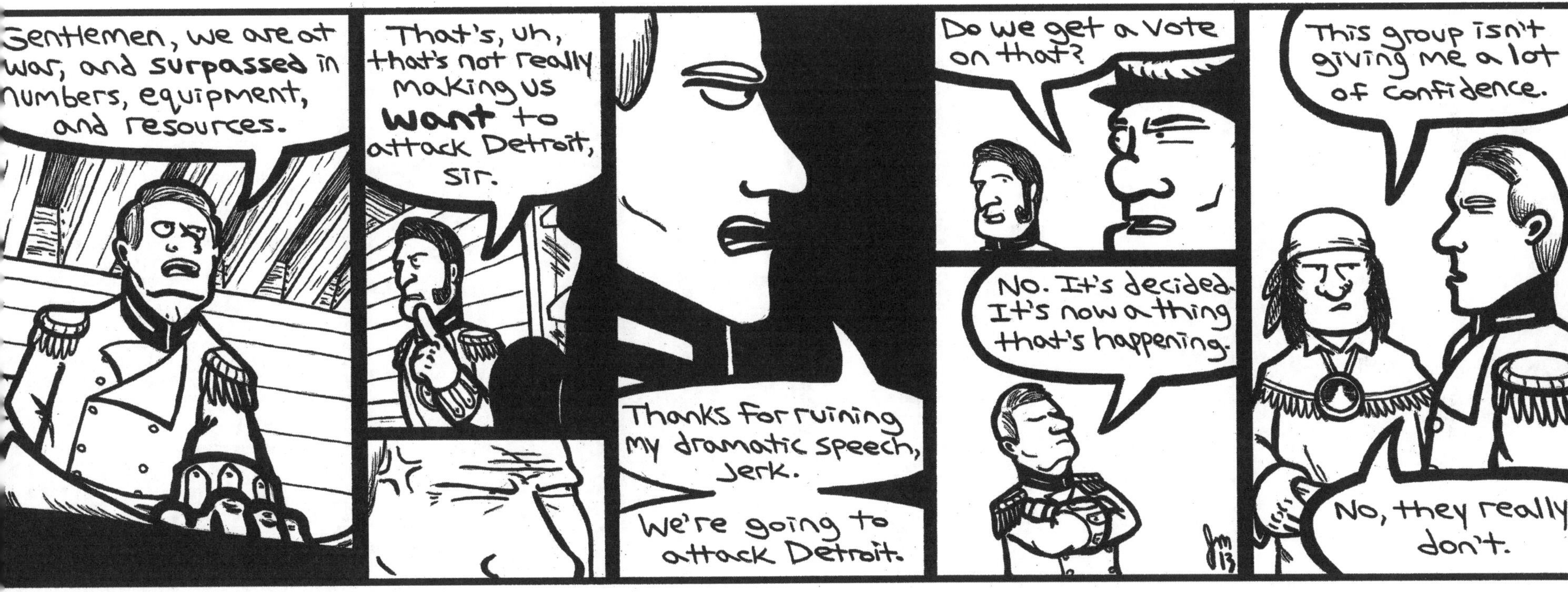
Gentlemen, we are at war, and **surpassed** in numbers, equipment, and resources.
That's, uh, that's not really making us **want** to attack Detroit, sir.
Thanks for ruining my dramatic speech, Jerk.
We're going to attack Detroit.
Do we get a vote on that?
No. It's decided. It's now a thing that's happening.
This group isn't giving me a lot of confidence.
No, they really don't.

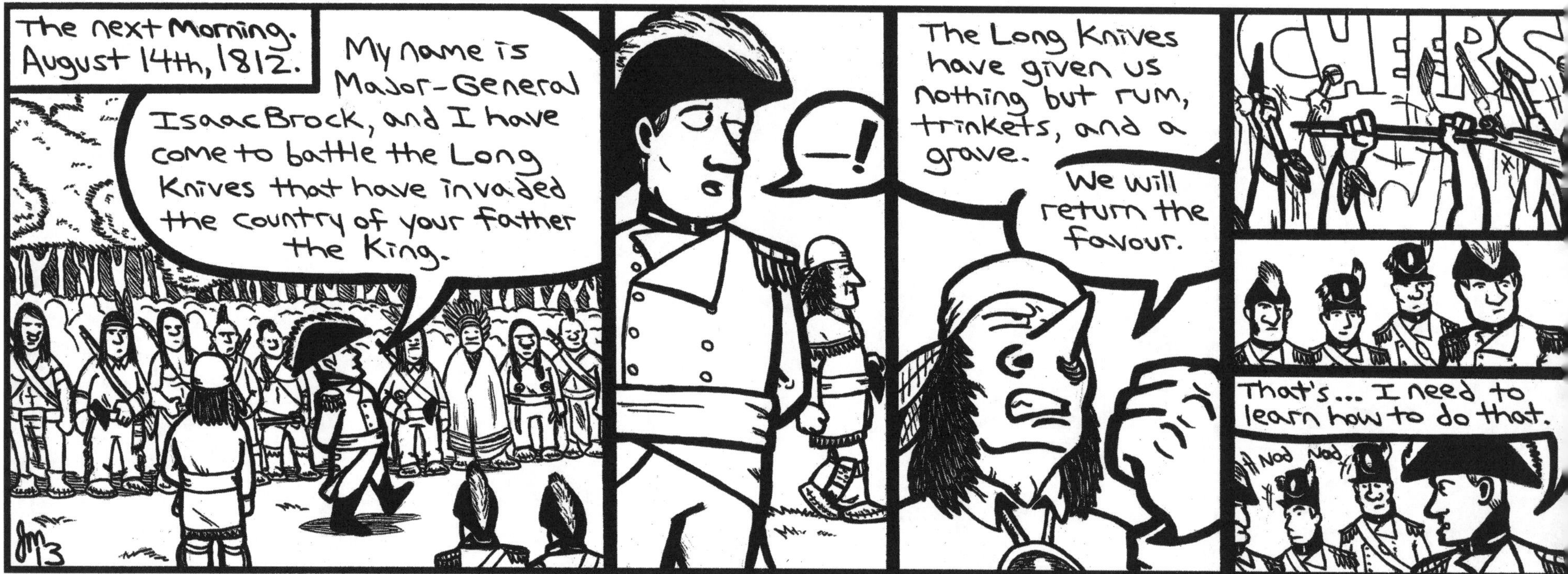

The next Morning. August 14th, 1812.
My name is Major-General Isaac Brock, and I have come to battle the Long Knives that have invaded the country of your father the King.
—!
The Long Knives have given us nothing but rum, trinkets, and a grave.
We will return the favour.
That's... I need to learn how to do that.
Nod Nod

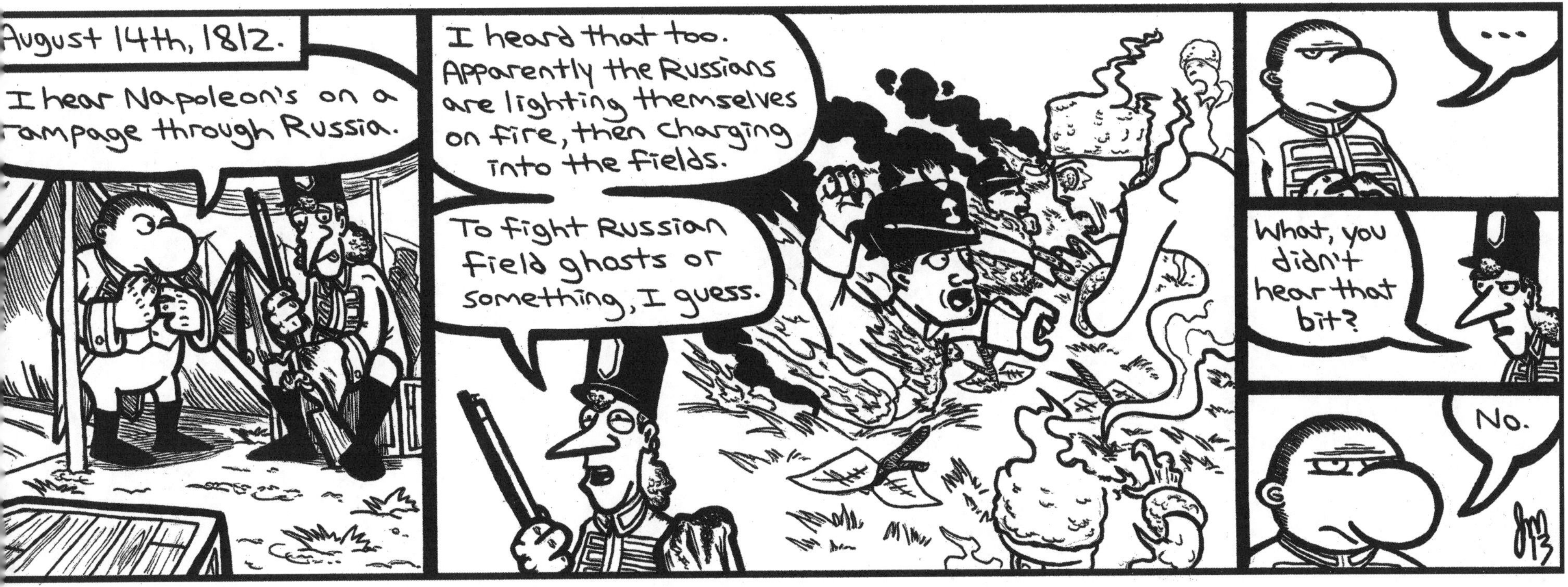
August 14th, 1812.
I hear Napoleon's on a rampage through Russia.
I heard that too. Apparently the Russians are lighting themselves on fire, then charging into the fields.
To fight Russian field ghosts or something, I guess.
...
What, you didn't hear that bit?
No.

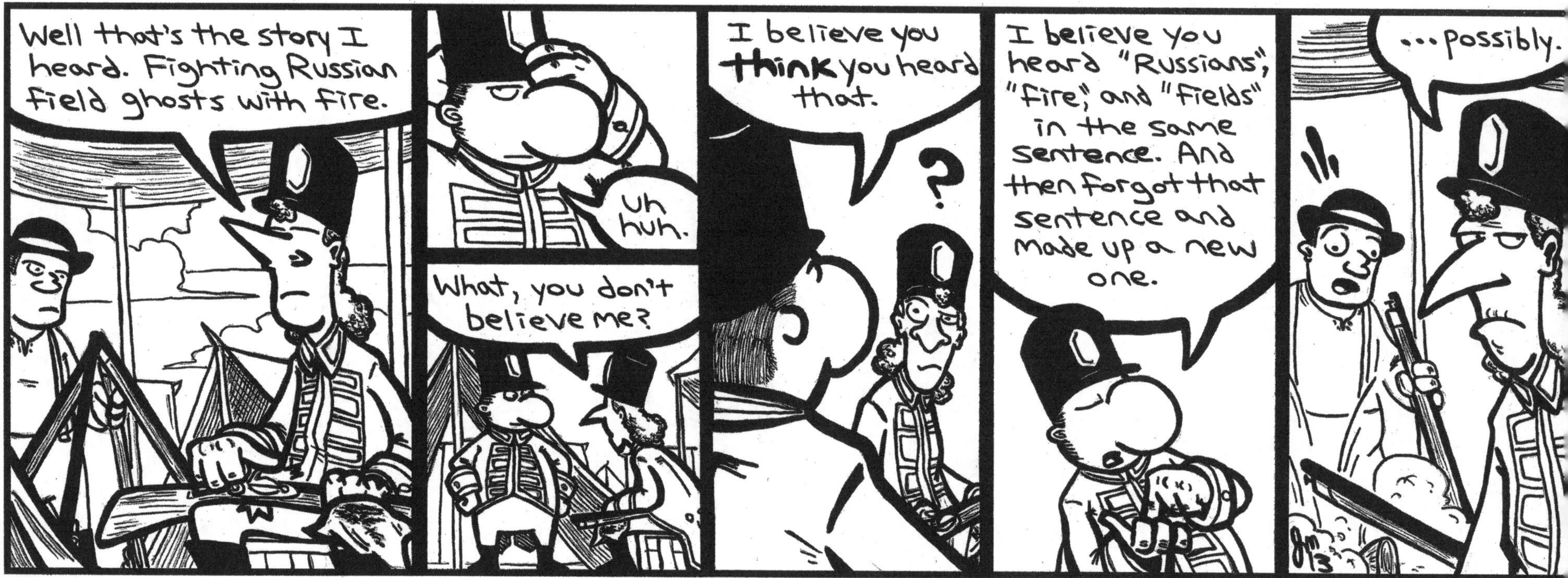
Well that's the story I heard. Fighting Russian field ghosts with fire.
Uh huh.
What, you don't believe me?
I believe you **think** you heard that.
?
I believe you heard "Russians", "fire," and "fields" in the same sentence. And then forgot that sentence and made up a new one.
...possibly.

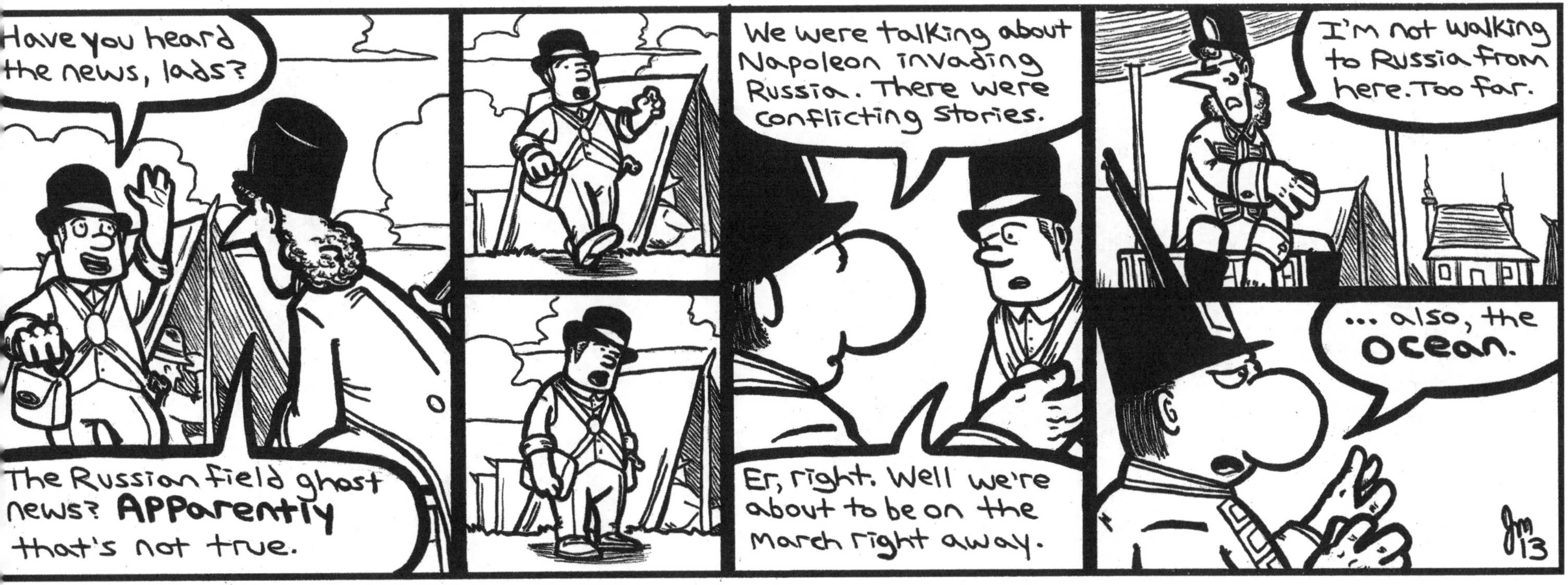
Have you heard the news, lads?
The Russian field ghost news? APPARENTLY that's not true.
We were talking about Napoleon invading Russia. There were conflicting stories.
Er, right. Well we're about to be on the march right away.
I'm not walking to Russia from here. Too far.
... also, the OCEAN.
JM 13

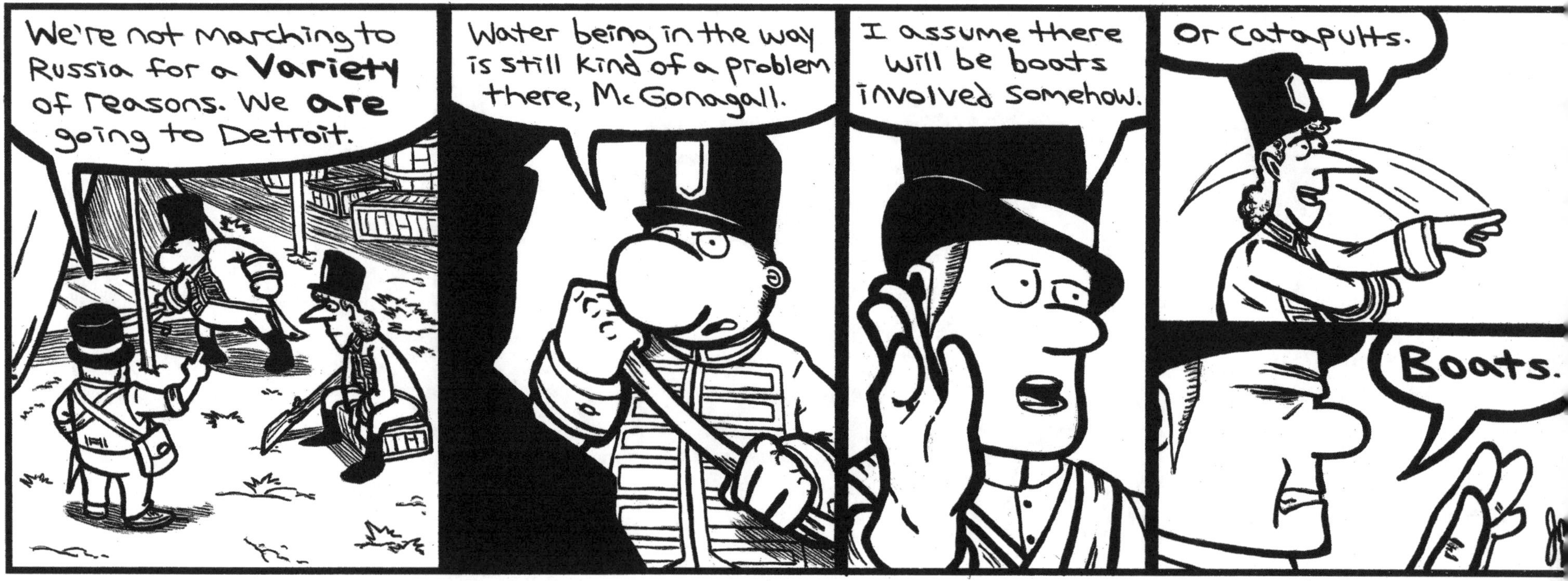
We're not marching to Russia for a variety of reasons. We are going to Detroit.
Water being in the way is still kind of a problem there, McGonagall.
I assume there will be boats involved somehow.
Or catapults.
Boats.

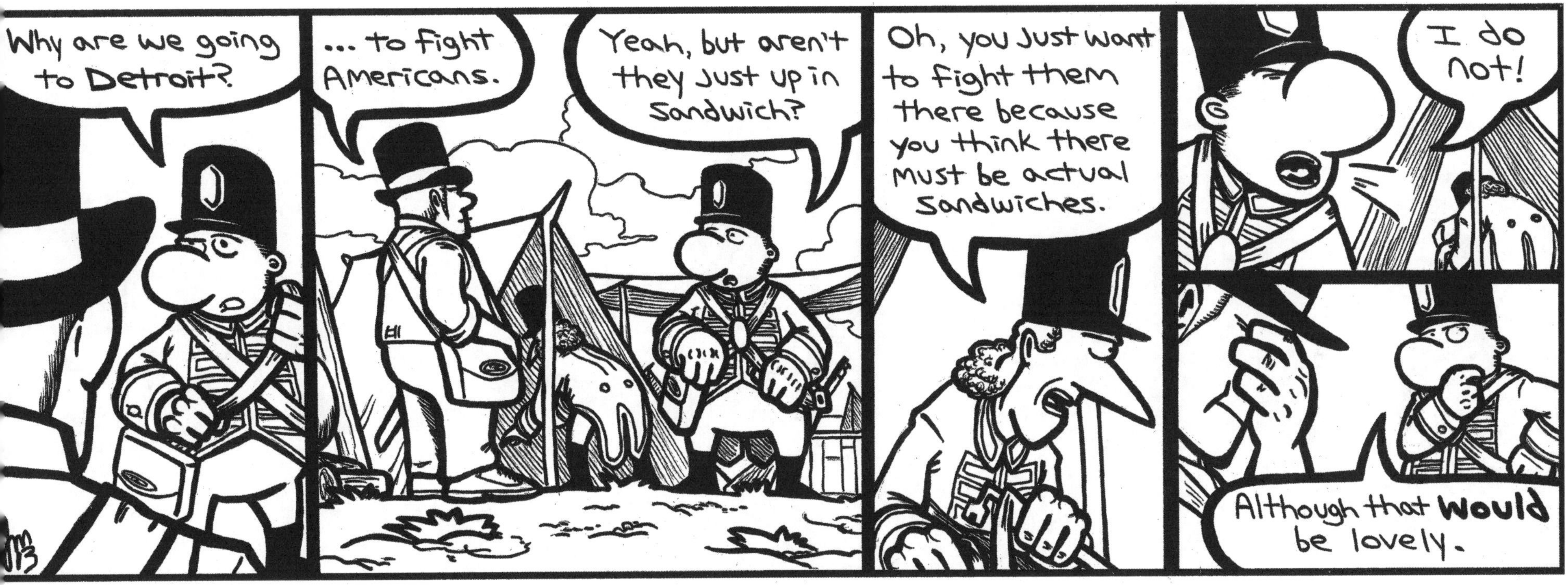
Why are we going to Detroit?
... to fight Americans.
Yeah, but aren't they just up in Sandwich?
Oh, you just want to fight them there because you think there must be actual sandwiches.
I do not!
Although that **would** be lovely.

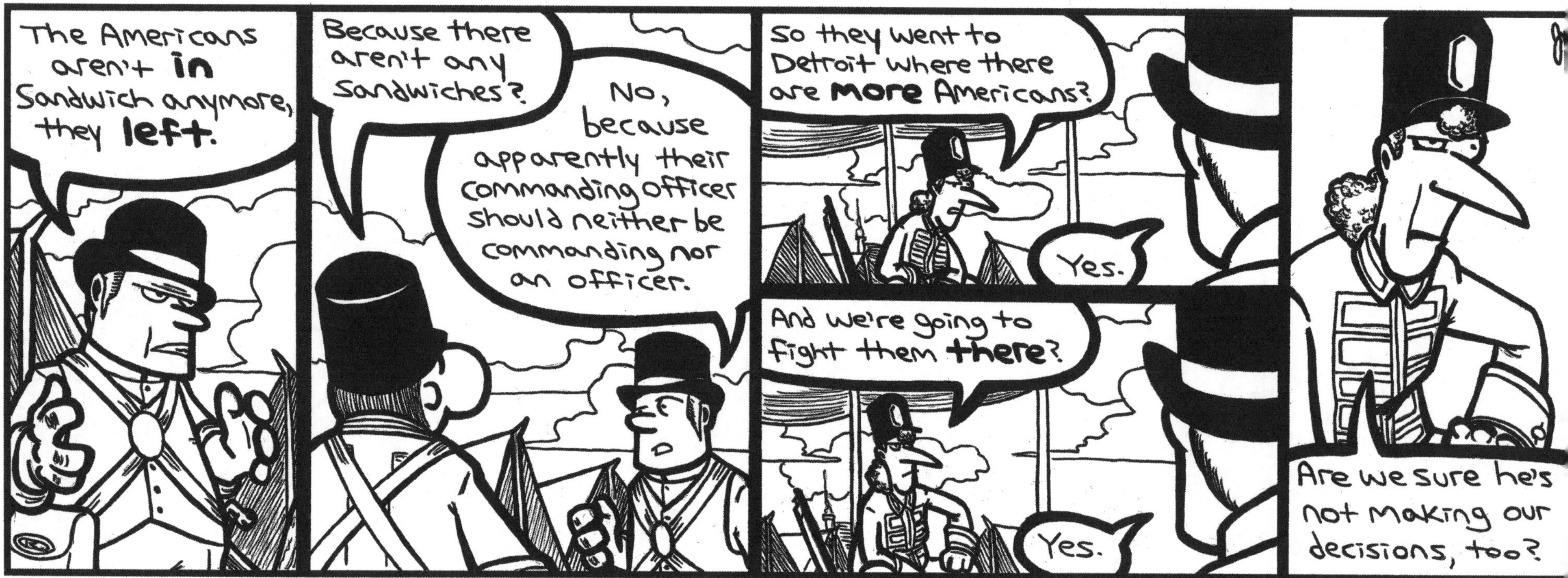
The Americans aren't **in** Sandwich anymore, they **left**.
Because there aren't any sandwiches?
No, because apparently their commanding officer should neither be commanding nor an officer.
So they went to Detroit where there are **more** Americans?
Yes.
And we're going to fight them **there**?
Yes.
Are we sure he's not making our decisions, too?

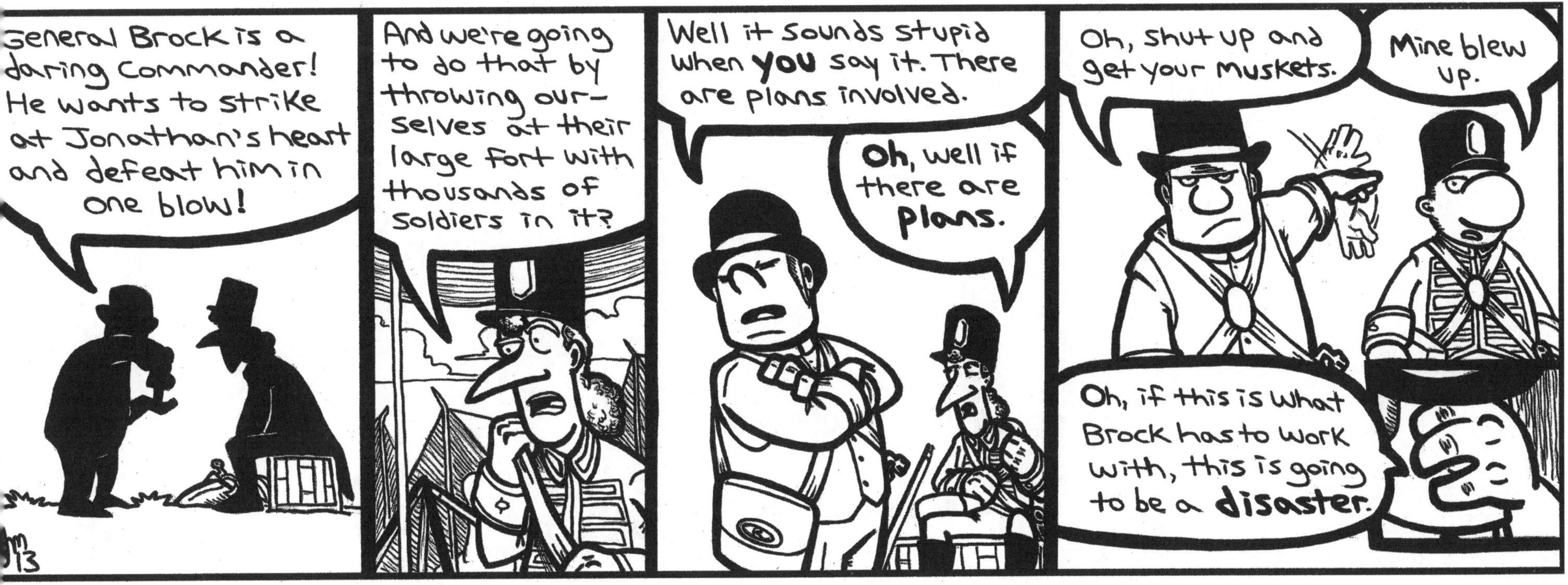
General Brock is a daring Commander! He wants to strike at Jonathan's heart and defeat him in one blow!
And we're going to do that by throwing ourselves at their large fort with thousands of soldiers in it?
Well it sounds stupid when **you** say it. There are plans involved.
Oh, well if there are **plans**.
Oh, shut up and get your muskets.
Mine blew up.
Oh, if this is what Brock has to work with, this is going to be a **disaster**.

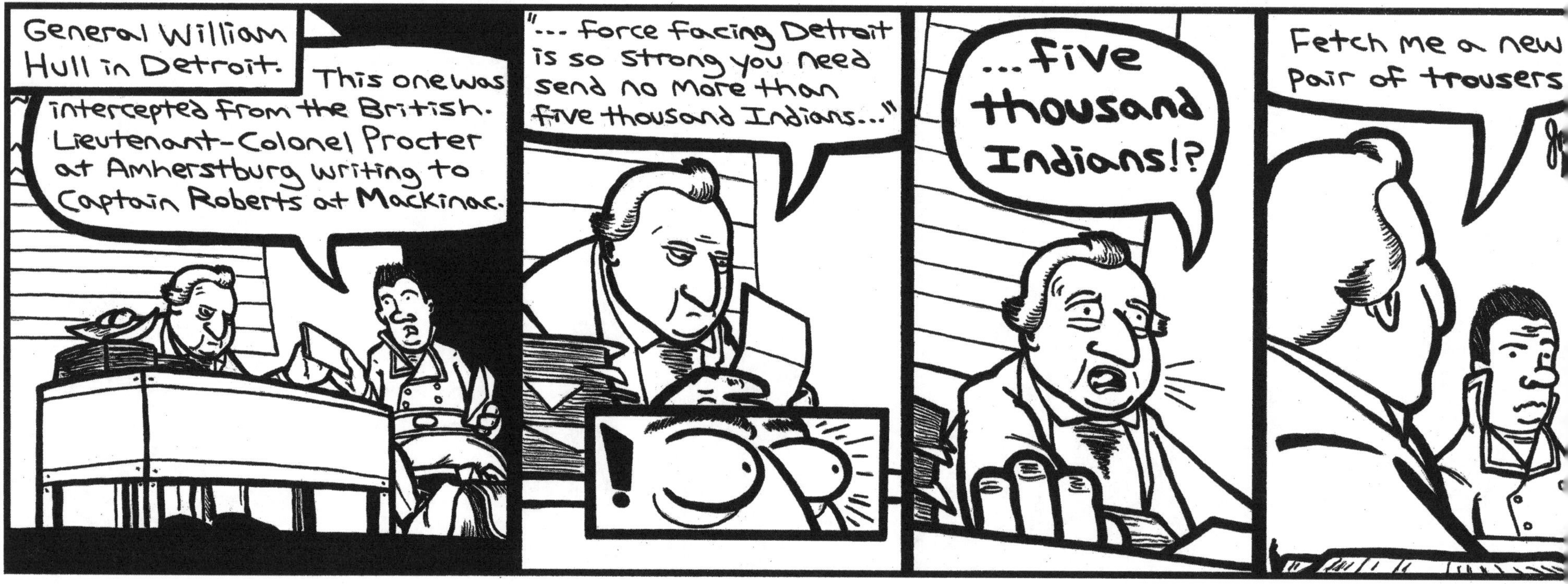
General William Hull in Detroit.
This one was intercepted from the British. Lieutenant-Colonel Procter at Amherstburg writing to Captain Roberts at Mackinac.
"... force facing Detroit is so strong you need send no more than five thousand Indians..."
!
...five thousand Indians!?
Fetch me a new pair of trousers

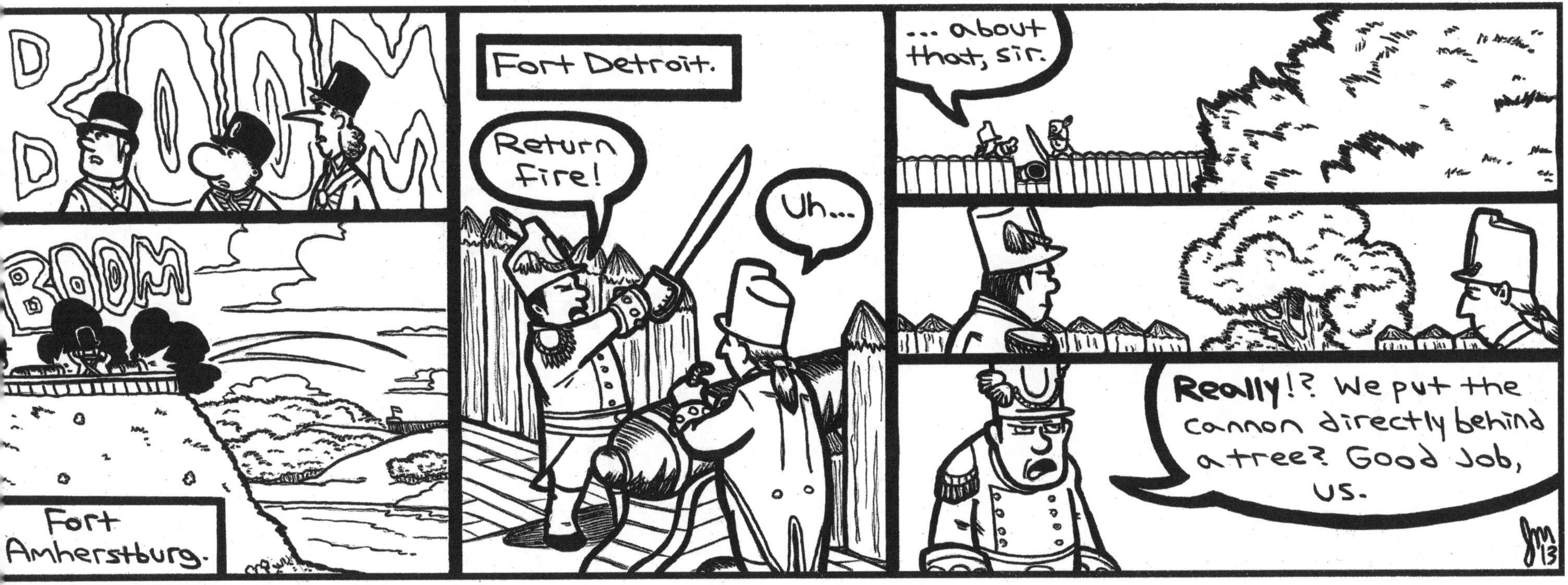

DOOM
DOOM
BOOM
Fort Amherstburg.
Fort Detroit.
Return fire!
Uh...
... about that, sir.
Really!? We put the cannon directly behind a tree? Good Job, us.
JM '13

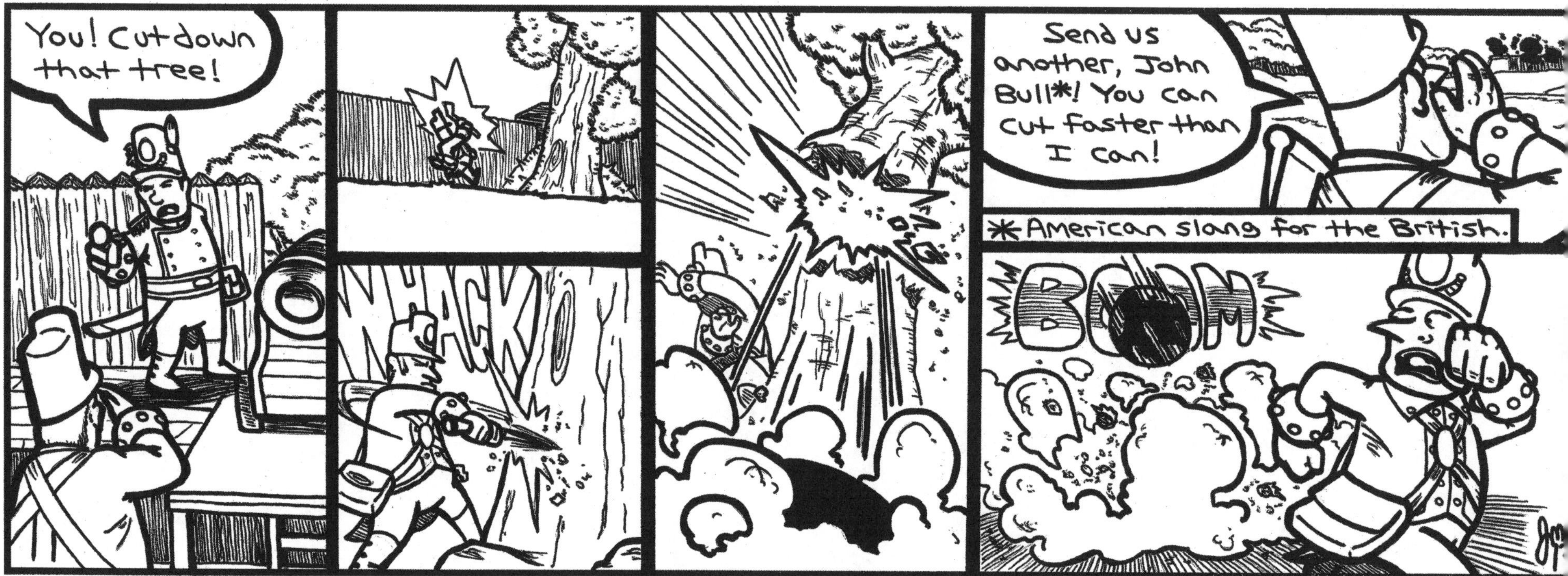
You! Cut down that tree!
WHACK!
Send us another, John Bull*! You can cut faster than I can!
*American slang for the British.
BOOM

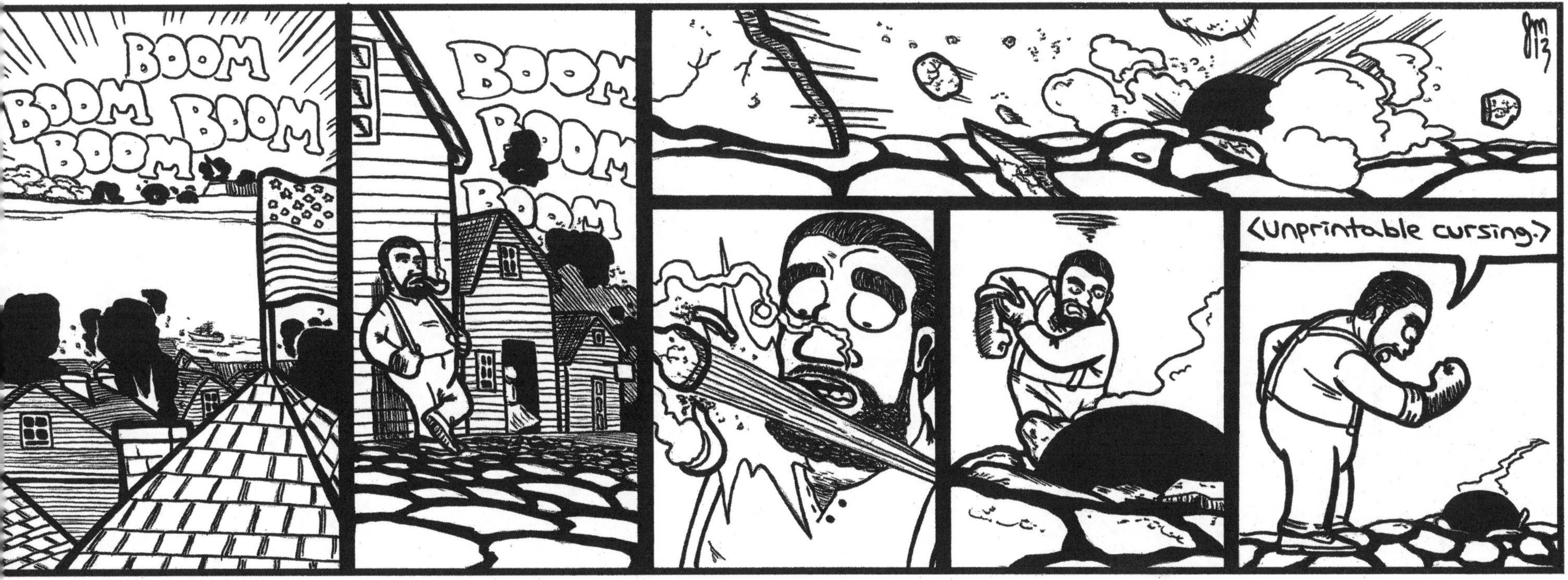
BOOM
BOOM BOOM BOOM
BOOM
BOOM
BOOM
BOOM
JM 13
<Unprintable cursing.>

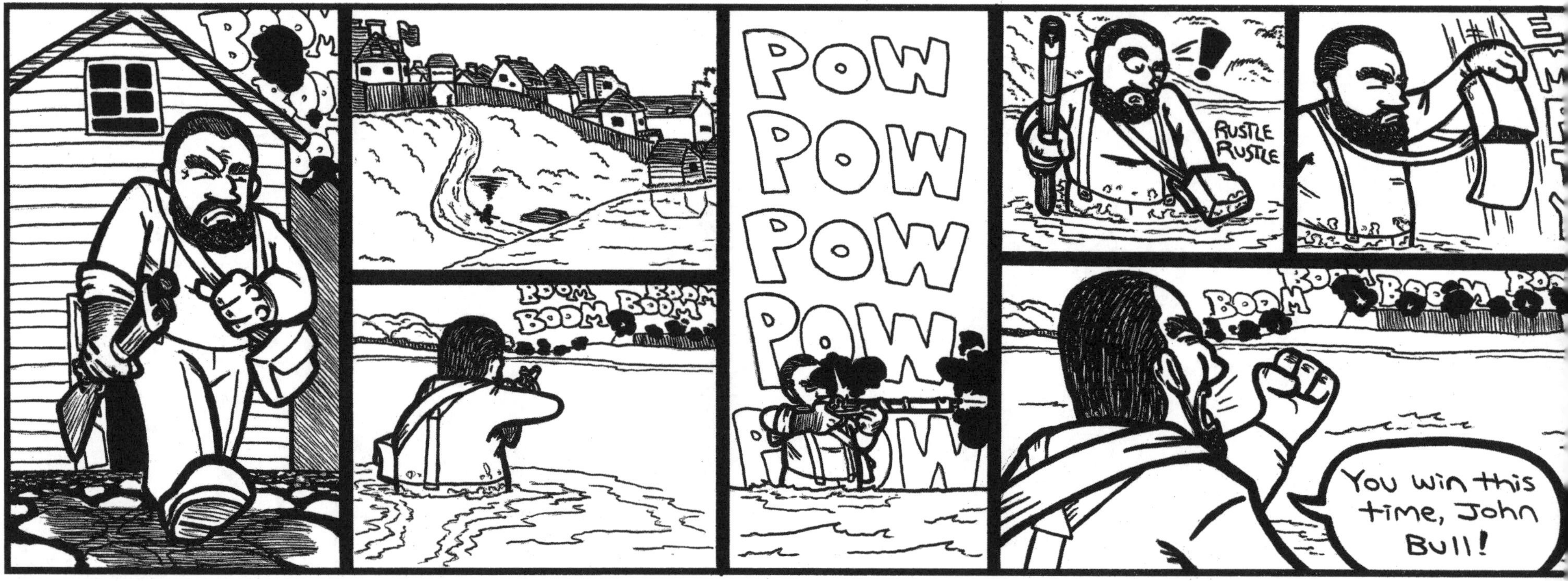
BOOM
BOOM BOOM BOOM BOOM
POW POW POW POW POW
RUSTLE RUSTLE
BOOM BOOM BOOM
You win this time, John Bull!

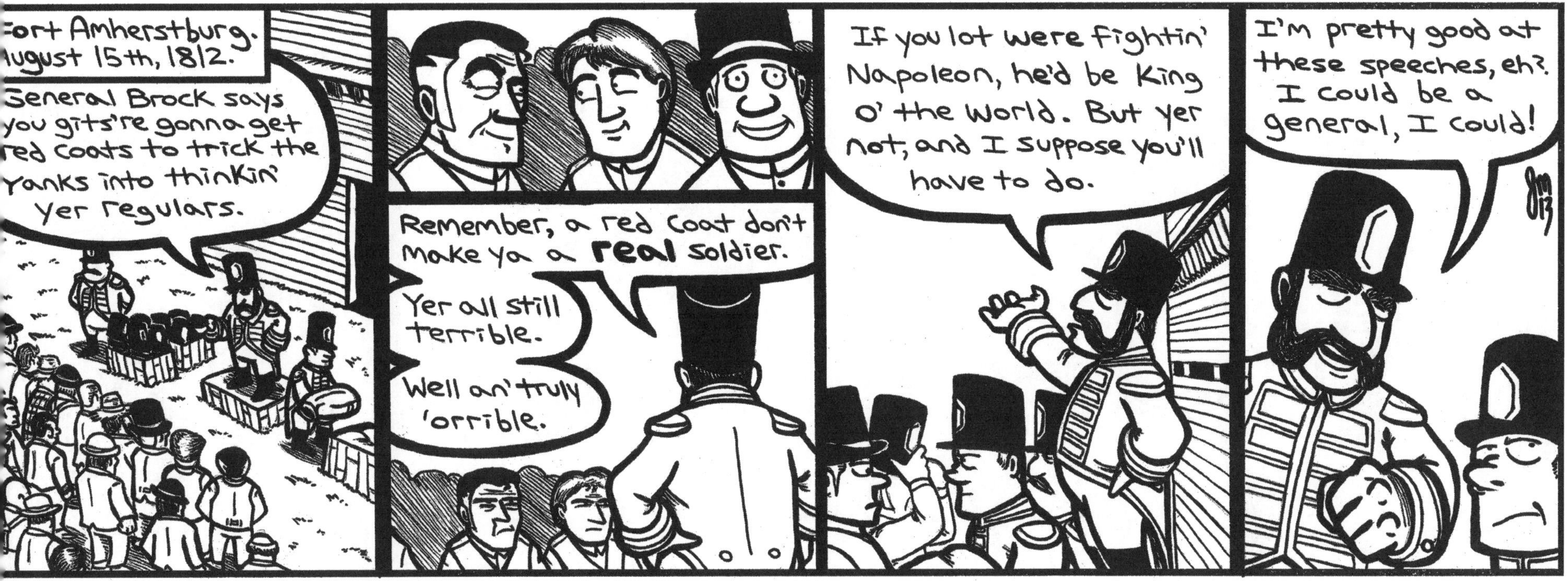

Fort Amherstburg.
August 15th, 1812.
General Brock says you gits're gonna get red coats to trick the yanks into thinkin' yer regulars.
Remember, a red coat don't make ya a **real** soldier.
Yer all still terrible.
Well an' truly 'orrible.
If you lot were fightin' Napoleon, he'd be King o' the world. But yer not, and I suppose you'll have to do.
I'm pretty good at these speeches, eh? I could be a general, I could!

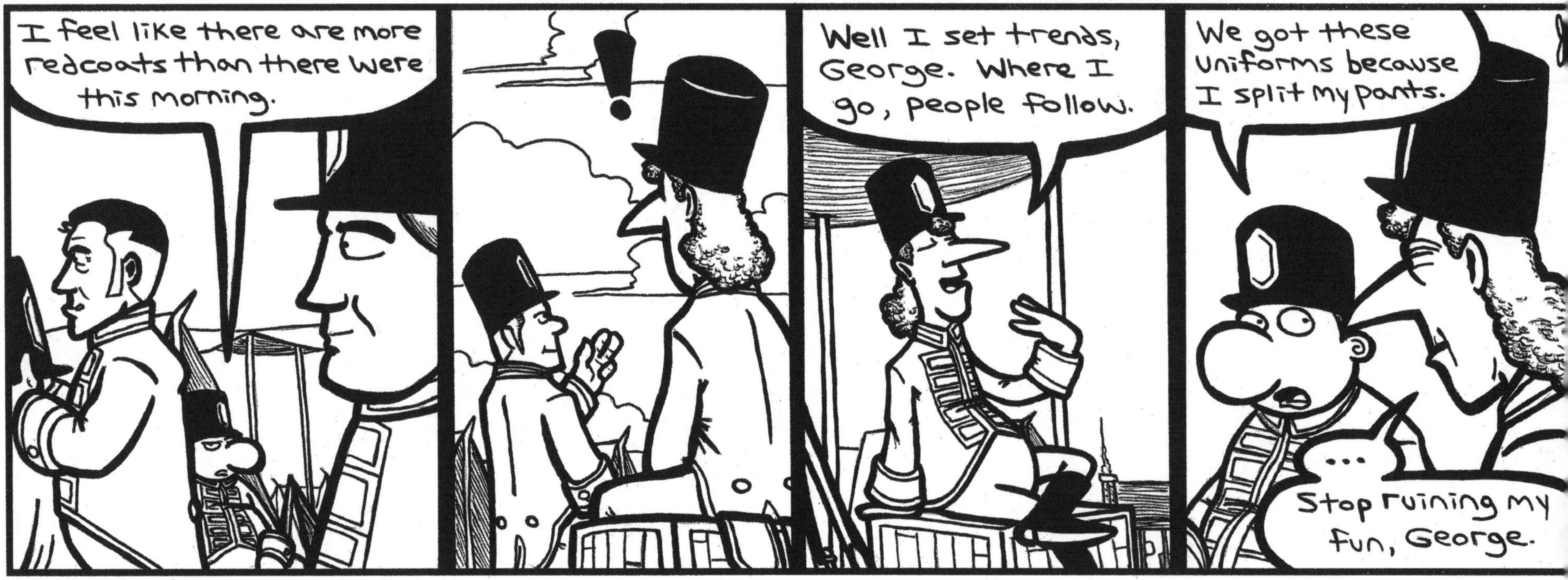
I feel like there are more redcoats than there were this morning.
!
Well I set trends, George. Where I go, people follow.
We got these uniforms because I split my pants.
...
Stop ruining my fun, George.

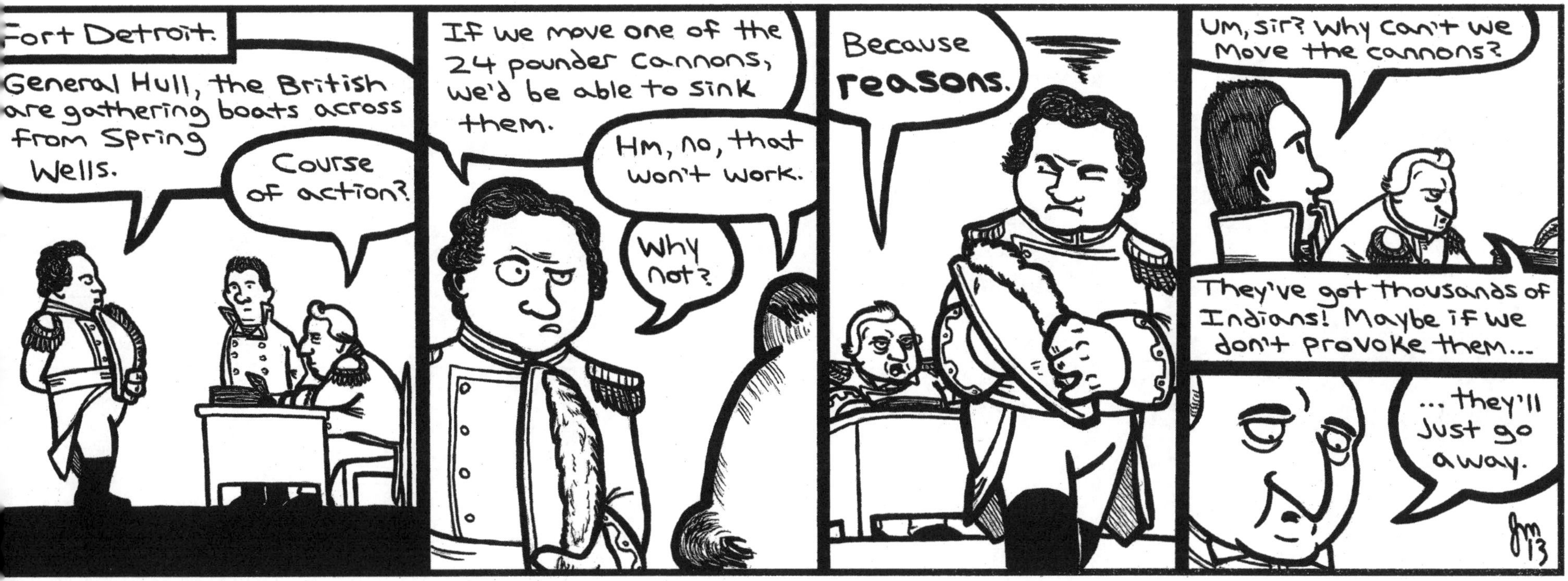
Fort Detroit.
General Hull, the British are gathering boats across from Spring Wells.
Course of action?
If we move one of the 24 pounder cannons, we'd be able to sink them.
Hm, no, that won't work.
Why not?
Because reasons.
Um, sir? Why can't we move the cannons?
They've got thousands of Indians! Maybe if we don't provoke them...
...they'll just go away.
JM 13

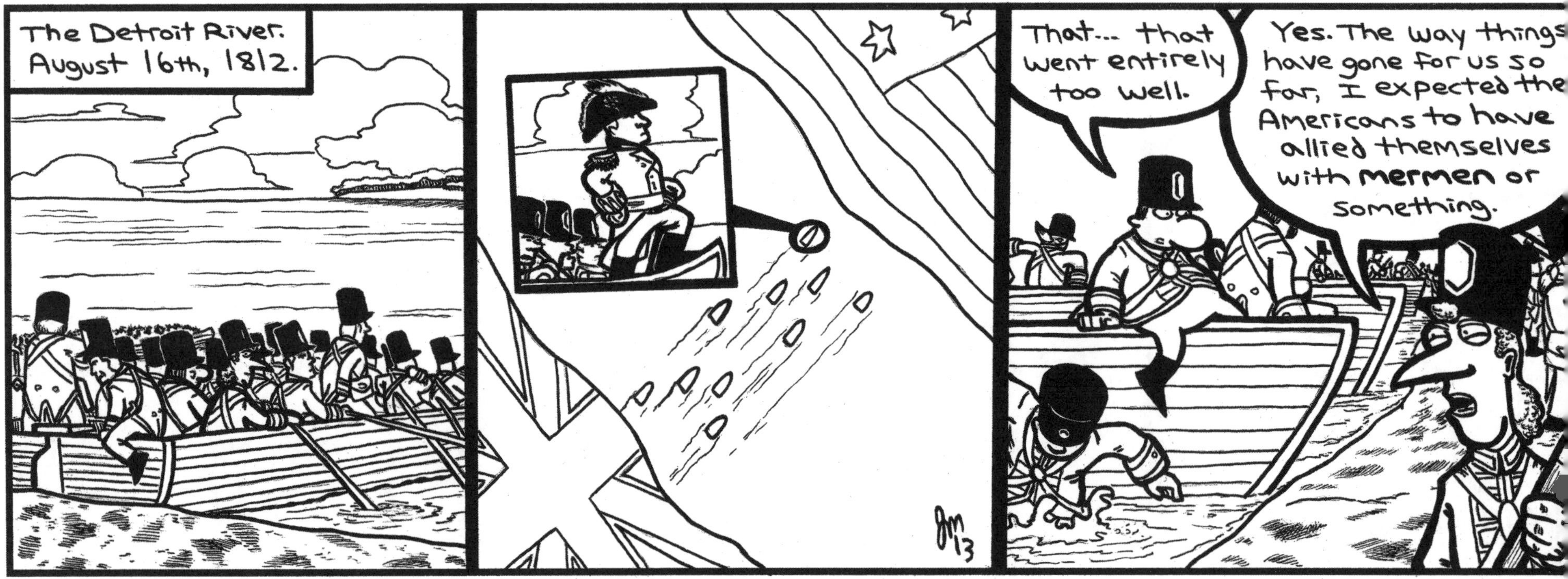
The Detroit River.
August 16th, 1812.
That... that went entirely too well.
Yes. The way things have gone for us so far, I expected the Americans to have allied themselves with **mermen** or something.

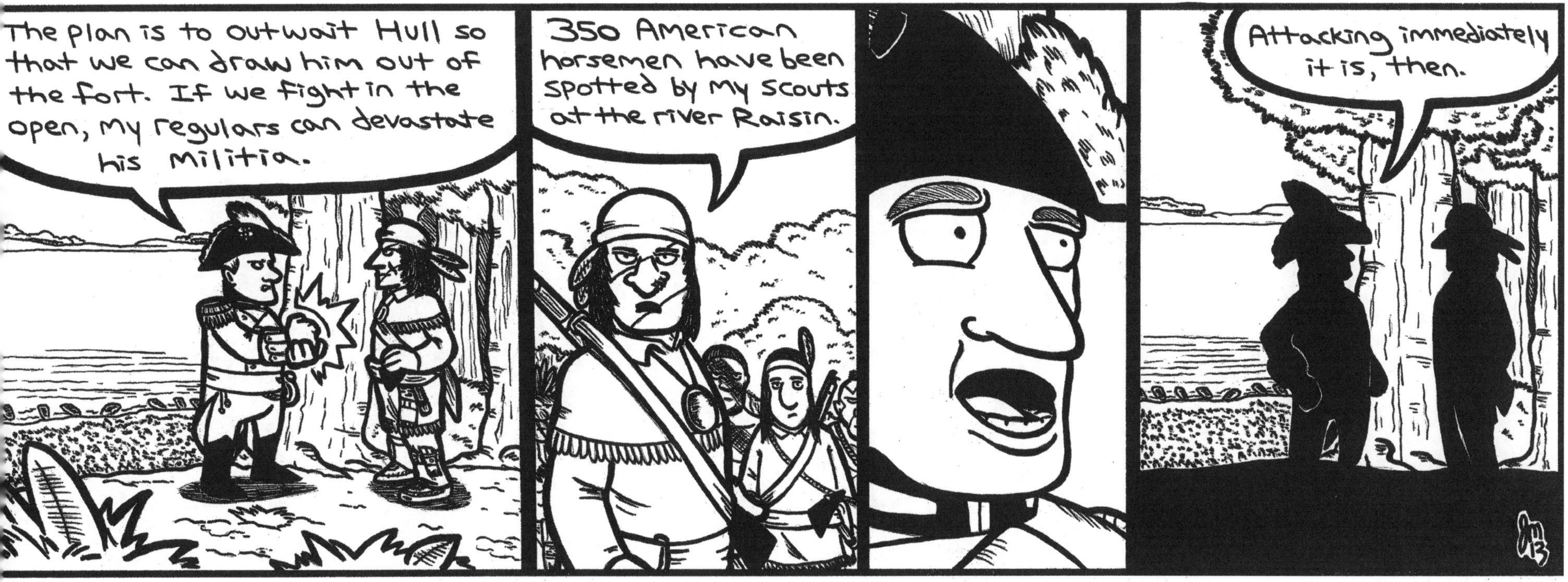
The plan is to outwait Hull so that we can draw him out of the fort. If we fight in the open, my regulars can devastate his militia.
350 American horsemen have been spotted by my scouts at the river Raisin.
Attacking immediately it is, then.

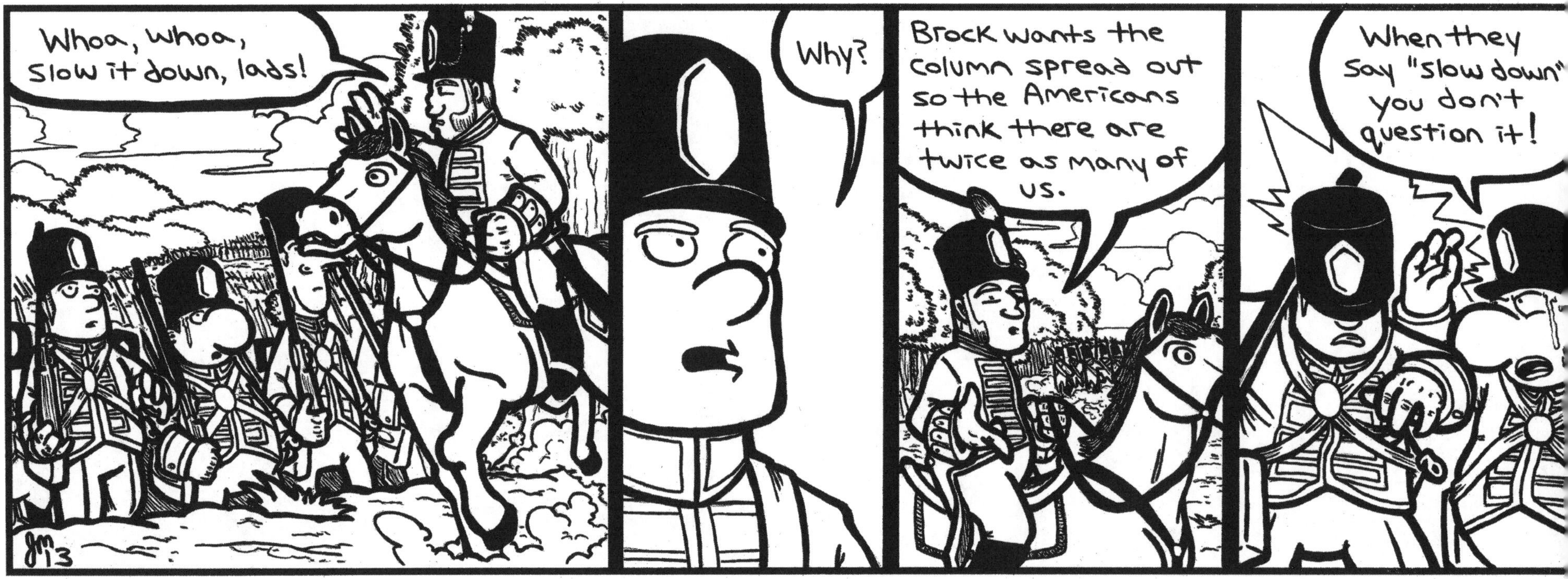
Whoa, whoa, slow it down, lads!
Why?
Brock wants the column spread out so the Americans think there are twice as many of us.
When they say "slow down" you don't question it!

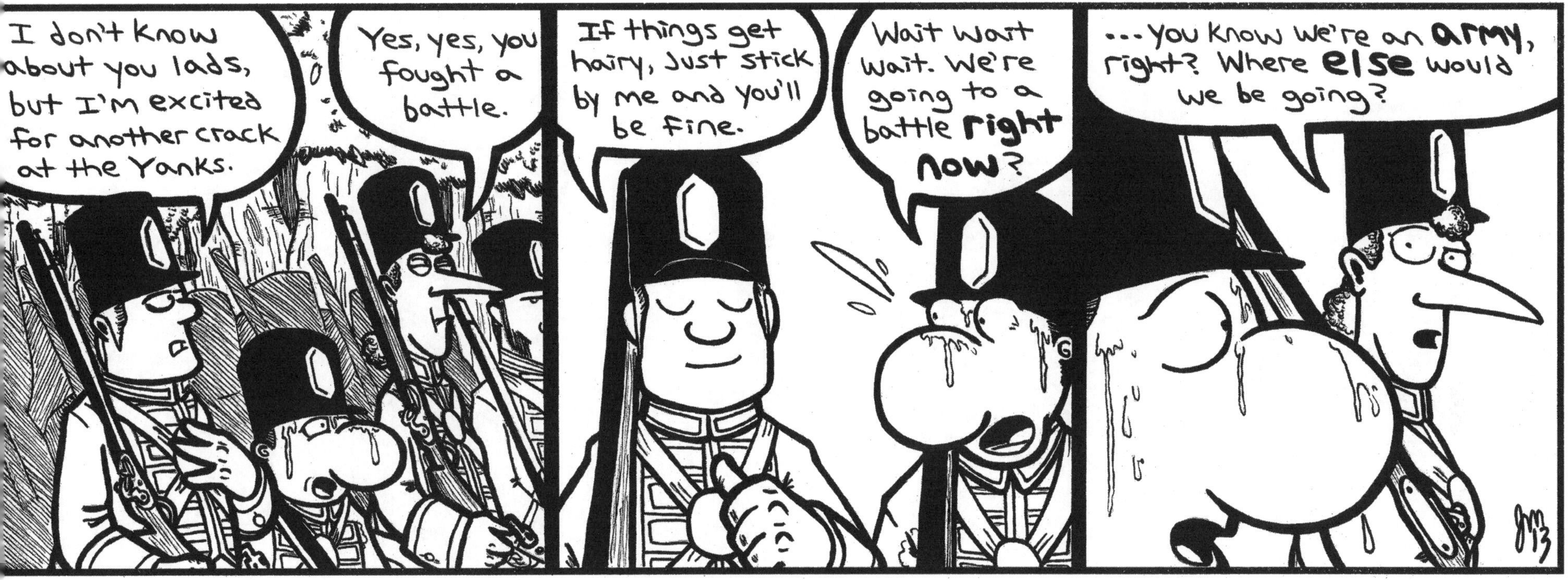
I don't know about you lads, but I'm excited for another crack at the Yanks.
Yes, yes, you fought a battle.
If things get hairy, just stick by me and you'll be fine.
Wait wait wait. We're going to a battle right now?
...you know we're an army, right? Where else would we be going?

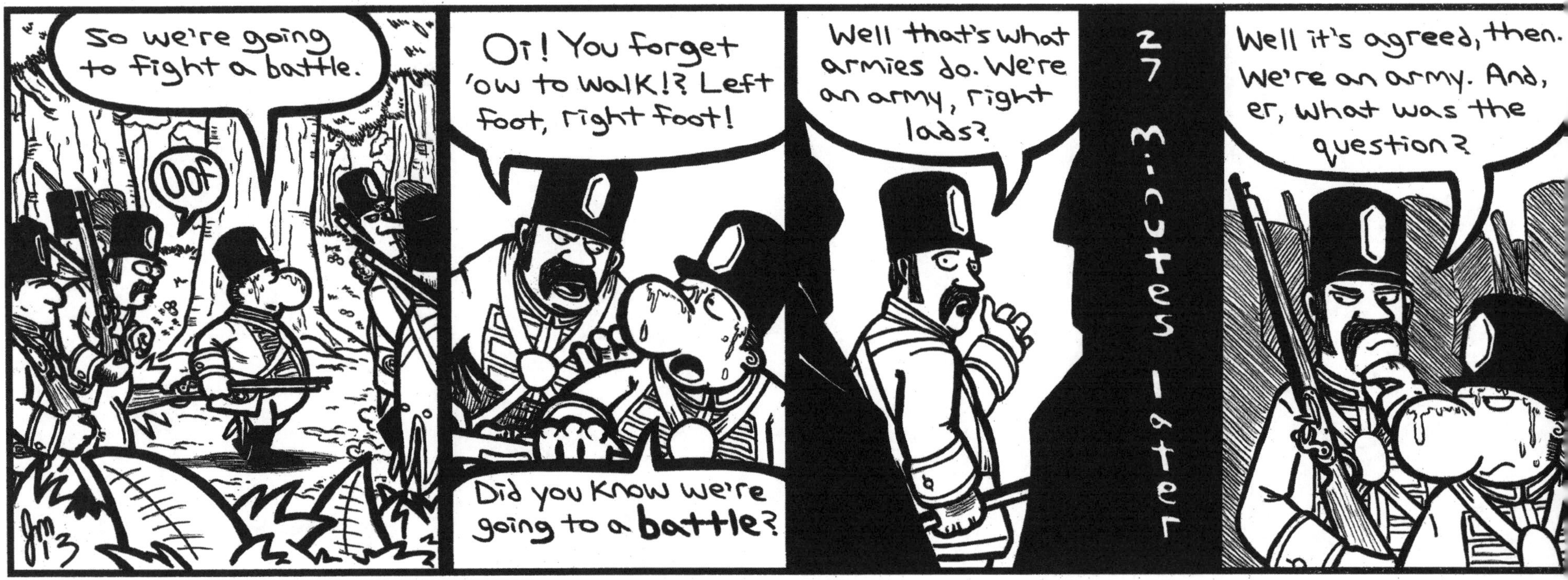
So we're going to fight a battle.
Oof
jm 13
Oi! You forget 'ow to walk!? Left foot, right foot!
Did you know we're going to a battle?
Well that's what armies do. We're an army, right lads?
27 minutes later
Well it's agreed, then. We're an army. And, er, what was the question?

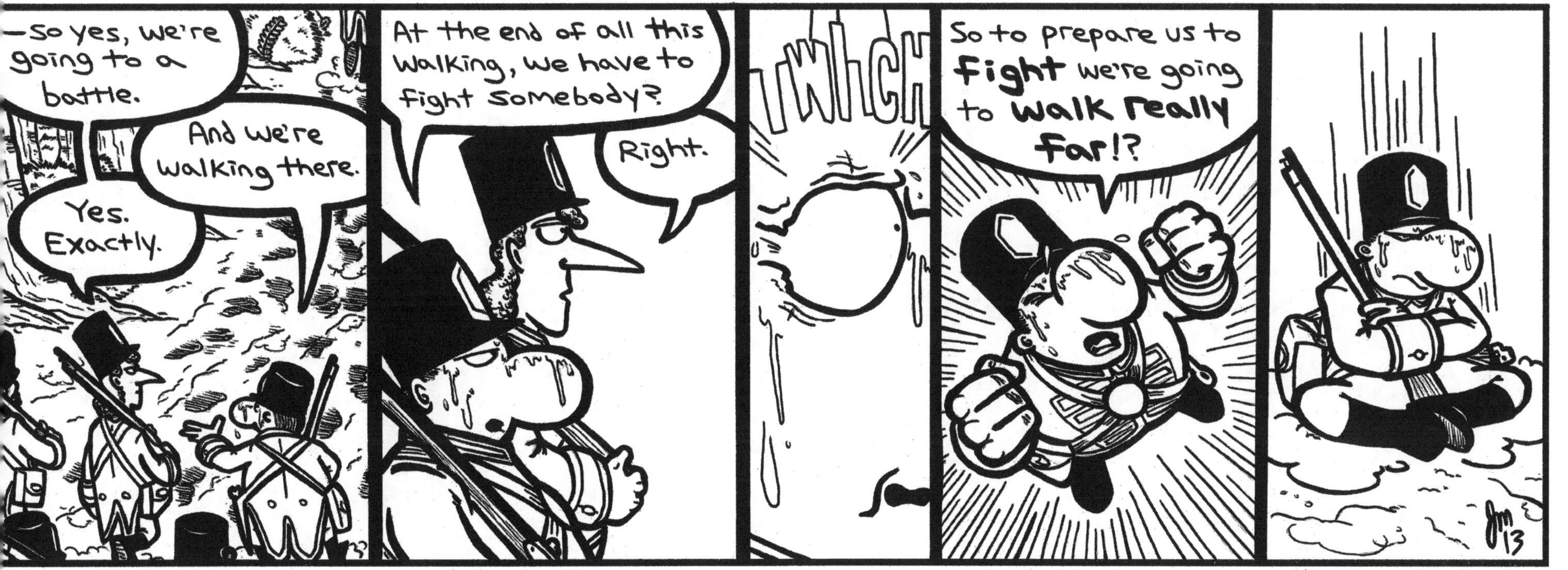
—So yes, we're going to a battle.
Yes. Exactly.
And we're walking there.
At the end of all this walking, we have to fight somebody?
Right.
TWITCH
So to prepare us to **fight** we're going to **walk really far!?**
JM 13

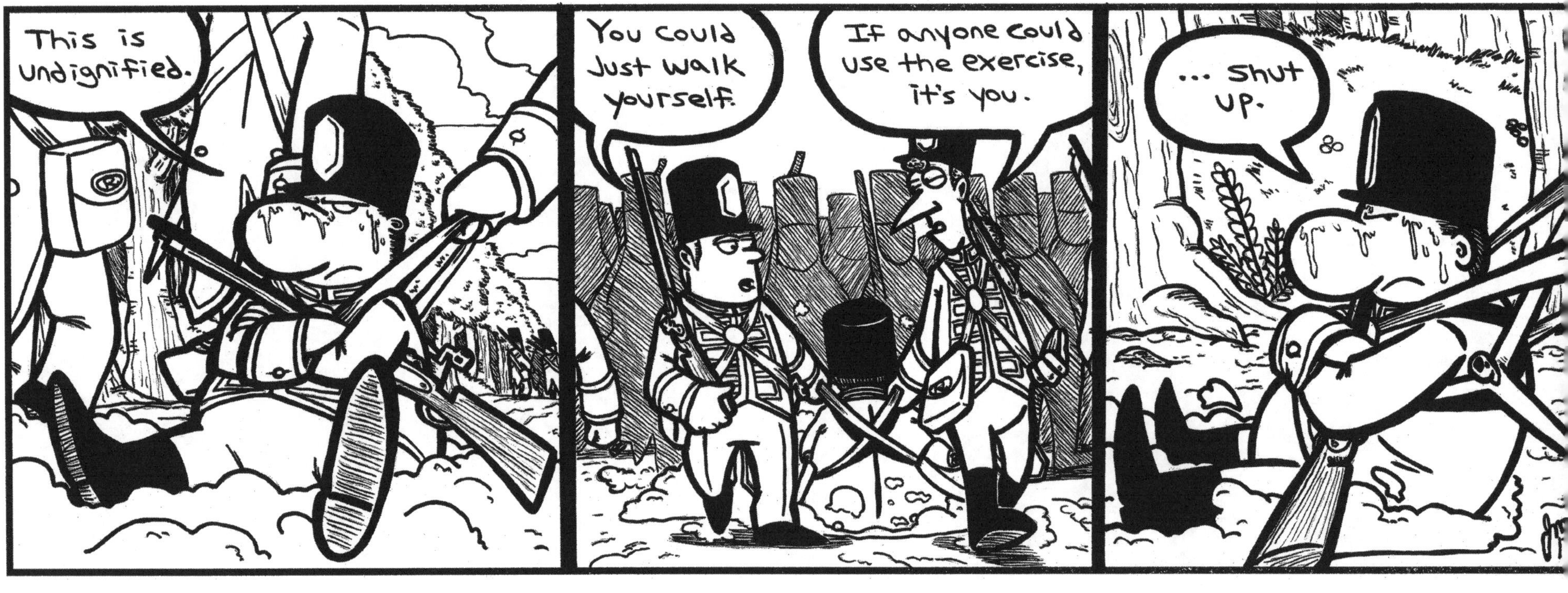
This is undignified.
You could just walk yourself.
If anyone could use the exercise, it's you.
... shut up.

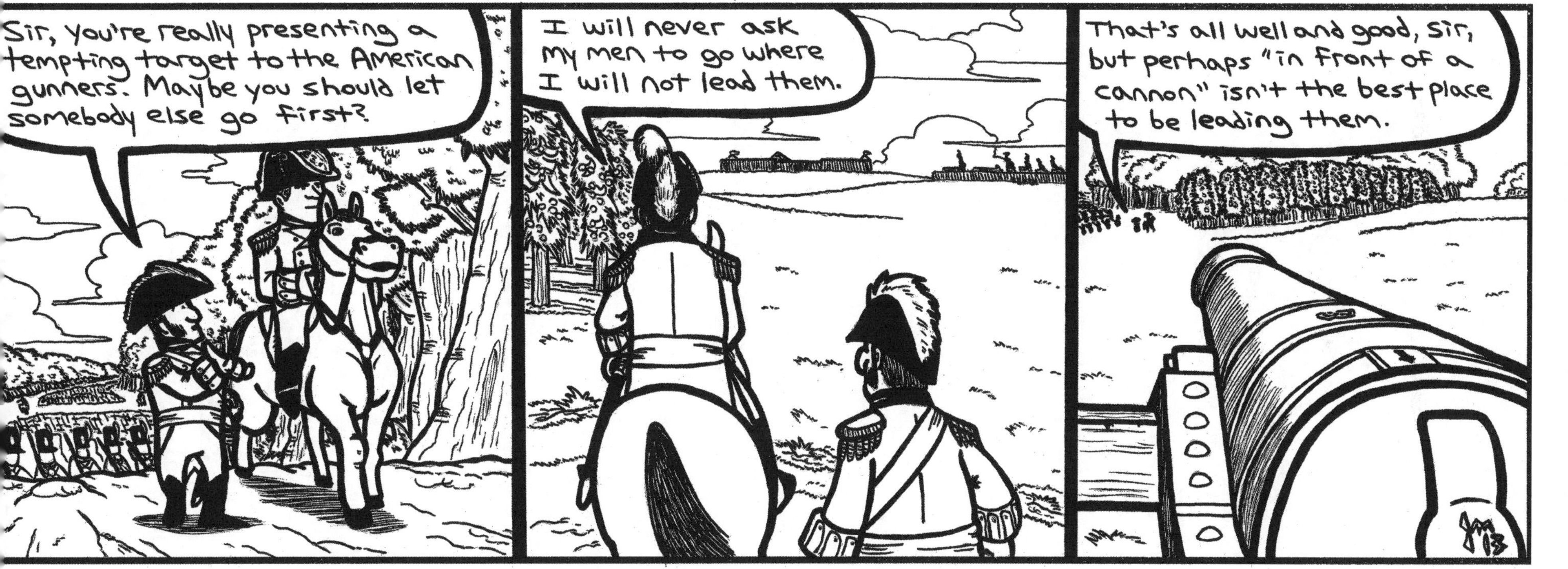
Sir, you're really presenting a tempting target to the American gunners. Maybe you should let somebody else go first?
I will never ask my men to go where I will not lead them.
That's all well and good, sir, but perhaps "in front of a cannon" isn't the best place to be leading them.
JM 13

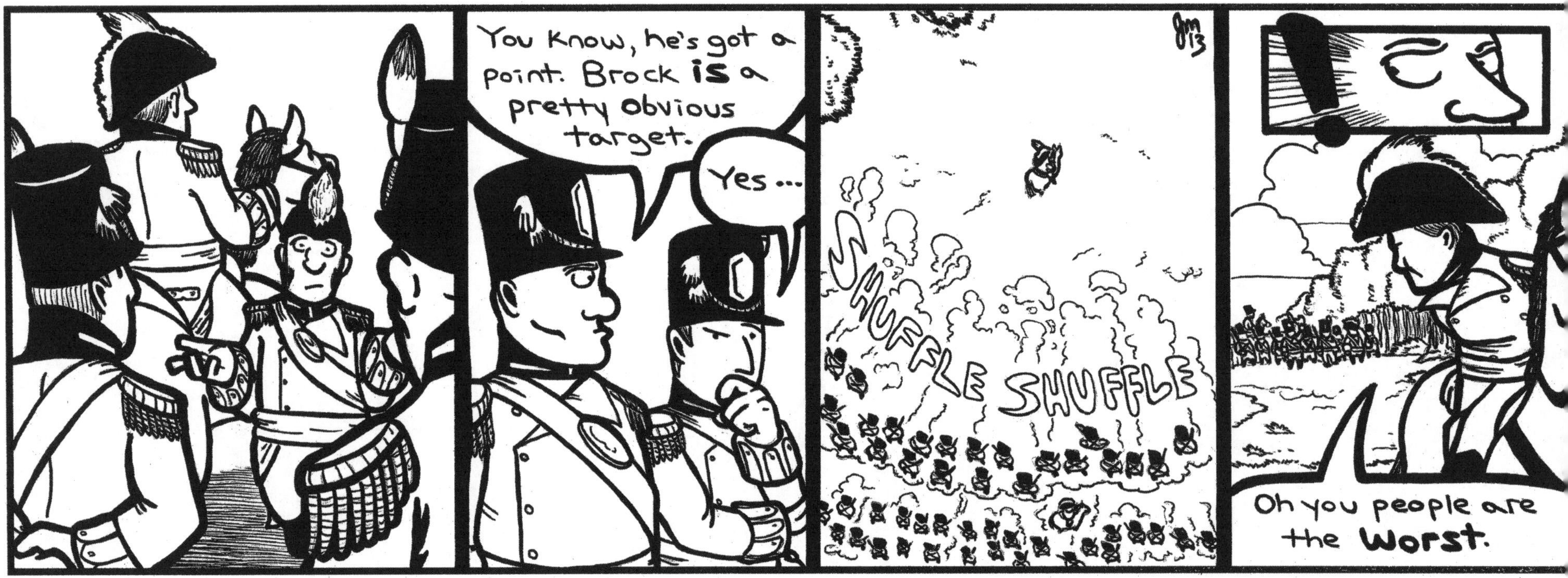
You know, he's got a point. Brock **is** a pretty obvious target.
Yes...
SHUFFLE SHUFFLE SHUFFLE
!
Oh you people are the **Worst**.

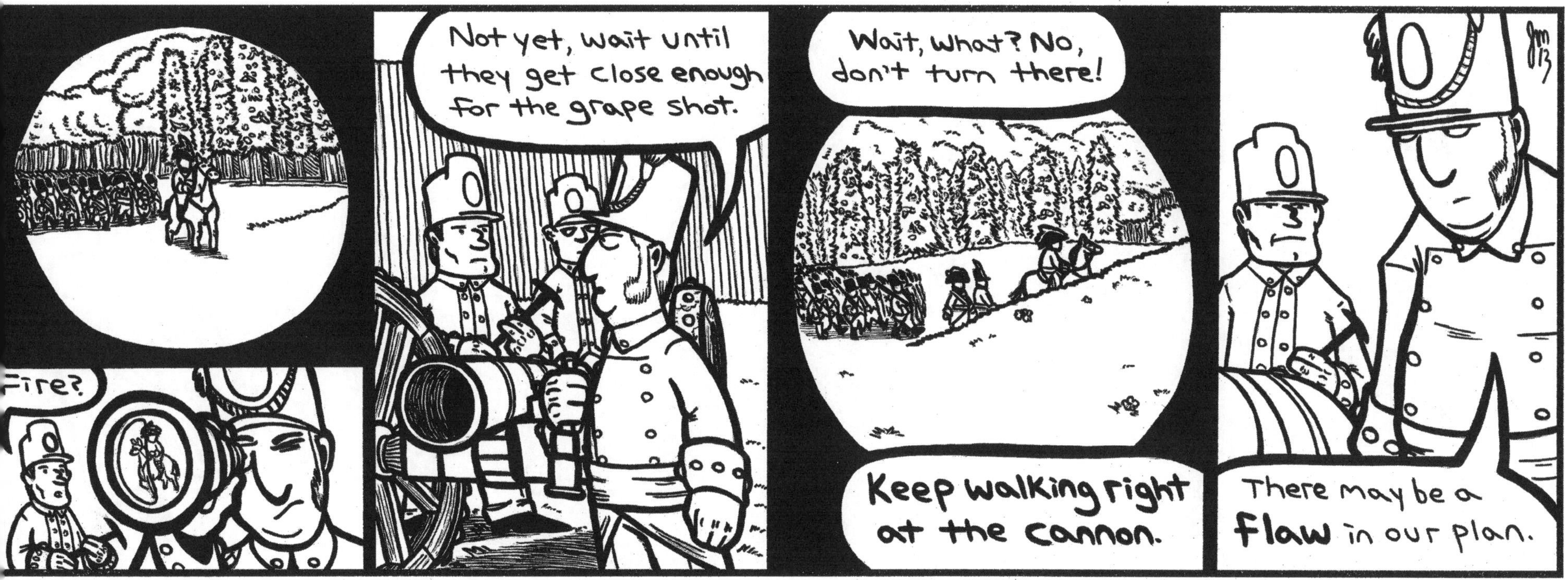

Fire?
Not yet, wait until they get close enough for the grape shot.
Wait, what? No, don't turn there!
Keep walking right at the cannon.
There may be a flaw in our plan.

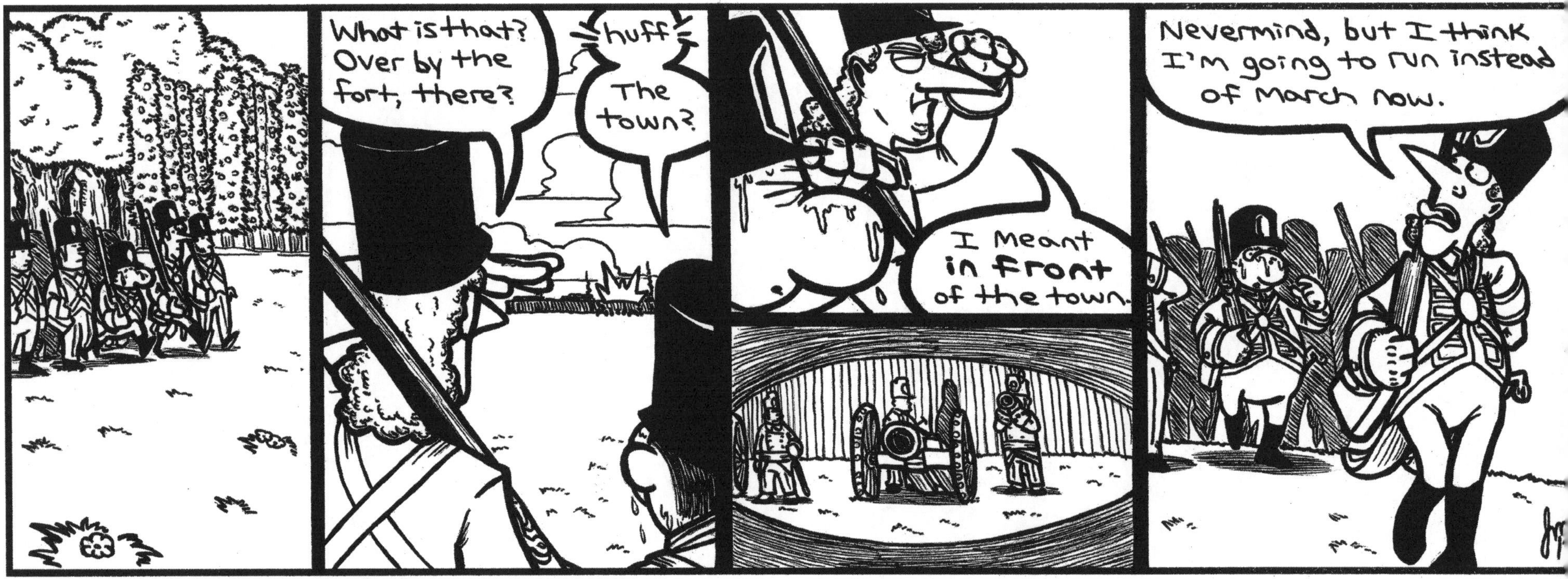
What is that? Over by the fort, there?
huff
The town?
I Meant **in front** of the town.
Nevermind, but I think I'm going to run instead of March now.

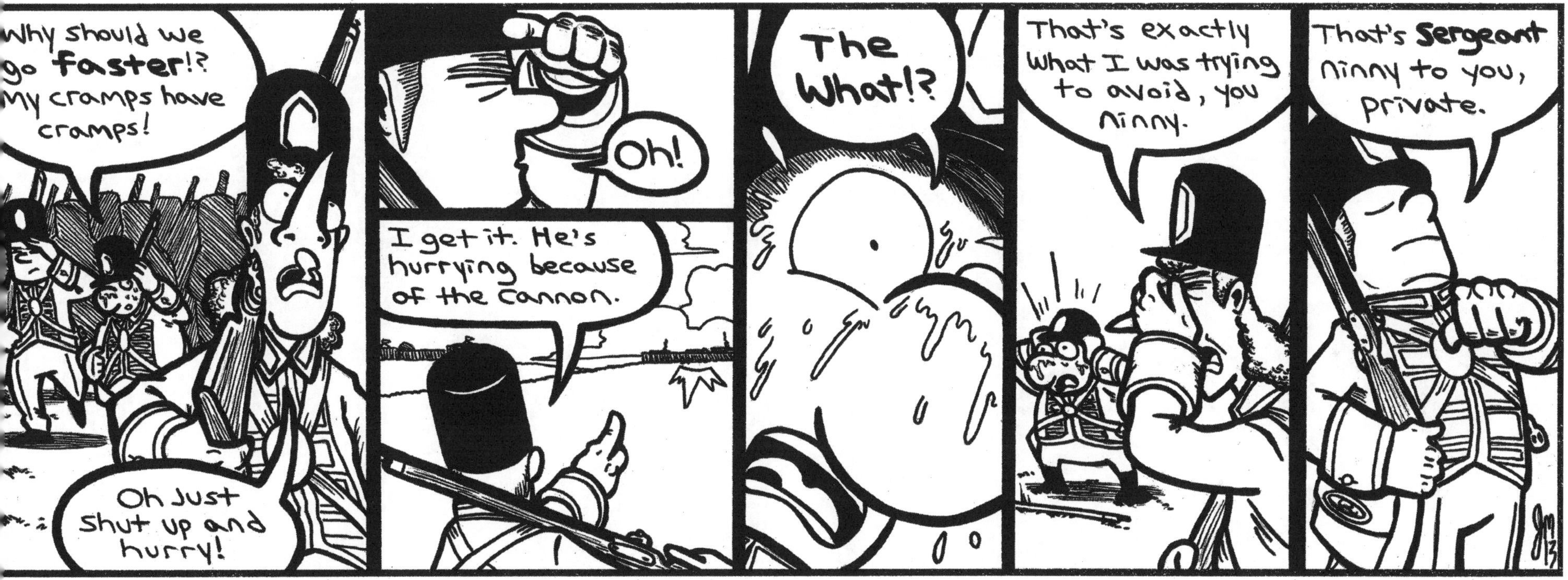
Why should we go faster!? My cramps have cramps!
Oh Just shut up and hurry!
Oh!
I get it. He's hurrying because of the cannon.
The What!?
That's exactly what I was trying to avoid, you ninny.
That's Sergeant ninny to you, private.

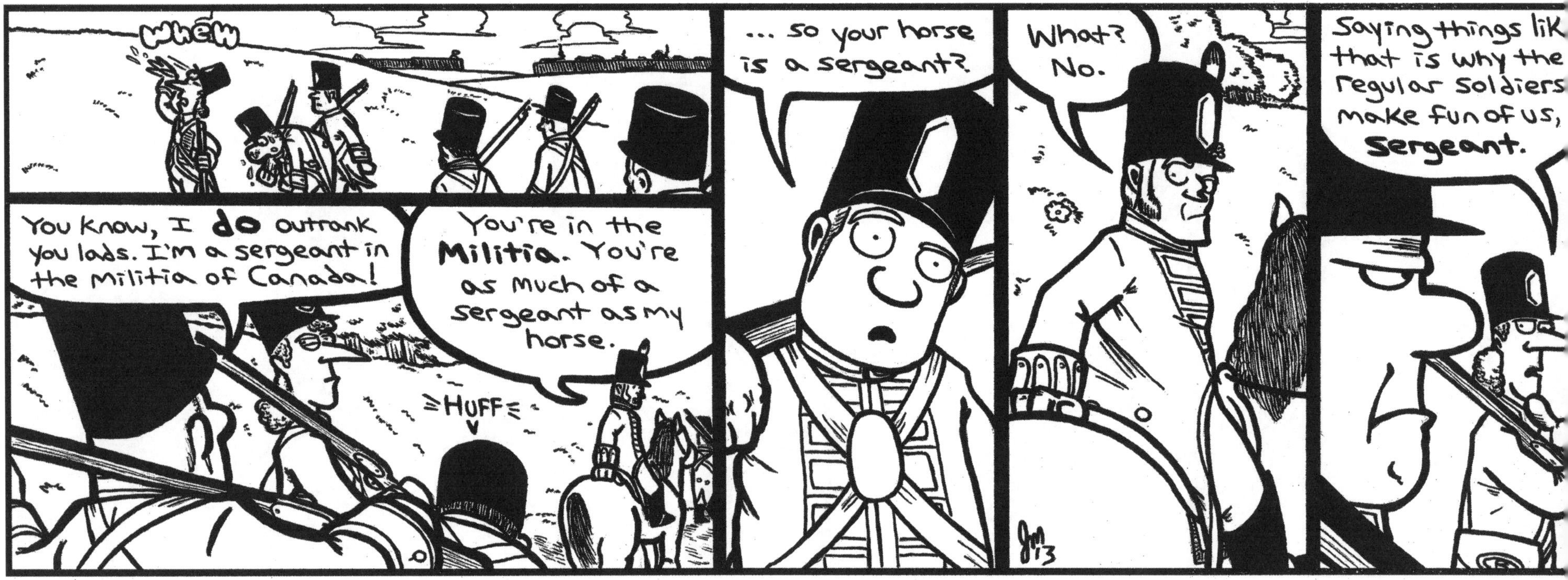
WHEW
You know, I **do** outrank you lads. I'm a sergeant in the Militia of Canada!
You're in the **Militia**. You're as much of a sergeant as my horse.
HUFF
... so your horse is a sergeant?
What? No.
Saying things lik that is why the regular soldiers make fun of us, **Sergeant**.

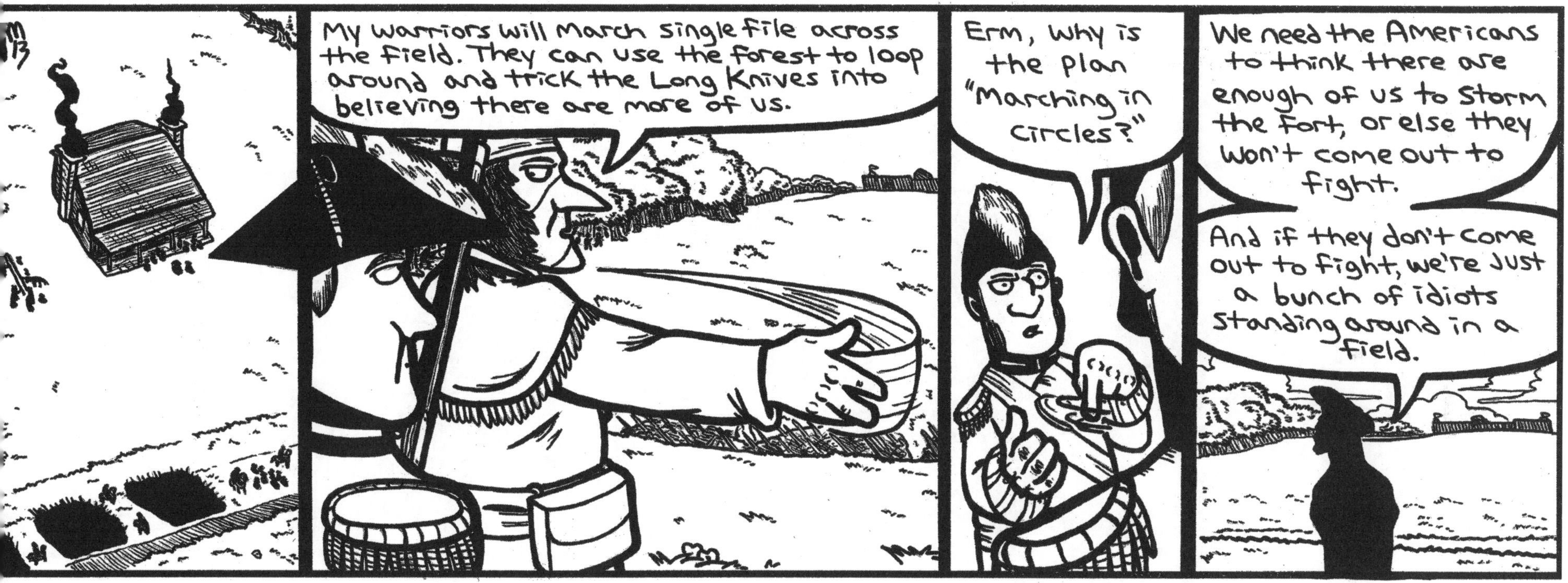
My warriors will march single file across the field. They can use the forest to loop around and trick the Long Knives into believing there are more of us.
Erm, why is the plan "Marching in circles?"
We need the Americans to think there are enough of us to storm the fort, or else they won't come out to fight.
And if they don't come out to fight, we're just a bunch of idiots standing around in a field.

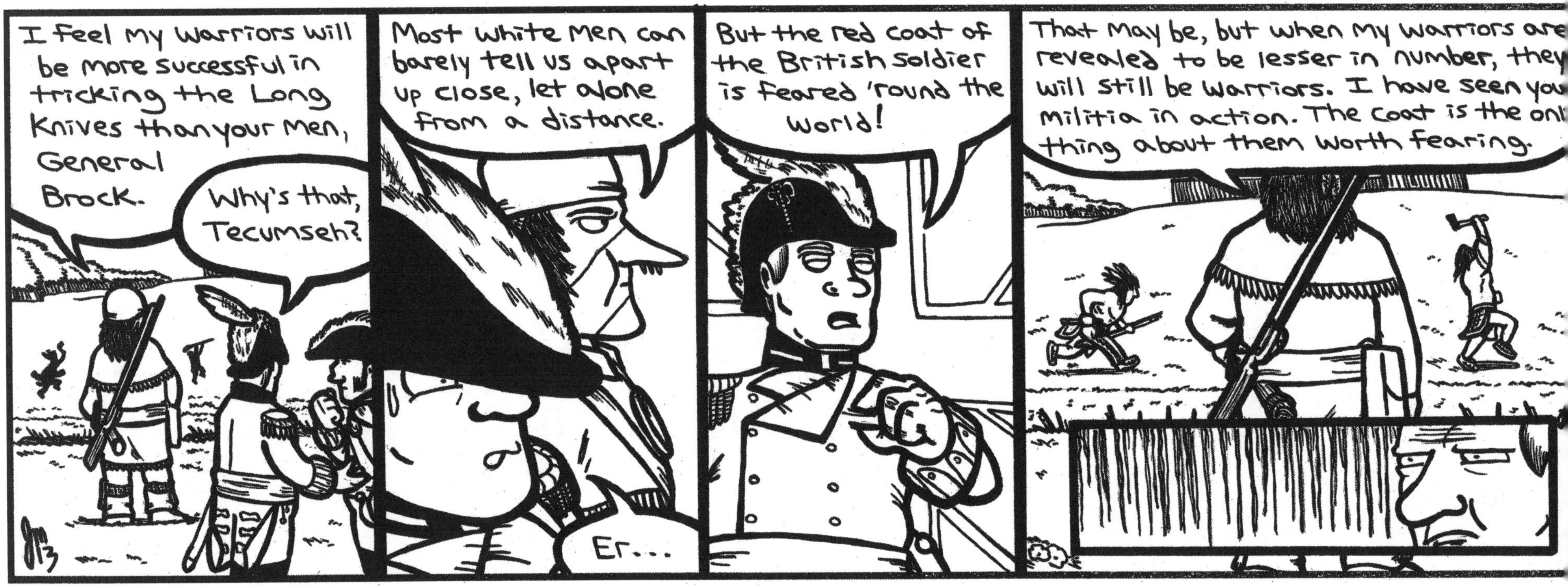
I feel my warriors will be more successful in tricking the Long Knives than your men, General Brock.
Why's that, Tecumseh?
Most white men can barely tell us apart up close, let alone from a distance.
Er...
But the red coat of the British soldier is feared 'round the world!
That may be, but when my warriors are revealed to be lesser in number, they will still be warriors. I have seen you militia in action. The coat is the onl thing about them worth fearing.

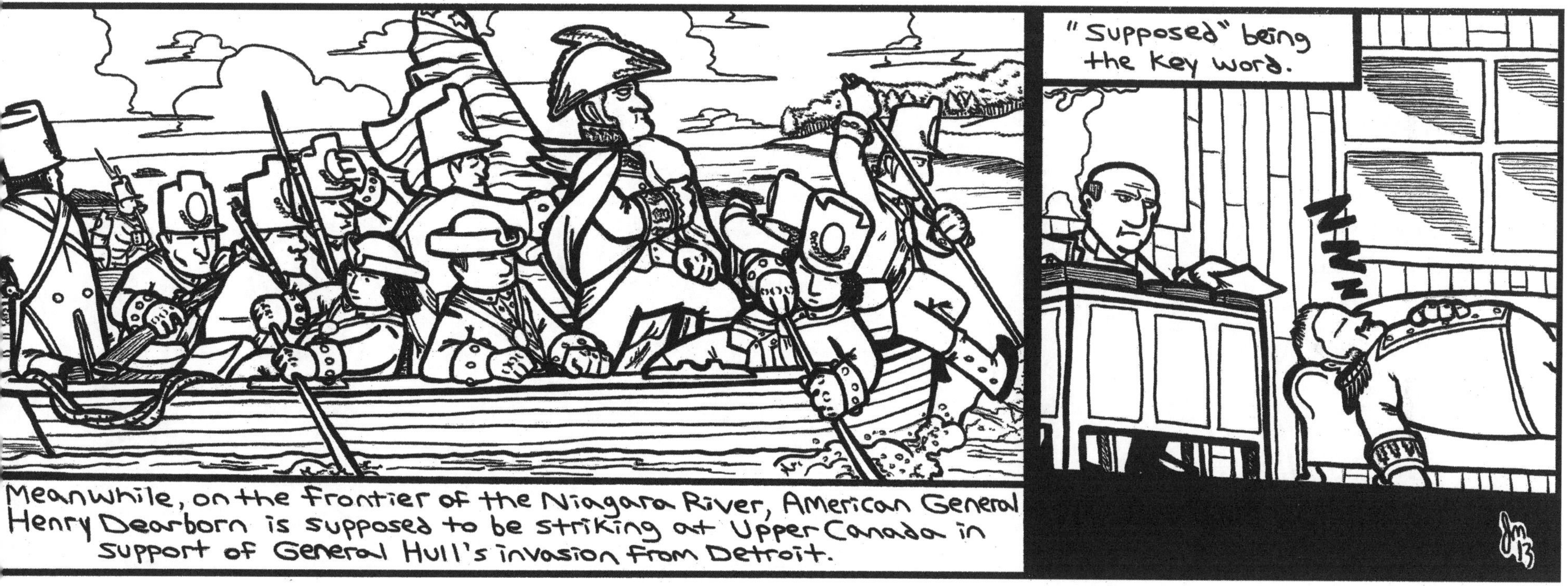
Meanwhile, on the frontier of the Niagara River, American General Henry Dearborn is supposed to be striking at Upper Canada in support of General Hull's invasion from Detroit.
"Supposed" being the key word.
NNN

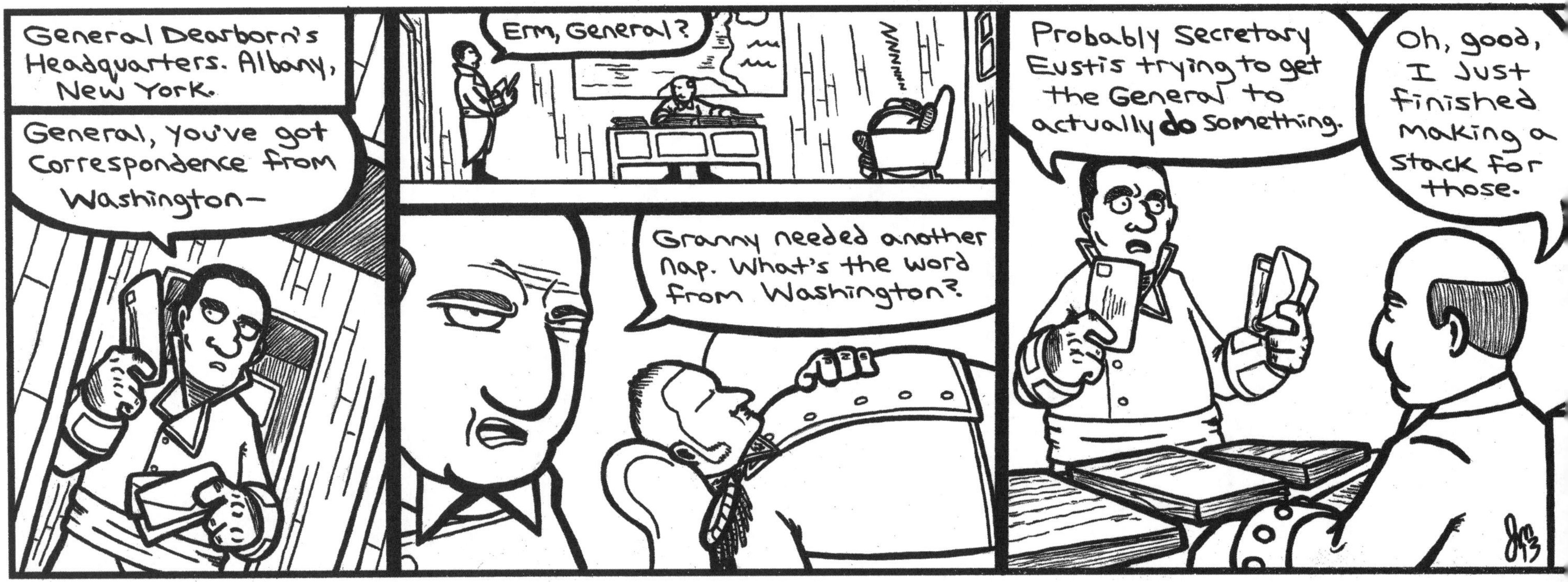
General Dearborn's Headquarters. Albany, New York.
General, you've got Correspondence from Washington–
Erm, General?
NNNNNN
Granny needed another nap. What's the word from Washington?
Probably Secretary Eustis trying to get the General to actually **do** something.
Oh, good, I Just finished making a stack for those.

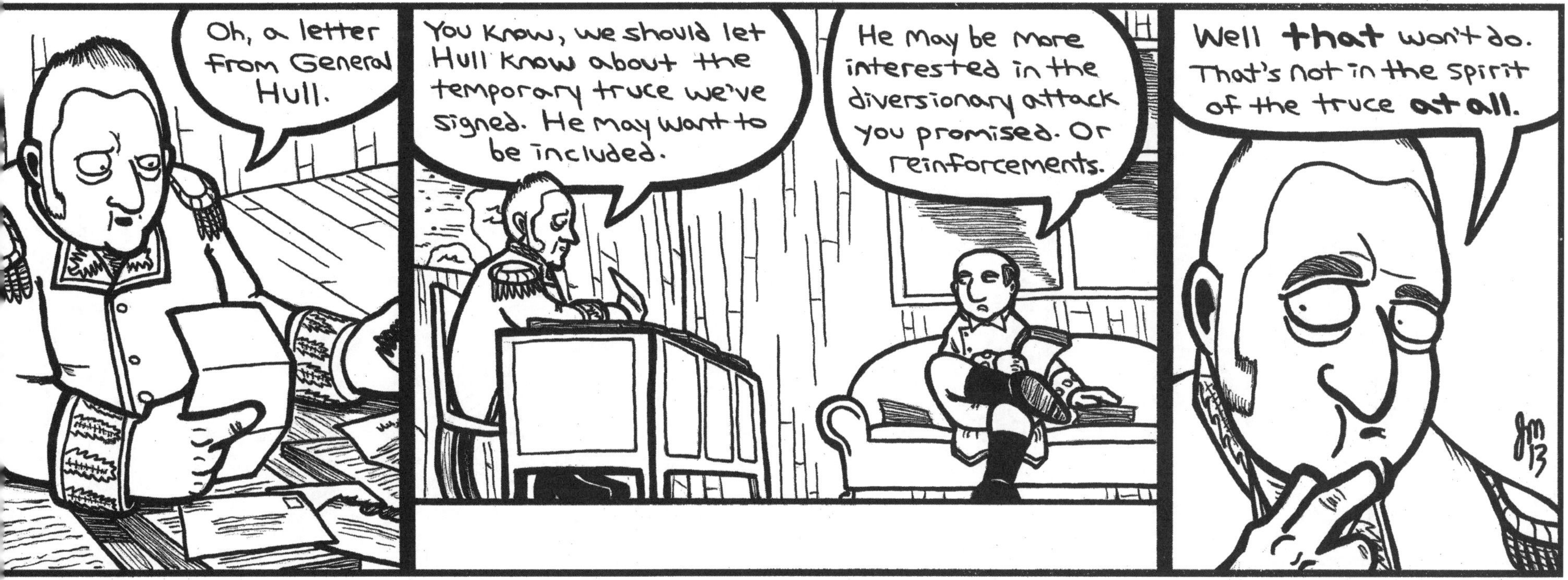
Oh, a letter from General Hull.
You know, we should let Hull know about the temporary truce we've signed. He may want to be included.
He may be more interested in the diversionary attack you promised. Or reinforcements.
Well **that** won't do. That's not in the spirit of the truce **at all**.

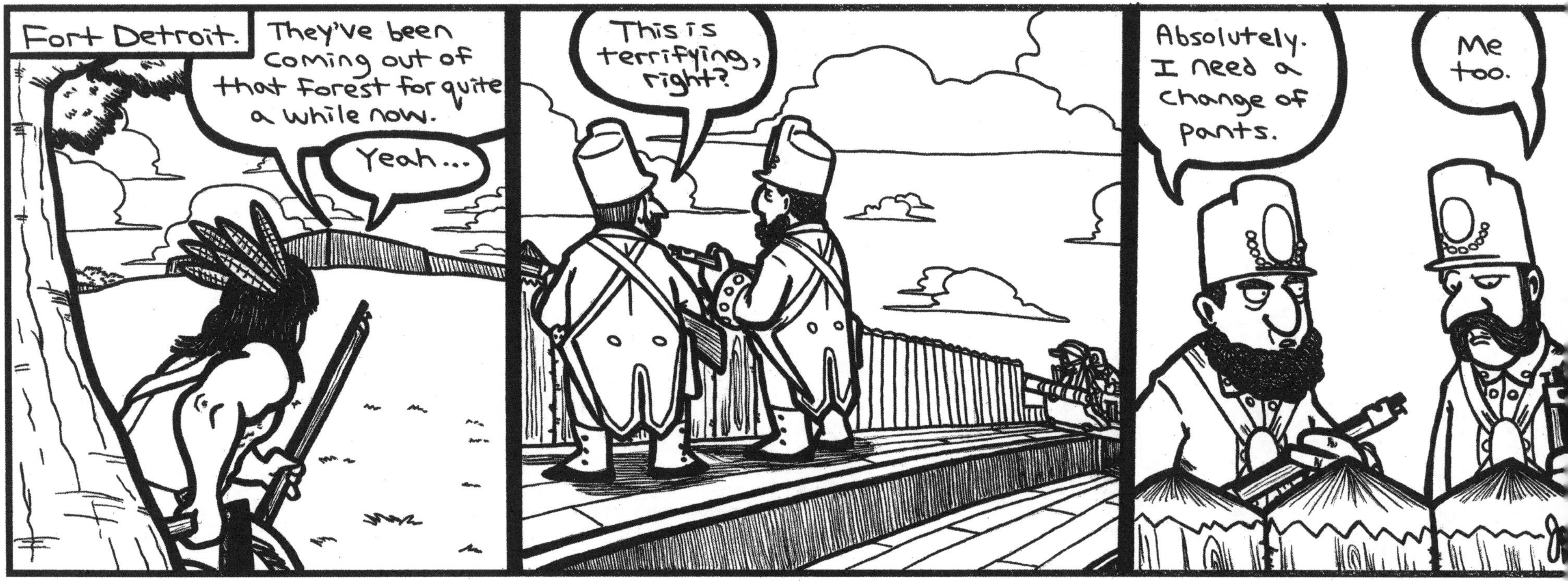
Fort Detroit.
They've been coming out of that forest for quite a while now.
Yeah...
This is terrifying, right?
Absolutely. I need a change of pants.
Me too.

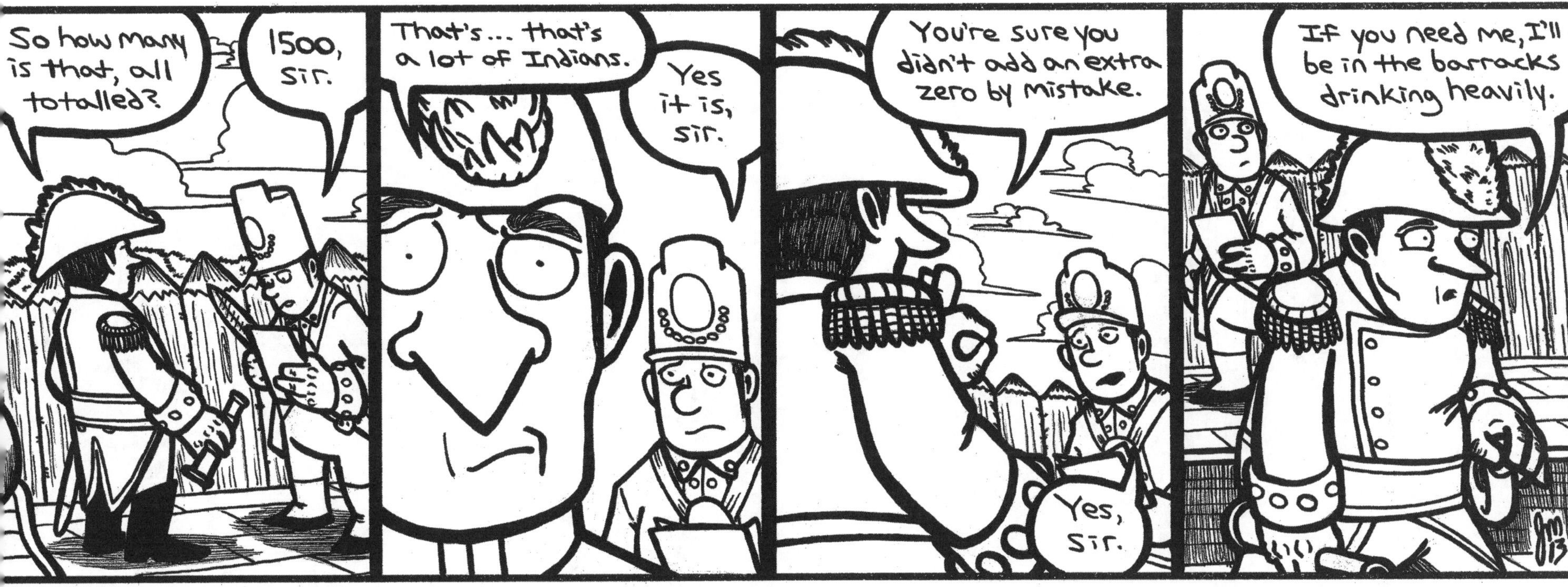
So how many is that, all totalled?
1500, sir.
That's... that's a lot of Indians.
Yes it is, sir.
You're sure you didn't add an extra zero by mistake.
Yes, sir.
If you need me, I'll be in the barracks drinking heavily.
JM 13

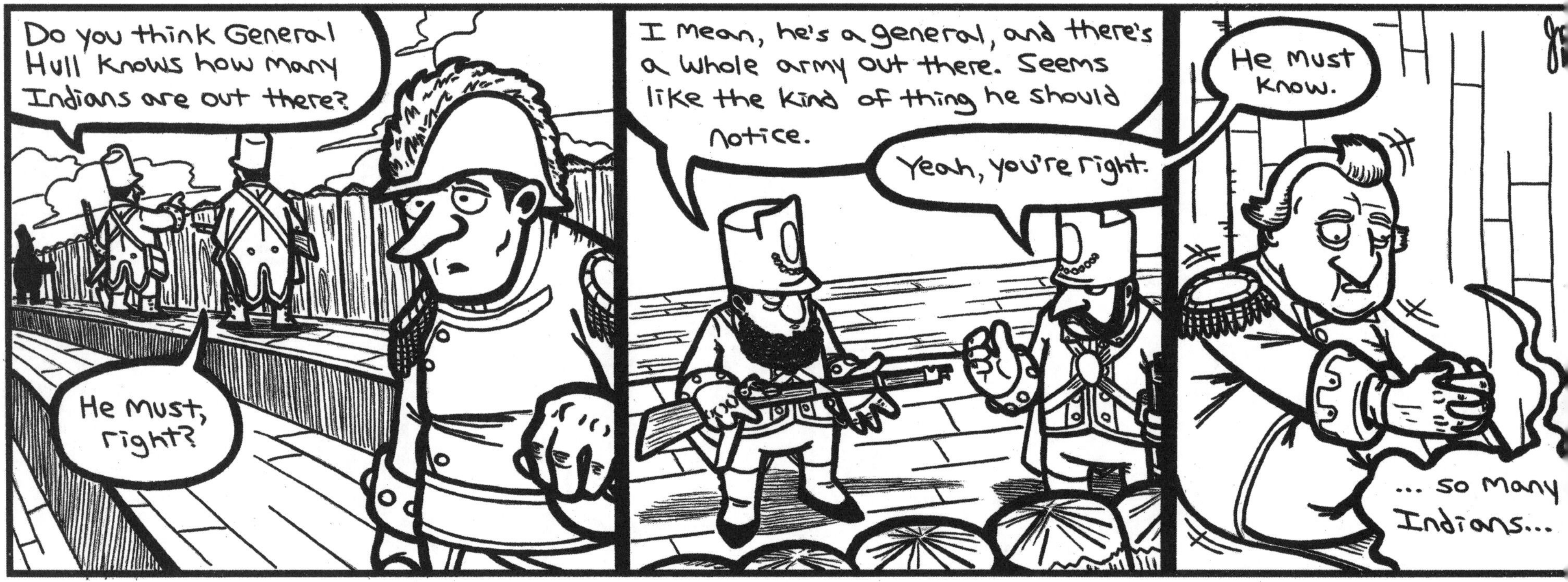
Do you think General Hull knows how many Indians are out there?
He must, right?
I mean, he's a general, and there's a whole army out there. Seems like the kind of thing he should notice.
Yeah, you're right.
He must know.
... so many Indians...

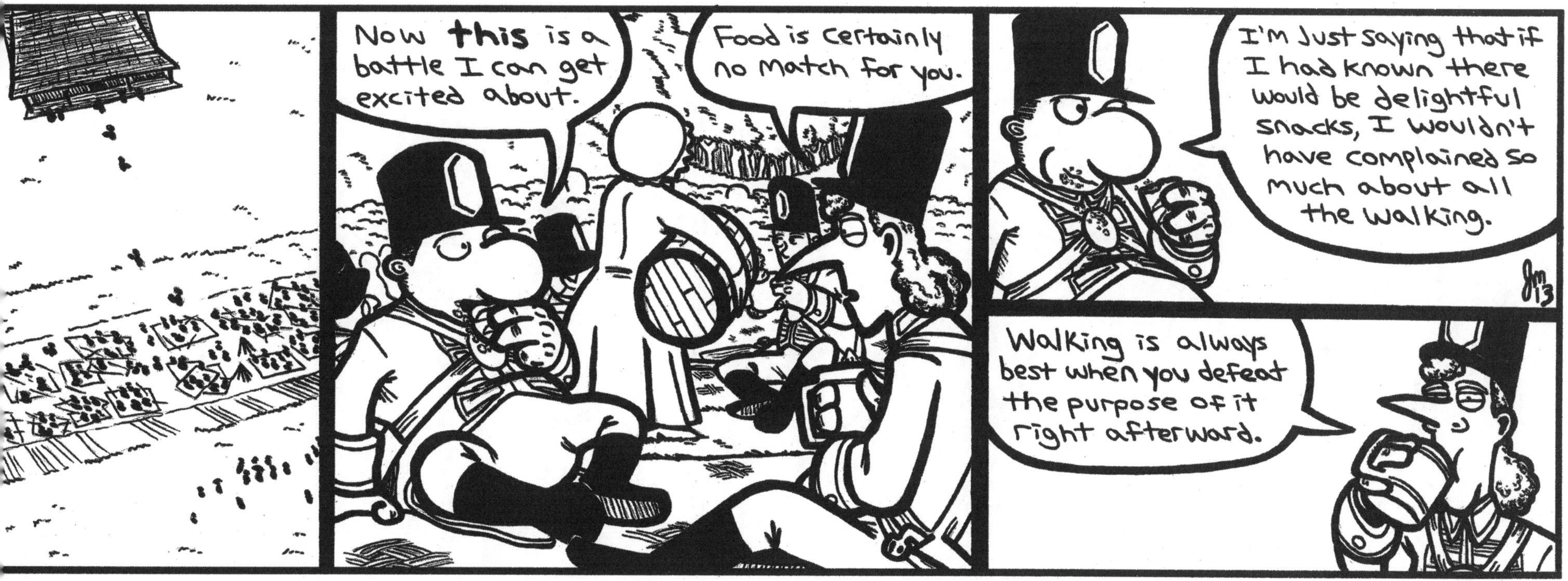

Now this is a battle I can get excited about.
Food is certainly no match for you.
I'm just saying that if I had known there would be delightful snacks, I wouldn't have complained so much about all the walking.
Jm 13
Walking is always best when you defeat the purpose of it right afterward.

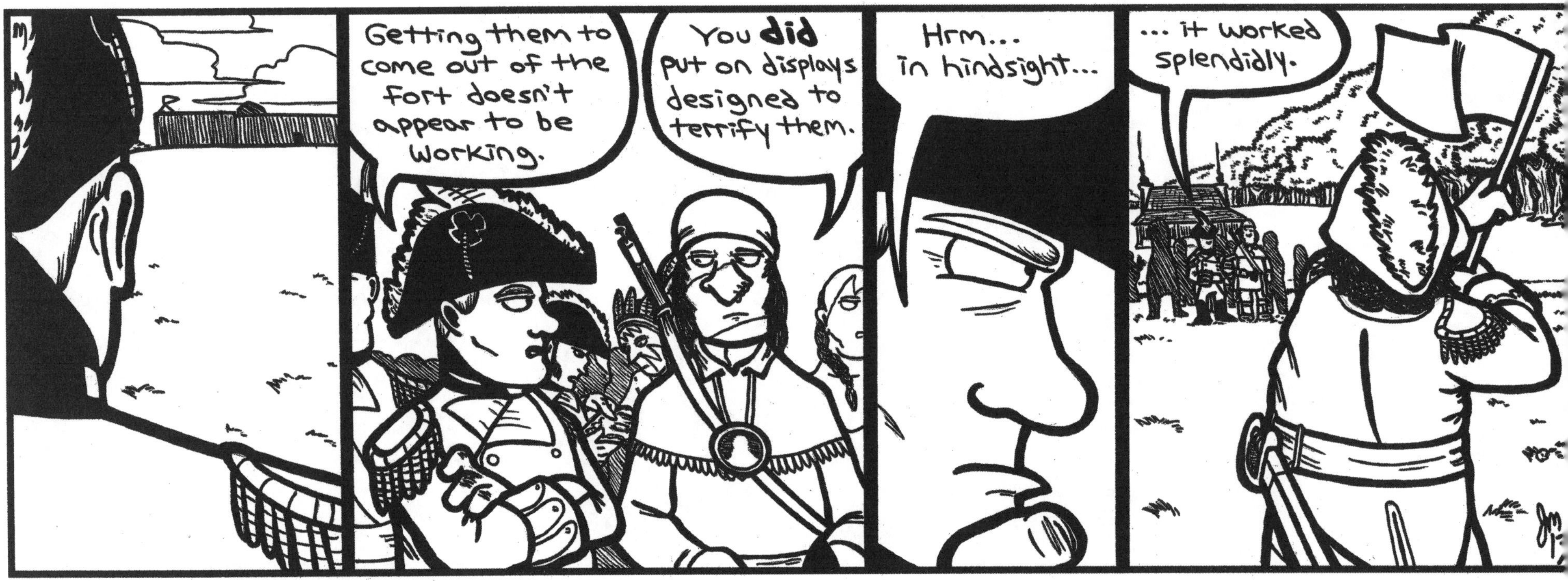
Getting them to come out of the fort doesn't appear to be working.
You **did** put on displays designed to terrify them.
Hrm... in hindsight...
... it worked splendidly.

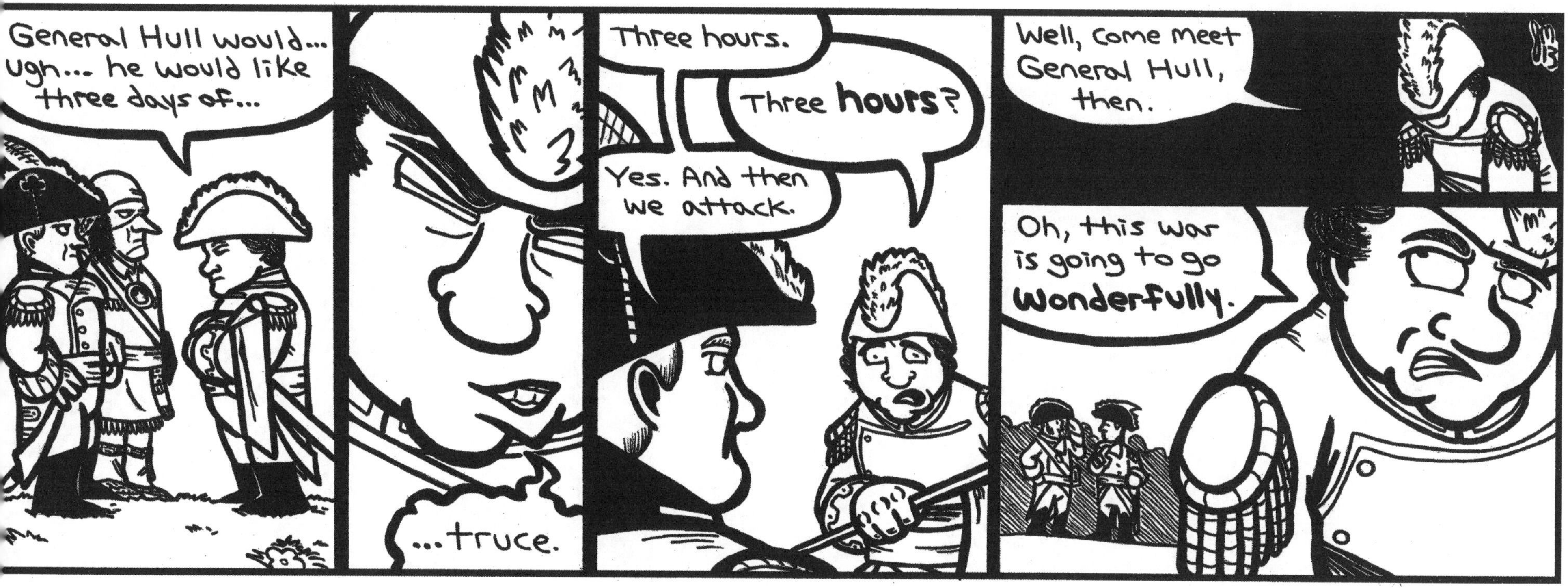
General Hull would... ugh... he would like three days of...
...truce.
Three hours.
Three **hours**?
Yes. And then we attack.
Well, come meet General Hull, then.
Oh, this war is going to go **wonderfully**.

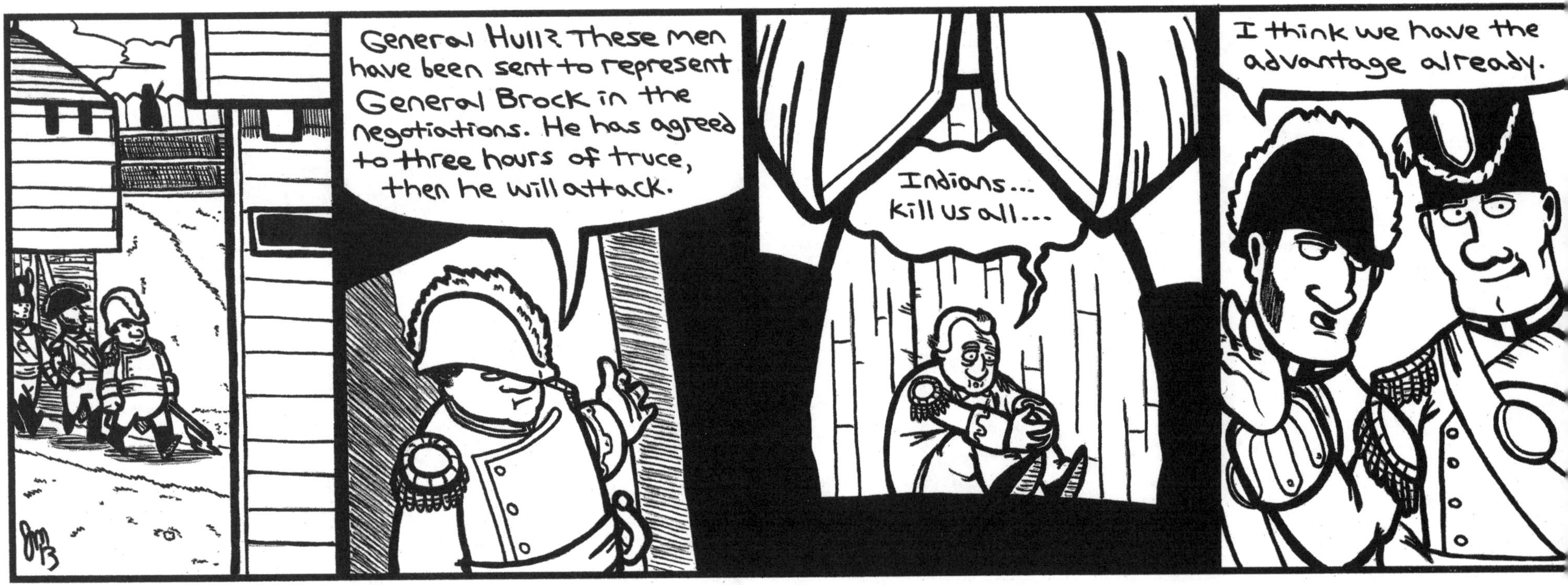
General Hull? These men have been sent to represent General Brock in the negotiations. He has agreed to three hours of truce, then he will attack.
Indians... kill us all...
I think we have the advantage already.

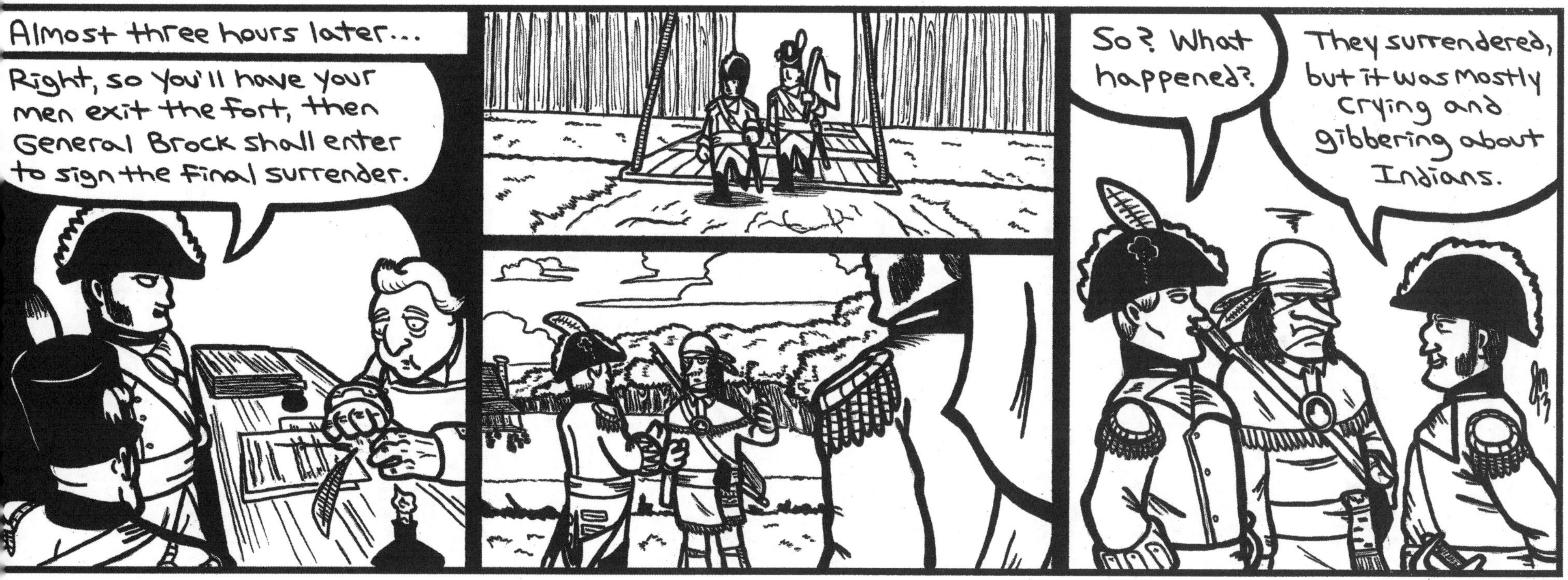
Almost three hours later...
Right, so you'll have your men exit the fort, then General Brock shall enter to sign the final surrender.
So? What happened?
They surrendered, but it was mostly crying and gibbering about Indians.

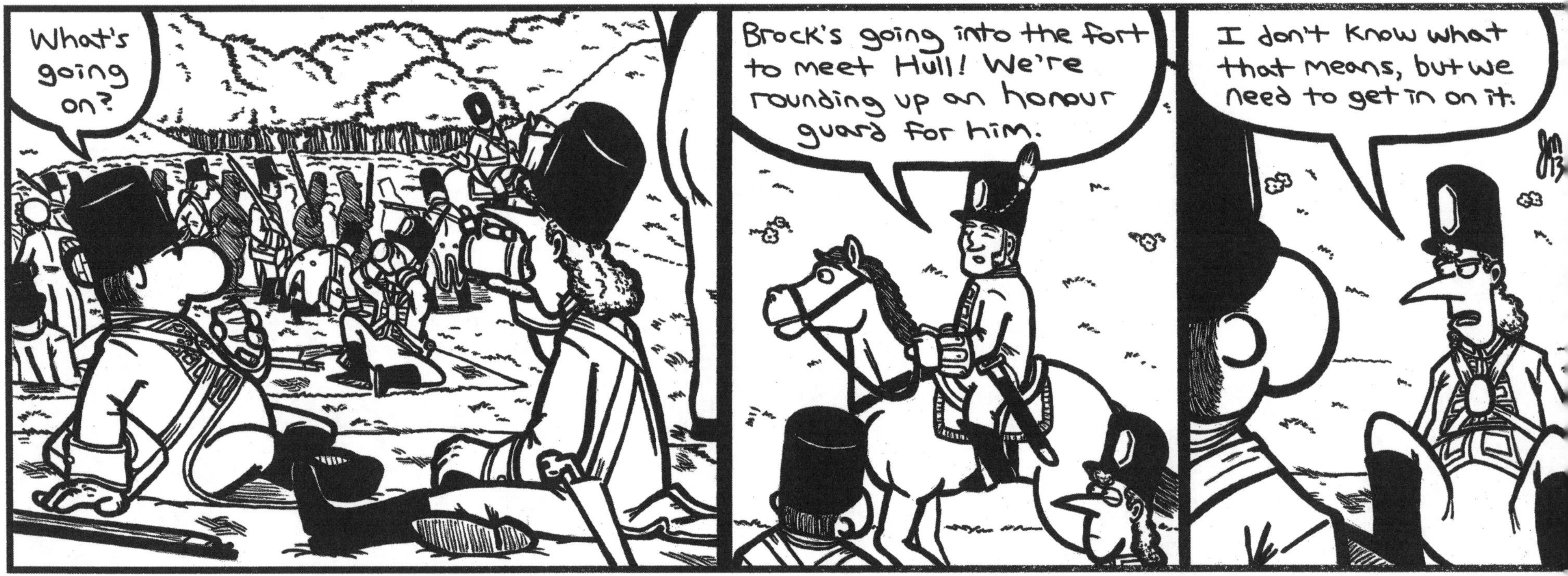
What's going on?
Brock's going into the fort to meet Hull! We're rounding up an honour guard for him.
I don't know what that means, but we need to get in on it.

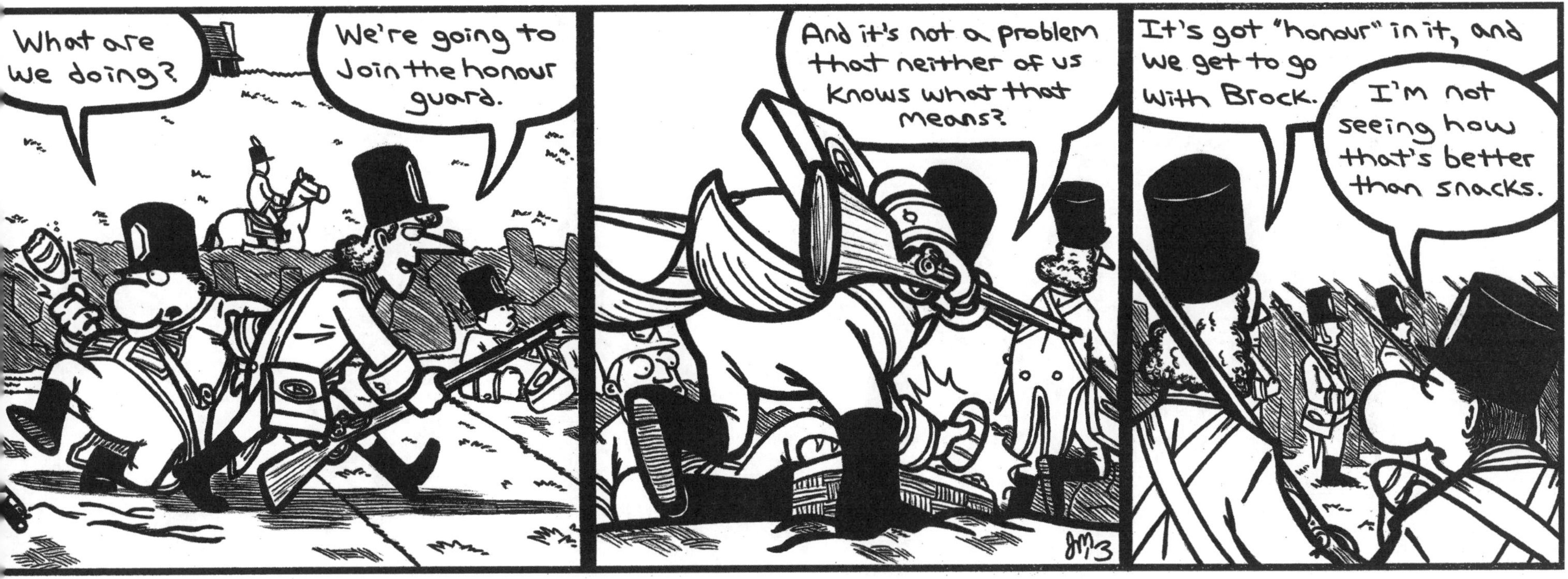
What are we doing?
We're going to Join the honour guard.
And it's not a problem that neither of us knows what that means?
It's got "honour" in it, and we get to go with Brock.
I'm not seeing how that's better than snacks.

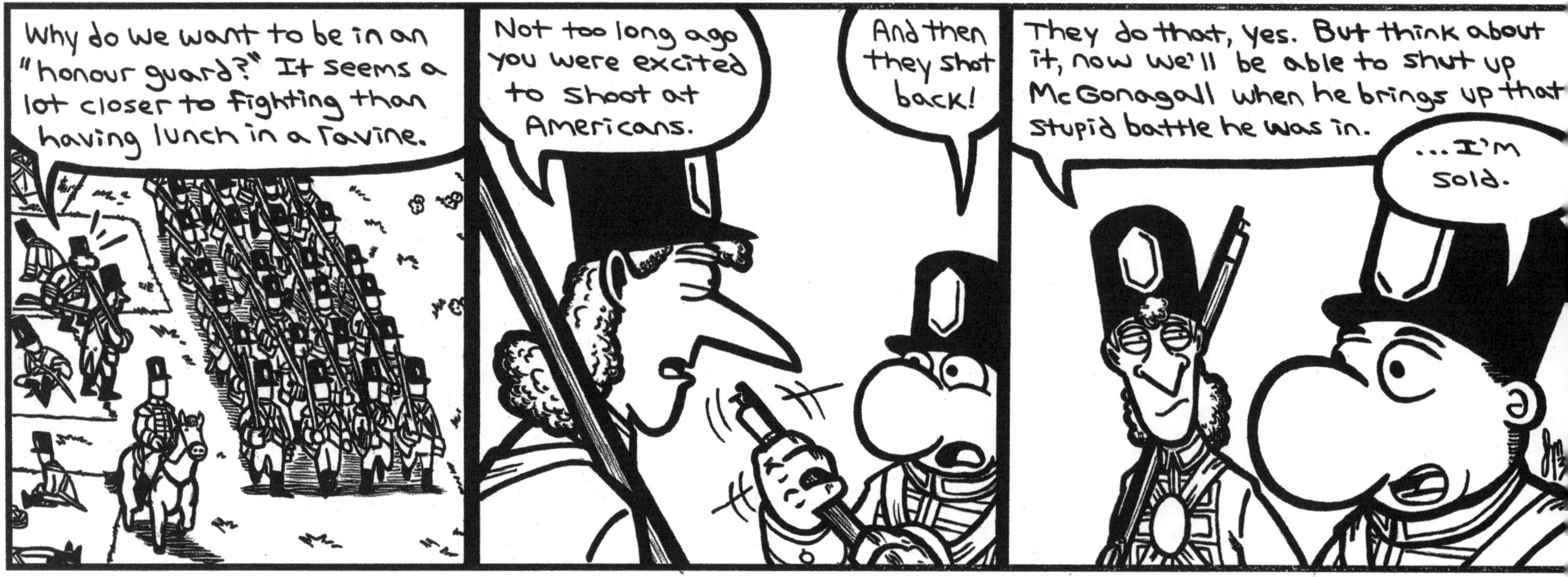
Why do we want to be in an "honour guard?" It seems a lot closer to fighting than having lunch in a ravine.
Not too long ago you were excited to shoot at Americans.
And then they shot back!
They do that, yes. But think about it, now we'll be able to shut up McGonagall when he brings up that stupid battle he was in.
...I'm sold.

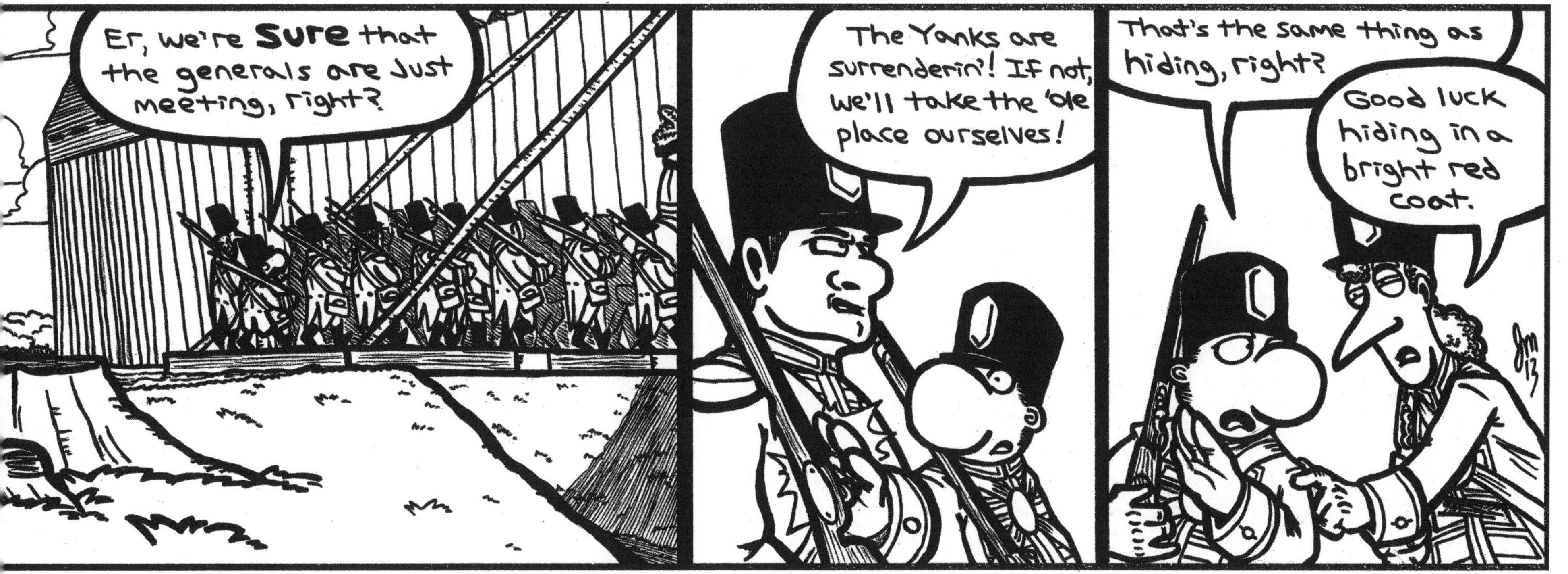
Er, we're SURE that the generals are just meeting, right?
The Yanks are surrenderin'! If not, we'll take the 'ole place ourselves!
That's the same thing as hiding, right?
Good luck hiding in a bright red coat.

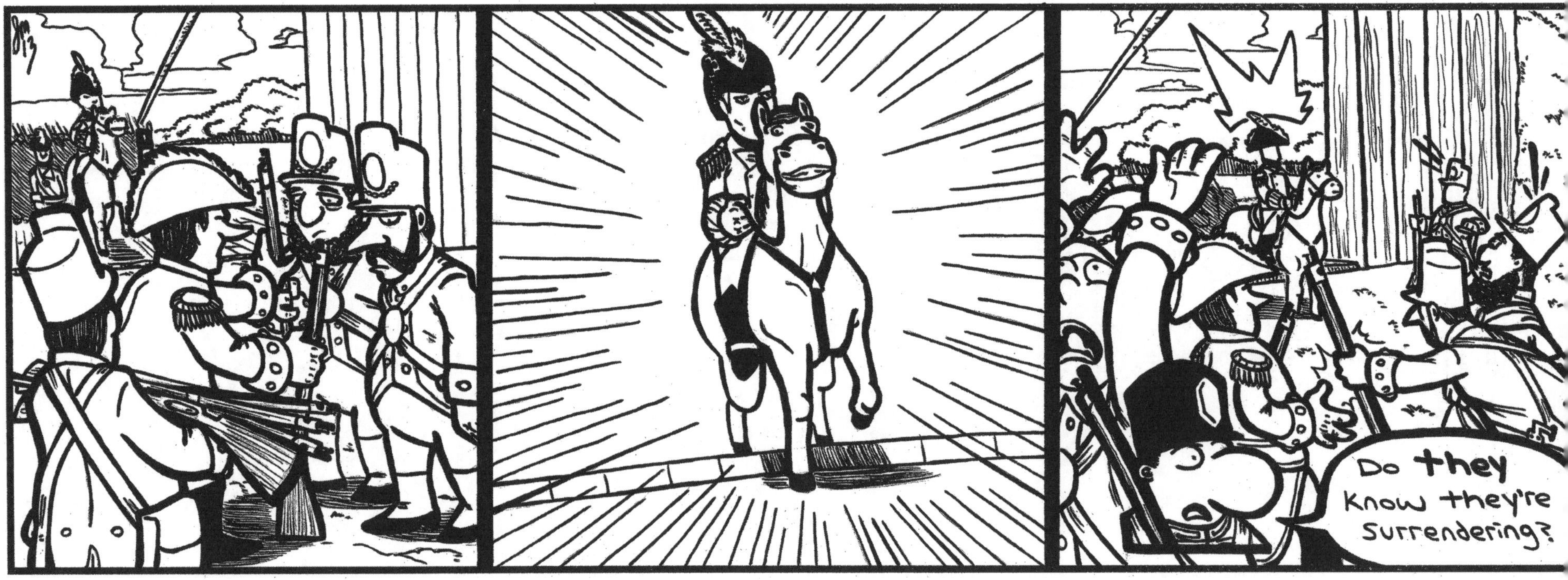
Do they know they're surrendering?

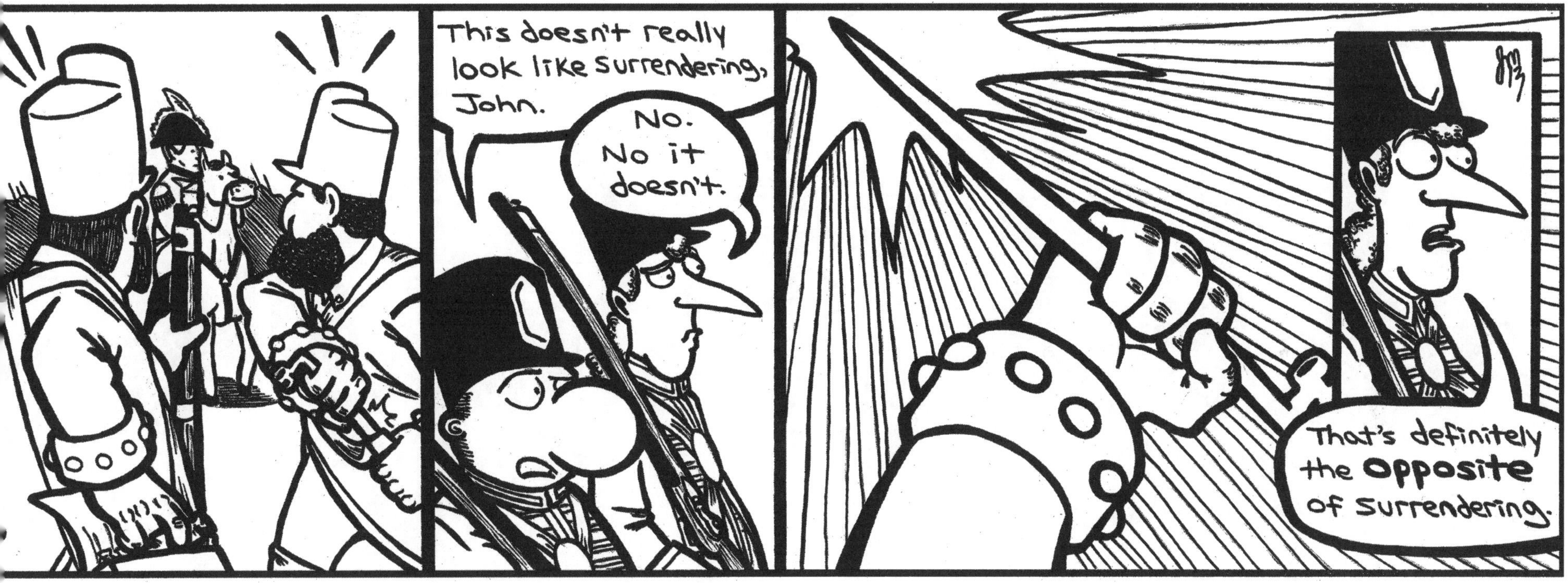
This doesn't really look like surrendering, John.
No. No it doesn't.
That's definitely the **opposite** of surrendering.

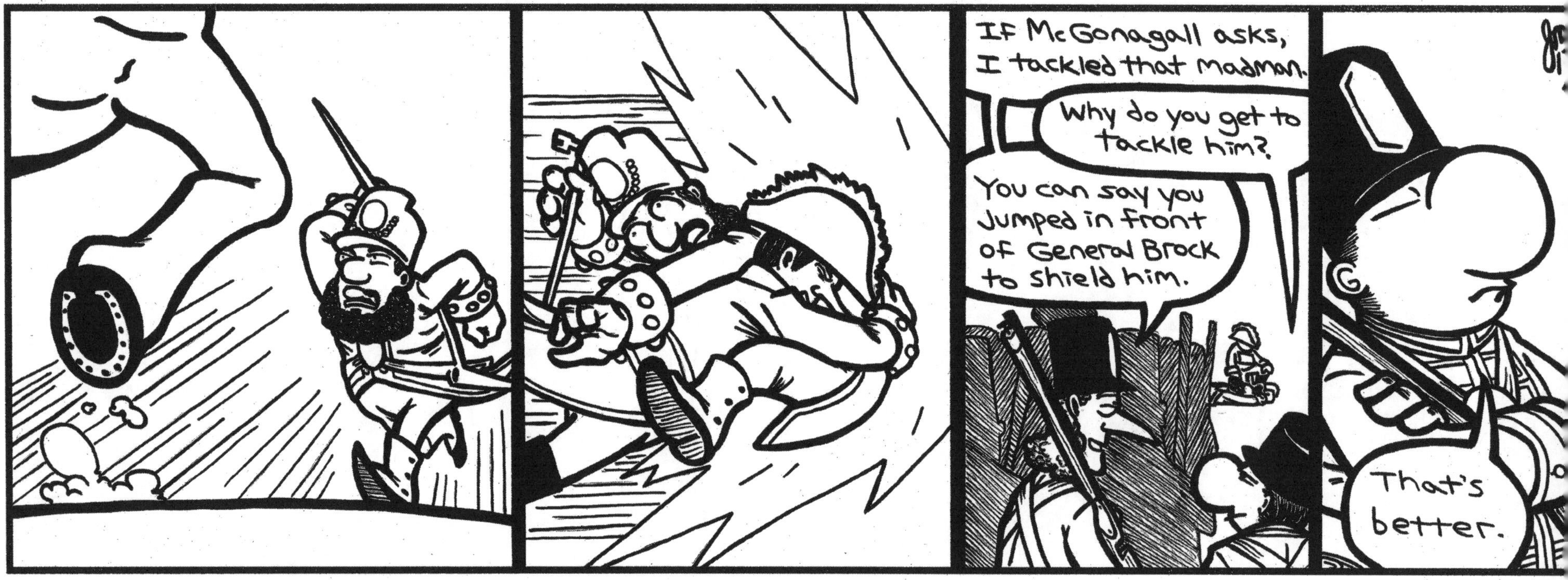

If McGonagall asks, I tackled that madman.
Why do you get to tackle him?
You can say you jumped in front of General Brock to shield him.
That's better.

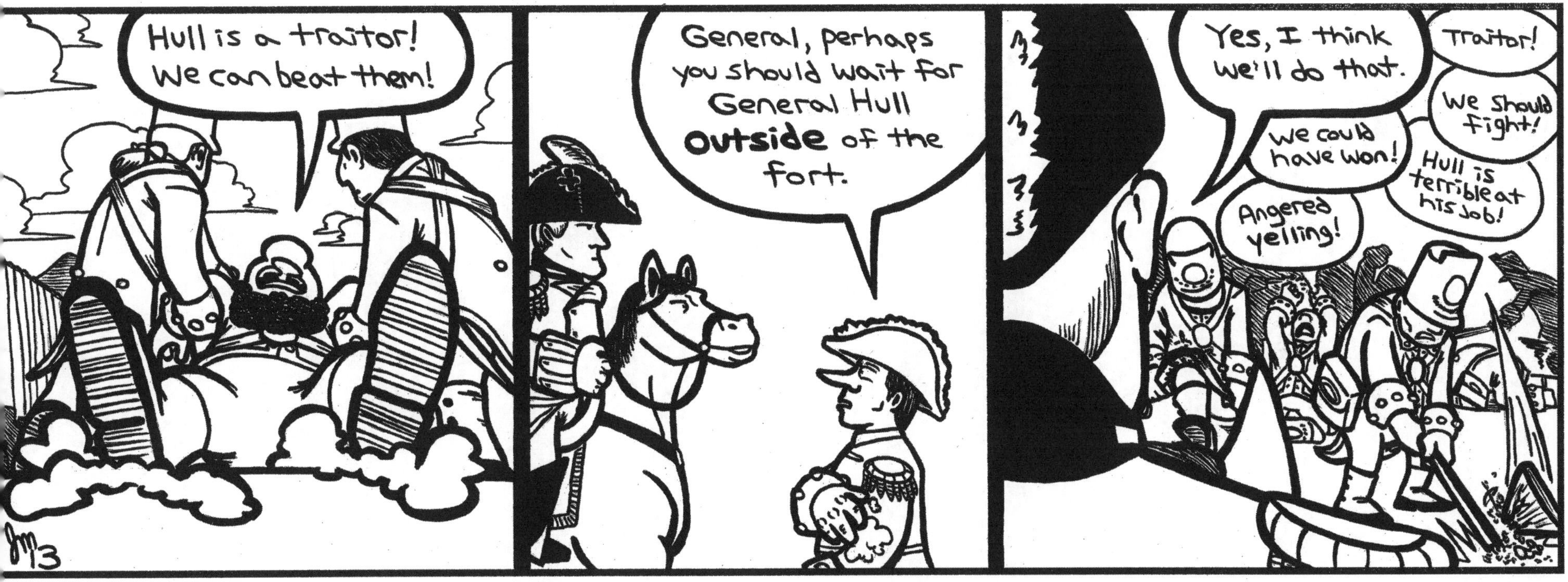
Hull is a traitor! We can beat them!
General, perhaps you should wait for General Hull **outside** of the fort.
Yes, I think we'll do that.
Traitor!
We should fight!
We could have won!
Hull is terrible at his job!
Angered yelling!

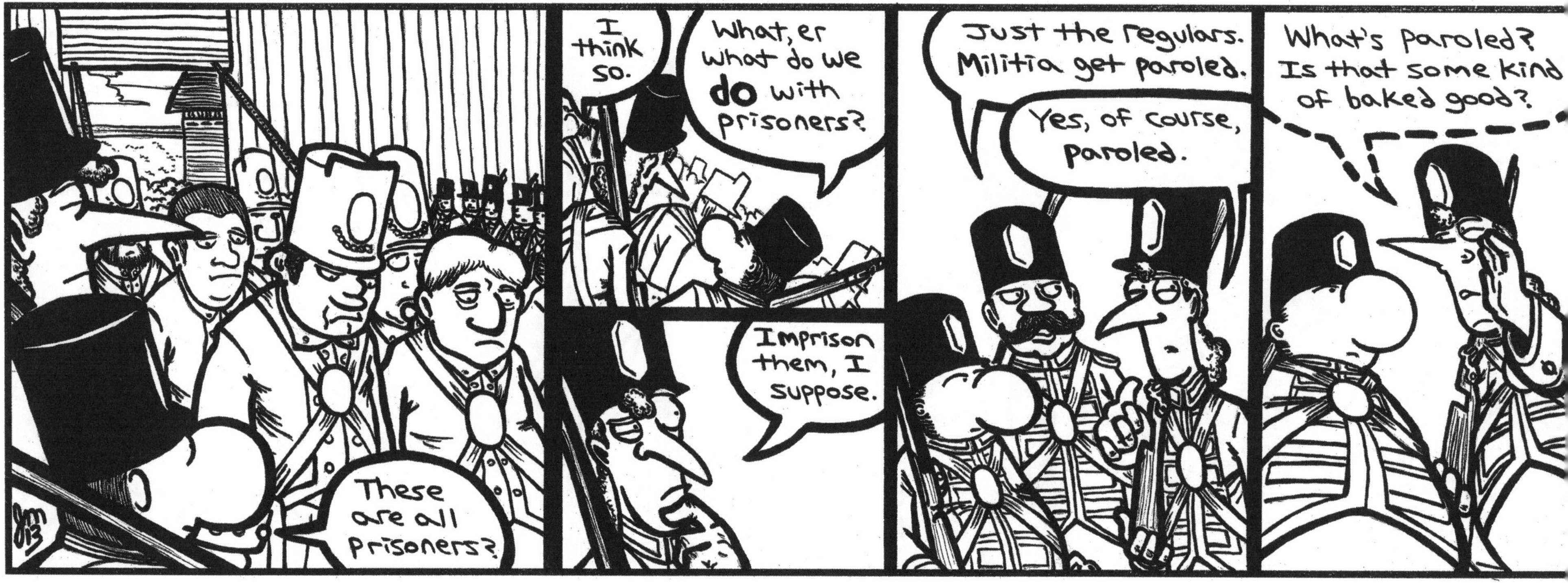
These are all prisoners?
I think so.
What, er what do we do with prisoners?
Imprison them, I suppose.
Just the regulars. Militia get paroled.
Yes, of course, paroled.
What's paroled? Is that some kind of baked good?
JM 13

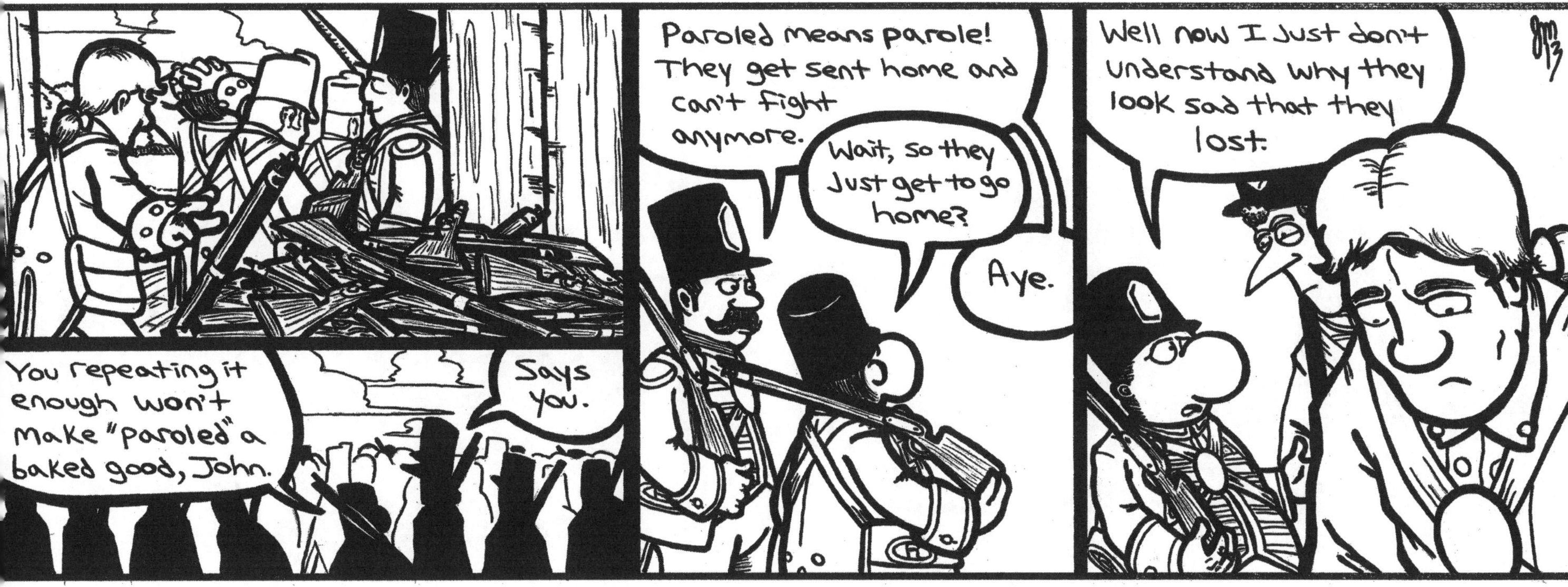
You repeating it enough won't make "paroled" a baked good, John.
Says you.
Paroled means parole! They get sent home and can't fight anymore.
Wait, so they Just get to go home?
Aye.
Well now I Just don't understand why they look sad that they lost.

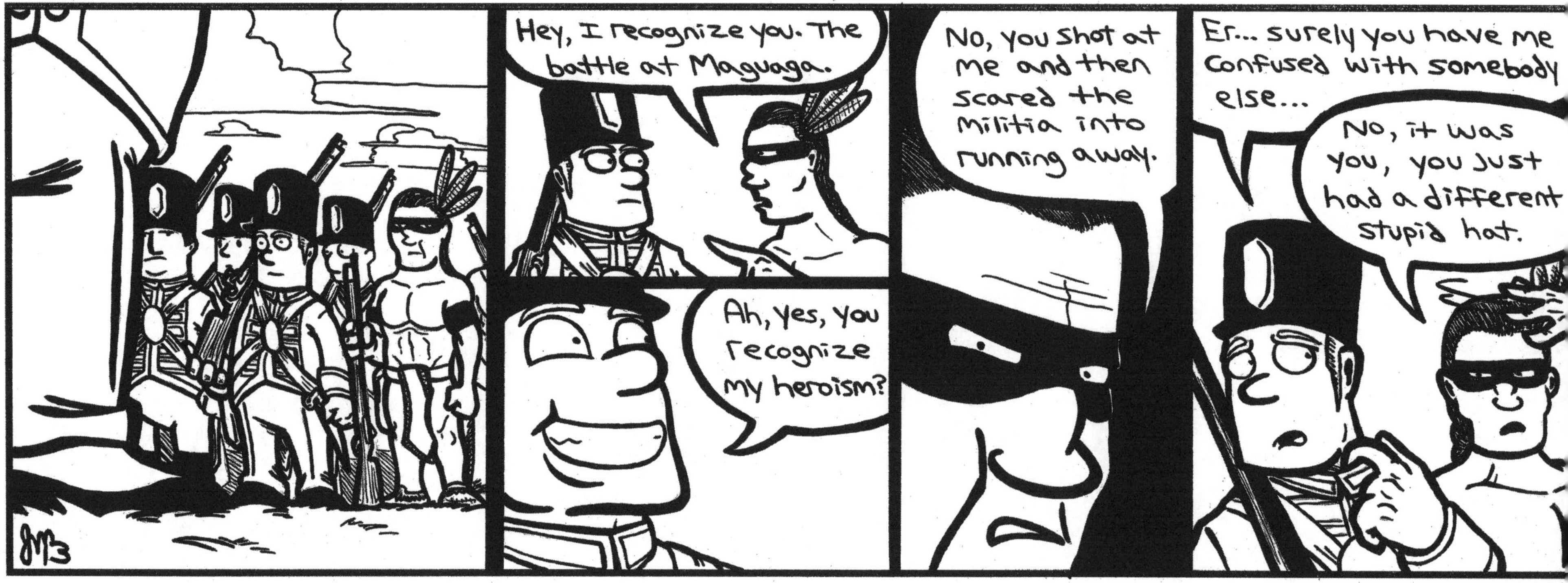
Hey, I recognize you. The battle at Maguaga.
Ah, yes, you recognize my heroism?
No, you shot at me and then scared the militia into running away.
Er... surely you have me confused with somebody else...
No, it was you, you just had a different stupid hat.

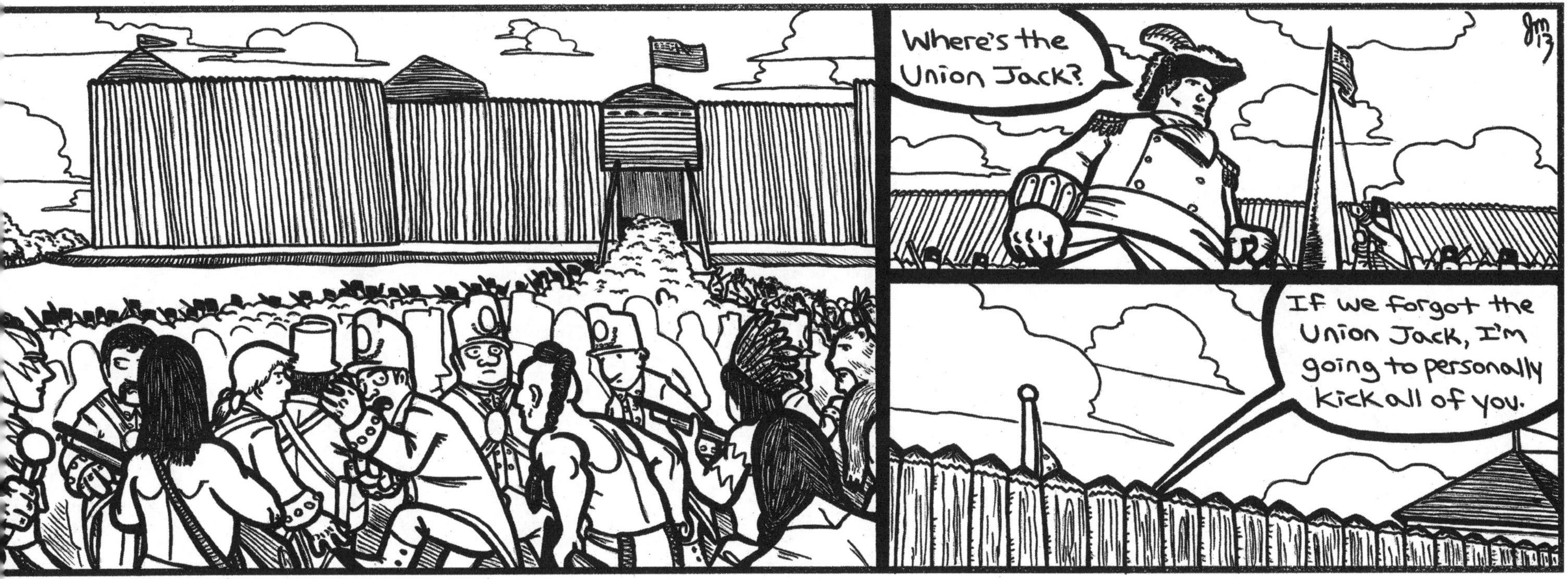
Where's the Union Jack?
If we forgot the Union Jack, I'm going to personally kick all of you.

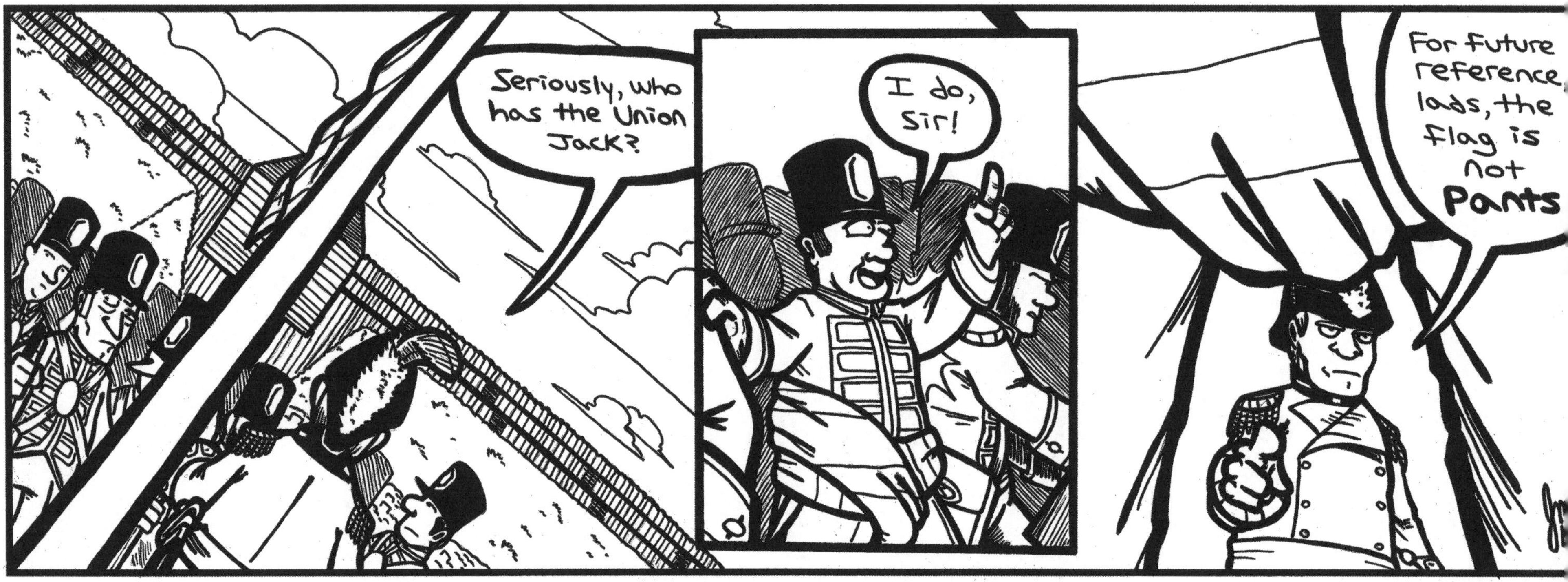
Seriously, who has the Union Jack?
I do, sir!
For future reference, lads, the flag is not **Pants**

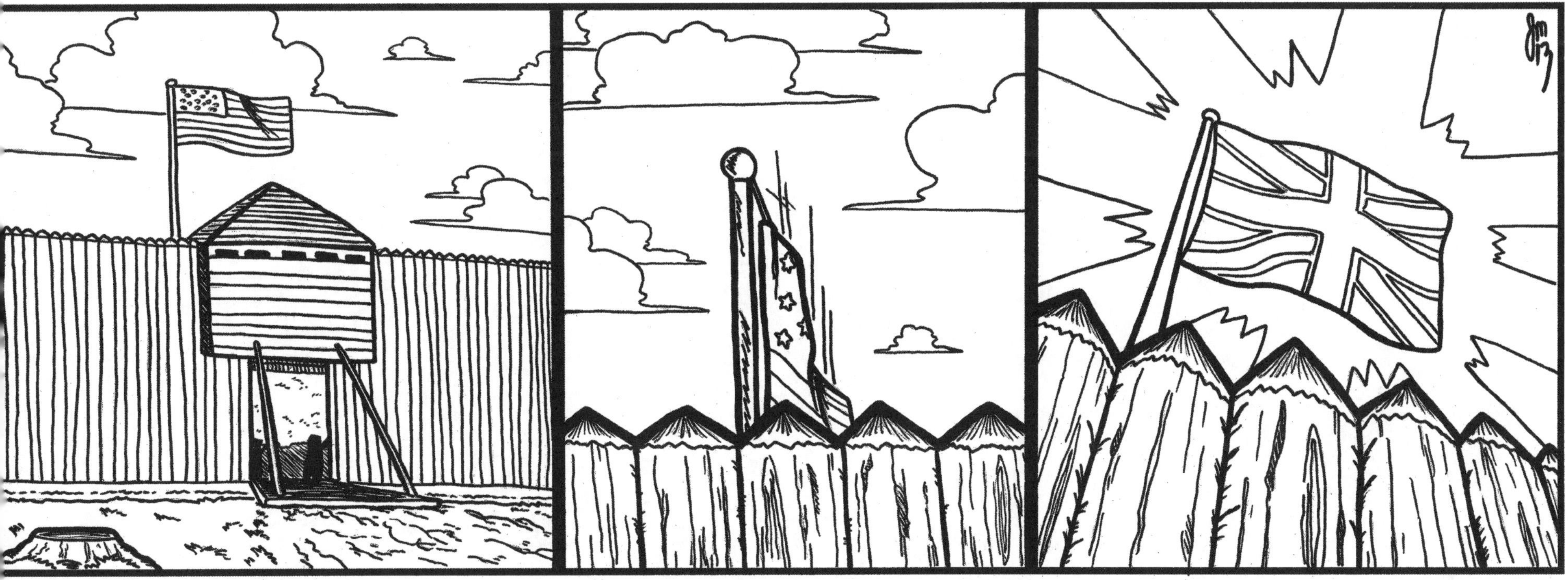

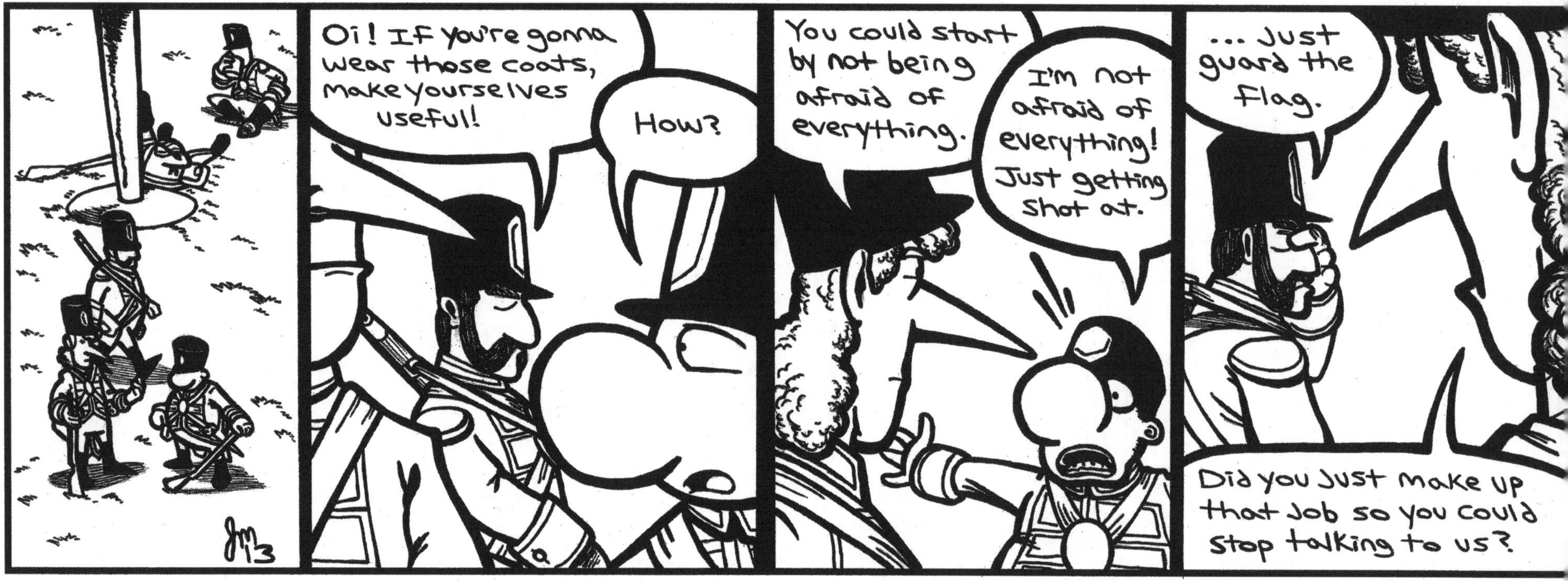
Oi! If you're gonna wear those coats, make yourselves useful!
How?
You could start by not being afraid of everything.
I'm not afraid of everything! Just getting shot at.
... Just guard the flag.
Did you just make up that job so you could stop talking to us?

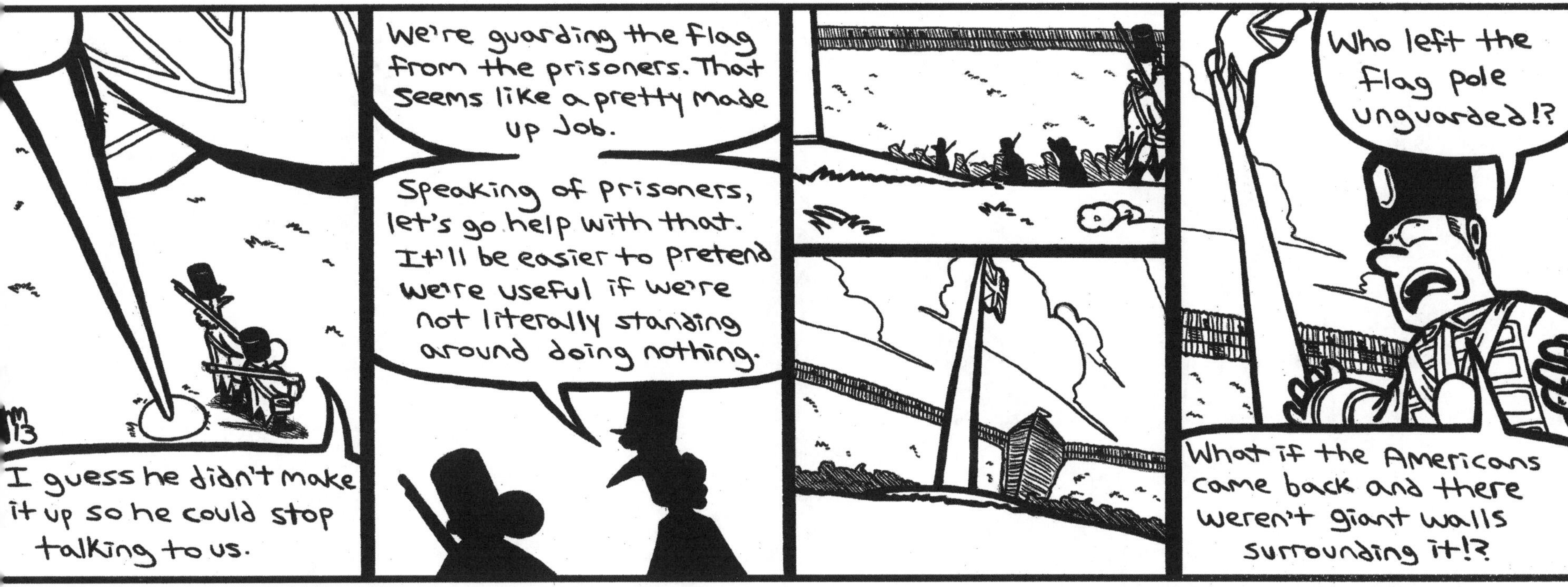
I guess he didn't make it up so he could stop talking to us.
We're guarding the flag from the prisoners. That seems like a pretty made up Job.
Speaking of prisoners, let's go help with that. It'll be easier to pretend we're useful if we're not literally standing around doing nothing.
Who left the flag pole unguarded!?
What if the Americans came back and there weren't giant walls surrounding it!?

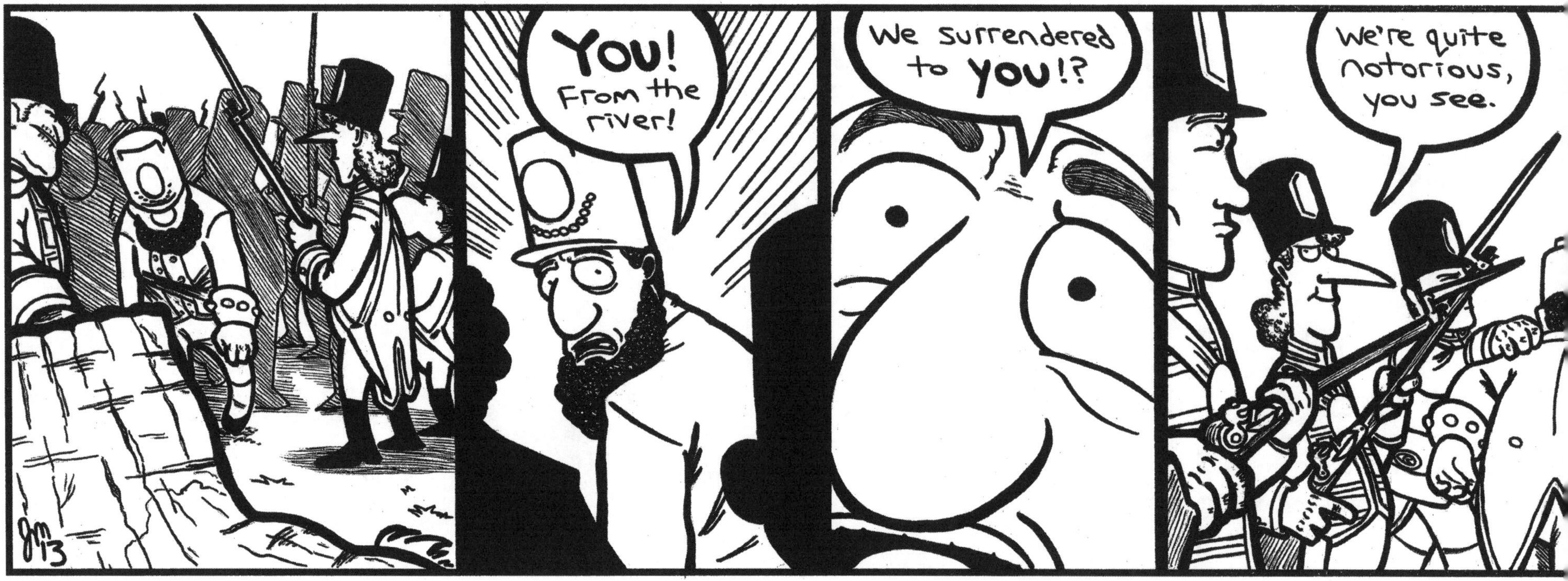
YOU! From the river!
We surrendered to YOU!?
We're quite notorious, you see.

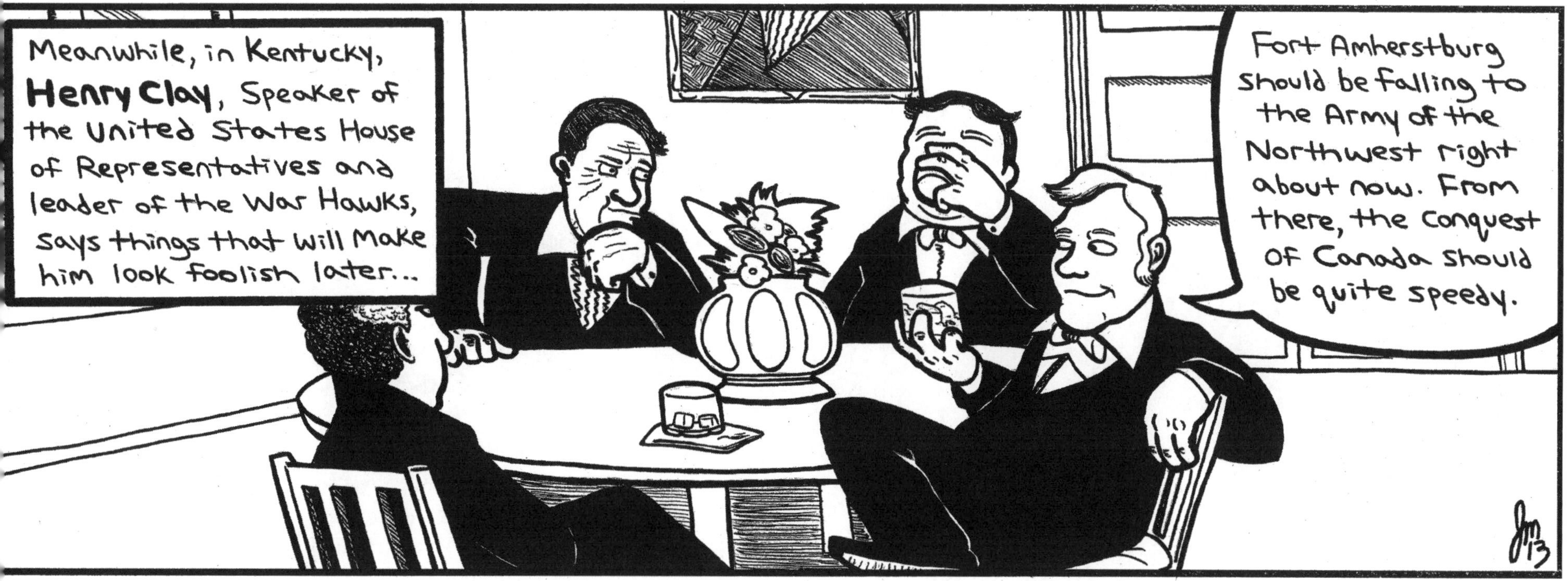
Meanwhile, in Kentucky, Henry Clay, Speaker of the United States House of Representatives and leader of the War Hawks, says things that will make him look foolish later...
Fort Amherstburg should be falling to the Army of the Northwest right about now. From there, the conquest of Canada should be quite speedy.

Other titles from Renegade Arts Entertainment

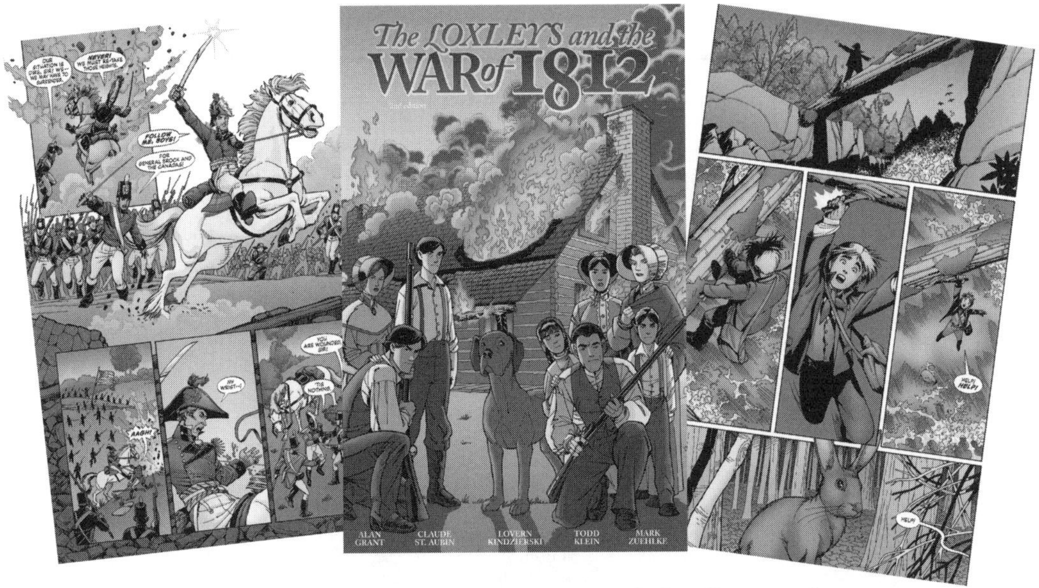
The LOXLEYS and the WAR of 1812
ALAN GRANT
CLAUDE ST. AUBIN
LOVERN KINDZIERSKI
TODD KLEIN
MARK ZUEHLKE
FOLLOW ME, BOYS!
HELP!

The Loxleys and the War of 1812 is a beautifully illustrated graphic novel telling a Canadian family's story as they are swept up in America's invasion. Written by Alan Grant, illustrated by Claude St. Aubin and Lovern Kindzierski, this is the only graphic novel to capture this period of Canadian History.
ISBN: 978-0-9921508-0-8

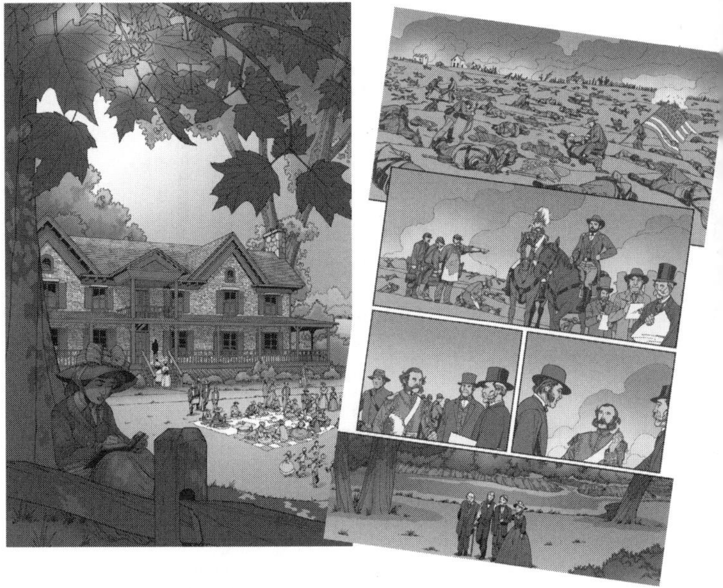

The Loxleys and Confederation catches up with the Loxley family as Canada once again is forced to adapt to the changes in America, this time the threat of another invasion and the sudden loss of almost all trade. Confederation takes young Lillian on a trip across Canada, the USA and even to Europe as Canada itself is born.
ISBN: 978-0-9921508-9-1